The Loony Bin Blues

Greg Johnson

iUniverse, Inc.
Bloomington

The author wishes to acknowledge use of the following copyrighted material:

Excerpt from "Casey Jones", lyrics by Robert Hunter, Copyright Ice Nine Publishing Company. Used with permission.

Excerpt from "Like a Rolling Stone", by Bob Dylan, Copyright 1963 by Warner Bros. Inc. Copyright renewed 1991 by Special Rider Music. All rights reserved. International copyright secured. Reprinted by permission.

Excerpt from "Bob Dylan's Dream", by Bob Dylan, Copyright 1965 by Warner Bros. Inc. Copyright renewed 1993 by Special Rider Music. All rights reserved. International copyright secured. Reprinted by permission.

Excerpt from Jitterbug Perfume, by Tom Robbins. Copyright 1984 by Tom Robbins. Published by Bantam Books.

iUniverse books may be ordered through booksellers or by contacting:

iUniverse
1663 Liberty Drive
Bloomington, IN 47403
www.iuniverse.com
1-800-Authors (1-800-288-4677)

ISBN: 978-1-4502-9379-2 (sc)
ISBN: 978-1-4502-9380-8 (ebook)

Printed in the United States of America

iUniverse rev. date: 02/17/2011

For Libby, Nick and Sarah

Author's Note/Acknowledgements

Once upon a time I sat down to write what was going to be a memoir about my years spent running group homes for teenagers, but when I fired up my laptop some wicked impulse took over and a novel started spilling out. While *The Loony Bin Blues* is based very loosely on my experiences as a social worker, the story and the characters are fictional, with the exceptions of Ann Warner and her late husband Buffy, the very real owners of the very real Howard's Pub in Ocracoke, North Carolina.

I owe many people thanks for their help. My brother-in-law Ed Meadows provided an insider's guide to Richmond and a place to sleep during my trips there. John Edgar, a student at William & Mary when I was writing *Loony Bin*, was willing to do research and footwork in exchange for an occasional free meal. My friend Denny Wood went along on a fact-finding mission to Ocracoke Island and spent a memorable night at the bar in Howard's Pub in the name of literature. Ronnie O'Neal, the captain of the Miss Kathleen, provided some basics about charter fishing on the island. Jim Lampos shared his experiences as a singer-songwriter on the grub 'n pub circuit, and his views on Pennsyltuckians. Julie Ford read the first draft and offered her insights ("Do you really mean to have two Chapter 18's?"). My wife Libby and friend Ann Benedict proofread several versions. Aaron Lancaster, Josh Nunley, DeWitt Shank, Steve Talbot, Sarah Johnson and Nick Johnson provided technical assistance. Lindsey Wood supplied the expression "pish posh" for Miss Beauregard. I owe Rich and Mimi Rice a big thank you for letting me write part of the story at their camp at an "undisclosed location" in the Adirondacks.

I'd also like to thank the hundred or so people who attended a public reading at the Greenbrier Valley Theatre and provided feedback at a crucial juncture in the story's development. I'm grateful to Don Rollins and Cathey Sawyer for facilitating this event, and especially grateful to the participant who said, "I laughed so hard I cried my mascara off." It was the review I needed to hear, and I tried to overlook the fact that her opinion might have been swayed by the three cases of wine the audience consumed during the event.

Finally, I'd like to say a word about Buffy Warner, the former West Virginia state legislator/free spirit/entrepreneur whose untimely death came as a shock to family and friends on Ocracoke and in West Virginia. When I first conceived *The Loony Bin Blues* and decided to set part of the story on the island, I planned to fictionalize Howard's Pub and its owners. On a whim I sent Buffy a copy of the lengthy first draft and asked if he and Ann would mind making cameo appearances in a novel. He replied in his typical Go-for-It fashion, and stayed in touch by e-mail and letter as the project unfolded. He rode out Hurricane Isabel in the interim, keeping his beach bar open with a generator, a feat that landed him in newspapers around the country. Following the tragic news of his accidental death on his boat, I again considered fictionalizing the pub's owners, but decided that his enthusiasm for the project deserves recognition. So among other things, *The Loony Bin Blues* is a small tribute to the spirit of the irrepressible Buffy Warner.

Greg Johnson
Lewisburg, West Virginia

Prologue

It all started with a song.

Chris Dewberry was standing backstage at the Cimiez Amphitheatre in Nice, France, with his hands shoved in his pockets and a Martin guitar slung over his back, thinking about how far three verses and a chorus had taken him. He'd written *Huck's Tune* when he was seventeen and tossed it in his guitar case. When his producer had insisted his first album needed another track he'd exhumed the song and cut it in one take. Ironically *Huck* had become his first hit, rising to Number One and lingering for three weeks. His management agency had hustled him off on a tour of North America, and now he was swinging across Europe, playing 28 gigs in 34 days.

Tonight he was singing in a stone bowl carved from Roman ruins in this ancient city on the Riviera. The home of the artist Henri Matisse loomed on a hill above the stage, and a few miles away lovers were strolling hand-in-hand along the Promenade des Anglais. Fifteen hundred concertgoers were growing restless, and he knew when he took the stage they'd start clamoring for *Huck's Tune*. He'd heard these requests in a dozen languages. He still couldn't get over how the whimsical little ditty he'd penned long ago on a summer afternoon in the backseat of his parents' Subaru had fired so many imaginations. Strangers would tell him the song had inspired them to set off on adventures. Tonight, far from his Virginia home, he was on one of his own. He'd asked his booking agent to sandwich Nice into his schedule, hoping he could flush out someone who lived nearby, an old friend who had the potential to bring some much-needed closure to this whirlwind chapter of his young life.

He was twenty-three and he'd already made more money than his history professor father had earned in his entire career at the College of William and Mary. The money was a pleasant by-product; ever since he was thirteen some mysterious force had compelled him to pick up a guitar and turn words and chords into songs, even when he wasn't being paid for it.

Earlier in the afternoon, after the sound check, he'd walked up to the Matisse museum to see what another artistic soul had produced in the course of a lifetime. He'd bought a poster of one of the painter's blue nudes, with a quote that said simply, *Sans passion, il n'y a pas d'art*, Without passion there is no art. He planned hang it in his recording studio for a little inspiration whenever the creative well ran dry.

In a few seconds he'd walk out under the stars and connect with these strangers the way troubadours had been doing for centuries. At the end of the first set he'd sing his anthem and French voices would join in:

I wish I had a raft so I could be like ol' Huck Finn
I'd light out for the territory where I've never been

The song had spilled from him six years earlier, at the end of an escapade that started in a psychiatric hospital where his parents had parked him in frustration. He'd never shared the story with anyone because it was long and complicated, and a pop song wasn't supposed to cast doubt on its composer's mental status. *Huck's* genesis still left him shaking his curly locks in disbelief. Fate was reminding him of his youthful indiscretions on a daily basis, but at least she was kind enough to pay him royalties.

The house lights dimmed and his band members took their places. He heard his name and applause and he strolled onto the stage with a smile to give Europe another taste of America's most popular export. A spotlight followed him to the mike and he raised his hands in greeting. "Bon soir, Nice!" He pointed to the orange disk peeking over the horizon. "I hate to argue with John Fogerty, but I see a good moon rising." He readjusted his playlist; he'd open the second set, the part where he came out by himself and did a low-key number, with Nanci Griffith's *Once in a Very Blue Moon*. He'd bring out Max to fake it on the cello. He was sure his classically trained cellist had never heard of the song, but Max could wing anything.

The Cimiez Amphitheatre was a perfect venue and the crowd seemed receptive. It was going to be a good night. If the right person was in the audience it was going to be stellar.

PART I
Richmond

Chapter 1

Six teenagers were sitting in a rough approximation of a circle, wearing expressions ranging from mild indifference to terminal apathy. Their therapist was running late, but with nowhere to go and nothing to do this didn't strike them as a troubling development. There were entertaining distractions, and Chris Dewberry was distracted by the silky pair of legs propped on the empty chair next to him.

Riverside Adolescent Psychiatric Center was a more interesting place than he'd expected, thanks in no small part to a golden goddess from Buckingham County named Sierra McGuire. Her presence at this treatment center, while entirely welcome, baffled him. After four weeks of listening to his peers' war stories he could recite their histories, pre-histories, alibis and extenuating circumstances. His roommate, Russell Moss, had been dealing pot at his high school. The group's only African American, Selena Booker, was a serial shoplifter. Fourteen-year-old Molly Potterfield had converted to Wicca to make a point to her Baptist preacher stepfather. Danny Roach and his outlaw brothers had borrowed a Hummer from the Maryland National Guard.

But for some mysterious reason Sierra was reluctant to reveal how she'd won her expense-paid vacation. She'd complained about her family's hard-knock life, but they didn't hospitalize 17-year-olds for being poor. He was determined to get to the bottom of this, but time was running out. He was scheduled for discharge in the morning. He'd been waiting for the right moment to bring up the subject in private, but privacy was hard to come by when you were being eyeballed 24-7 by a team of helpful adults.

The door flew open and their therapist, Kate Oxley, breezed in and took her seat. "Sorry I'm late, guys. I was talking with Dr. Garcia and I lost track of the time. I'm sure you won't object if we have an abbreviated session."

"I object," Chris said. "I insist on the full boring, fruitless fifty minutes my parents are paying for."

"We'll try to cram fifty minutes worth of fruitlessness into ten," she promised. "Does anyone have an issue they'd like to discuss?"

Danny Roach tipped his chair back, folded his tattooed arms and glowered. "I hate this damn shit-hole. I want out."

Selena rolled her eyes. "Roach, time they let you out you'll be on Viagra."

Kate sized up her young rebel-without-a-clue, who always seemed to have a bandanna on his head and a chip on his shoulder. "Would you mind expressing your views in a more socially acceptable manner, Roach?"

"That's bullshit. This whole place is bullshit."

"You're here for an psychological evaluation, Roach," Russell refreshed his memory. "They can keep you as long as they want. Enjoy it while you can. They're not going to let you get away with stealing government property. You'll probably go to a lock-up when you leave here."

"I'm already in a lock-up!" Roach said in exasperation. "I'm tired of talkin' about my feelin's."

"So you're angry and frustrated?" Kate asked him.

"Yeah. "

"You just shared your feelings."

Roach hated this kind of adult trickery. "Man, I don't belong in this place. I'm normal."

"Normal," the word rolled off Molly's blackened lips with disdain. "Who wants to be normal?"

Chris studied her raccoon eyes and decided she hadn't mastered her Goth makeup yet. "Don't worry, Molly, no one's going to mistake you for normal. You look like you just rolled off an embalming table."

Roach sensed he was losing his audience. "Will somebody tell me when I can leave?"

Molly twirled a strand of her jet-black hair around a finger. "What's the rush? We're all here because our homes suck."

"Yeah, but this place sucks worse."

Kate usually let her group members hash these things out themselves, but she decided she needed to speed things along. "Where are you from, Roach?"

"Oxen Hill, Maryland."

"I guess you've got lots of friends there?"

"I hang with my bros."

"The same bros who wrecked the military vehicle?"

"You got it."

"But if you leave here without finishing the program, isn't the State of Maryland going to charge you with felonies?"

"They gotta catch me first. If you don't let me out, I'm breakin' out." Chris yawned. Molly studied her ebony fingernails.

"Yeah, right," Russell summed up the group opinion.

"People bust out of these places," Roach felt sure.

"Yeah, and the cops know right where to find them," Russell said. "Home sweet home."

"Buffalo Mound, Maryland," Chris added.

"Oxen Hill, you asshole."

"Sorry, man. I knew it had something to do with a hairy beast and a bowel movement."

"Eat shit, Dewberry."

"I've been eating it three times a day for the past month, just like you."

Kate turned to Sierra. "Sierra, everyone else seems to be full of advice this morning. Do you have anything you'd like to say to Roach?"

Anticipation hung in the air as the resident babe ran her fingers through her golden tresses and considered Roach's dilemma. "Roach, you'll get out of here a lot quicker if you just keep your stupid mouth shut."

The mouth in question fell open. Kate decided it was time to wrap things up. "Thanks for sharing, everyone. We'll take up where we left off tomorrow."

As they straggled out of the room, Chris was thinking about Sierra's advice. She was obviously keeping her own mouth shut about something. He had 24 hours to find out what.

On the floor below the therapy room Norman Chase was sitting in his elegantly appointed office, gazing meditatively out the picture window and congratulating himself on his life of service to problem children.

Thanks to problem children every morning he could drive through the Riverside Adolescent Psychiatric Center's wrought iron gates in his silver Ferrari and enter a kingdom where he was lord. Problem children were responsible for his handcrafted mahogany desk, his tufted leather presidential chair and his commanding view of the manicured lawn that swept gently down to the James River. In one of life's strange, sweet ironies, the same surly teens who'd given their parents migraines and their teachers ulcers had given him a townhouse in Richmond's Fan District, a beach cottage in Duck, North Carolina, and a ski chalet in Snowshoe, West Virginia.

Fifteen years earlier Norman had been selling drugs for Abbott Labs, making his rounds in a run-down Chevy, calling on doctors and pushing pills. One morning he was visiting a psychiatrist in a hospital ward when a group of young people caught his eye. They were sitting in a circle, having some kind of meeting. Curious, Norman engaged the doctor in a little friendly chitchat. In the process he discovered a branch of medicine that didn't require expensive machines, surgical procedures or even hospital gowns, a branch that smelled suspiciously profitable. Soon he was knocking on doors in the Commonwealth's health care bureaucracy, armed with grim statistics about a younger generation spinning hopelessly out of control, and a proposal to open a 45-bed facility to address their needs. They gave him his license and he was off and running, energetically gathering young misfits with vague diagnoses like Oppositional Defiant Disorder and Cannabis Abuse, and billing insurance companies for umpteen bottles of pills and countless hours of talk. Now, thanks to all those pills and all that talk, he was a very wealthy man. People were impressed he'd chosen such a humanitarian line of work. "Yes, I find it extremely rewarding," he'd say.

He thought the name Riverside Adolescent Psychiatric Center had a touch of class, but the medical community had an affinity for acronyms, so they called his little hospital RAP. Whenever someone introduced him as the CEO of RAP he felt like a hip-hop deejay, but he held his tongue. As long as they kept sending him referrals they could call him the CEO of CRAP for all he cared. There were days it would have been an appropriate title.

He heard someone at his door. He took his feet off the desk and pretended to be going over some budget figures. "Come in."

Kate Oxley poked her head in. "Mr. Chase, do you have a minute? There's something I'd like to discuss."

His clinical director was one of the few staff members Norman deemed worthy of his time, since she carried her own workload plus most of his. He was worried that this energetic young psychologist would head for greener pastures and force him to have to go back to captaining the ship of fools in his employ. He shoved his paperwork aside. "You know I've always got time for you, Kate."

She took a seat in one of the wingback chairs that faced his aircraft carrier of a desk. "We need to talk about Dr. Garcia."

Norman's eyebrows shot up in mock surprise. "Garcia? What about him?"

"He's not working out."

"Oh, really? What makes you say that?"

"He can barely speak English! He doesn't seem to know much about psychiatry either. Maybe he's Mexico's answer to Sigmund Freud, but you couldn't prove it by me. He's not connecting with these kids."

Norman had anticipated problems with this new psychiatrist, but Dr. Garcia had one overriding qualification: he was willing to work for peanuts. He gave her a paternal look. "Kate, I've always thought of you as an open-minded person. Don't you think you're being a little culturally biased?"

Her mouth fell open. "I'm *not* culturally biased," she resented this accusation. "I don't care where he's from – he's a lousy excuse for a professional."

"Give the poor guy a break," Norman said. "Put yourself in his shoes. What if you had to deal with your patients in Spanish?"

"I wouldn't try to diagnose and treat people if I couldn't understand them."

"We didn't hire him to teach Shakespeare. We hired him to write prescriptions and sign off on treatment plans."

"Every psychiatrist you've hired has been worse than the one before! And they're all from Chihuahua!"

"My amigo Ernesto runs an employment agency down there."

"Maybe you need to get a new amigo. I don't intend to be here when it all comes crashing down." She left her chair and headed for the door.

Norman rushed after her. "I hope you're not thinking of leaving us, Kate," he said anxiously. "You know how much we value your contributions. If you leave you'll only hurt the kids. Remember - it's all about the kids!"

Chapter 2

It was a perfect spring morning, and Andrew Boone had taken the top and doors off his new Jeep Wrangler to soak up the sun. As he followed Riverside Drive's winding path and watched the sun play on the James River he wondered how his parents had ever convinced him to trade the life of a fishing guide for the life of an urban wage slave. He'd left their Rappahannock County farm, picked up a bachelor's in social work from Virginia Commonwealth University and joined the rat race. The Boone family finally had a college graduate, but the grad had a nagging suspicion that he was supposed to be knee-deep in the Upper James, trolling for smallmouth bass.

His cubicle at Child Protective Services seemed like a tiny prison, so he spent most of his time in the field, which he defined as anyplace but his office. This morning he was meeting with a young man in a treatment center and giving him some bad news. He put on his blinker, turned in the hospital's gated entrance and explained his business to the security guard.

A few minutes later he was sitting in a conference room, facing a 16-year-old named Russell Moss. "Call me Andrew," he tried to put him at ease. "I'm not big on the mister stuff. I'm from Child Protective Services. Do you know what that is?"

"Bodyguards for rich kids?" Russell guessed.

He laughed. "I wish. We investigate abuse and neglect. When we find young people in those situations we try to help them out." He watched the young man's expression morph from mild wariness to full-fledged suspicion.

"What's this got to do with me?"

"Why don't you tell me why you're here?"

"I was selling weed at school," he said with a shrug. "The cops brought in a drug dog named Officer Sniffy and he found four baggies in my locker.

They gave me a lawyer and she told me to plead to possession and agree to come here. I go back to court in two weeks. They're supposed to give me probation and send me home."

Andrew studied his client. There wasn't any good way to convey what he had to tell him. "Russell, you're not going home when you leave here."

The young man looked stunned. "What do you mean?"

"Judge Murphy asked CPS to investigate your home situation."

"What's to investigate? We live in a crappy place. My mom's a drunk and a pothead. So what? It's not classified information."

"And you were helping yourself to her stash and recycling it at school to cover the rent?"

"Yeah. I don't even use the shit myself."

"I believe you," Andrew said. "I've heard the same story from your teachers and your school counselor. They think pretty highly of you. They showed me some of the pictures you took for the school paper and the yearbook. The judge understands your situation and he doesn't have any problem giving you probation, but he's not going to let you serve it under the supervision of a parent with a substance abuse problem. He wants us to place you in foster care until your eighteenth birthday."

"Eighteen! That's a year-and-a-half from now!"

"You'll have a hearing in two weeks. They'll give your mother a lawyer and she'll have a chance to explain her side of things."

"Yeah, like she'll really win that one."

"She probably won't. That means we've got two weeks to find you a new home. We can go over your options now, or I can give you some time to get used to the idea and come back tomorrow."

"I'll never touch weed again," he bargained. "I'll get a job. I'll flip burgers at Mickey D's. I'll go to church and sing in the choir. Whatever it takes. I don't want to go to some foster home. Don't screw my life up like this."

"What about school?" Andrew asked him. "Richmond expelled you for a year. If you're living in another district you can go back in September. Doesn't that make more sense than sitting out your senior year?"

"I don't want to graduate from some place I've never been. You're punishing me for my mom's problems."

Andrew was tempted to remind him that his mother wasn't the one selling drugs to minors, but he let it slide. "Listen, Russell, I know it's probably hard for you to believe, but we're trying to help you. You've got a rough situation and you deserve better."

"If you really want to help me, leave me alone."

"Unfortunately that's not an option."

"If you put me in a foster care I won't stay there."

"You can't go home and you've got to live somewhere," he gave him the bottom line. "I'll let you get used to the idea and I'll come back in the morning and we'll talk about it. You like to fish?"

"No."

"I'll get permission to take you out. We'll go down to the Pony Pasture, throw our lines in the water and try to figure out the next eighteen months of your life."

"Who put you in charge of my life?" He stood up, shoved his chair and stomped angrily out of the room.

Soon Andrew was back in his Jeep, retracing the path of the James River and thinking about his job. The abuse and neglect cases he investigated were usually pretty clear-cut, but this one bothered him. He'd met the boy's mother. Grace Moss was a hopeless addict, but harmless. There was a live-and-let-live part of him that wanted to leave this young man to his own devices. It was the same part of him that was still knee-deep in the Upper James, trolling for smallmouth bass.

Dr. Garcia looked up from his patient's file. "Creez?"

"That's Chris," the patient corrected him.

"You are feeling better, Creez?"

"No, I'm feeling shitty."

"Sheety?"

"Yeah, sheety. I'm supposed to go home tomorrow. I'm not ready. I think I need another week or two." He glanced at the diploma on the wall. "Universidad de Correspondencia? Is that a big school?"

"Si. Berry beeg."

"What part of Mexico are you from?"

"I am being from Chihuahua."

"I thought a Chihuahua was a dog."

"Si." Now that he'd established rapport with his patient, Dr. Garcia was ready to get down to business. "The peels are being good for you, no?"

"The what?"

"The Buspar. You are not..." The doctor hesitated. He pulled out a pocket dictionary and paged through it until he found what he wanted. "Sad, gloomy?"

"I was never sad, gloomy. I was pissed."

"Peezed?"

The name on the file caught Chris's eye. "Are you sure you don't have me mixed up with Chris Wilson? The dude on Unit Five who slit his wrists? That's his file. I'm Chris Dewberry."

The doctor examined the label. "Ees wrong Creez?"

"I'm Chris *Dewberry*. Do I have to keep taking the pills, or were those for Chris Wilson?"

"Ees making you better, no?"

He shook his head. "No, I don't like them."

"You are not doctor of the psychiatry, Creez. I am doctor of the psychiatry. You take peels."

"Yeah, whatever." Tomorrow he was going home and the peels were going down the toilet.

Kate was sitting in a corner of the hospital dining room reading the *Times-Dispatch* when she looked up and saw Russell Moss heading her way with a grim look. She expected an earful now that he knew a foster home was in the works. He reached her table. "Mind if I join you?"

"You'll ruin your reputation if your friends see you eating with staff members, Russell."

He took a seat on the opposite bench. "When they take you out of your school in handcuffs and stick you in a psycho ward you don't have a reputation left to ruin. I need a big favor, Kate. I need to get in touch with my mom. She doesn't have a phone. Our landlord's got one, but he's old and he forgets to give her messages. Can you go by our apartment and ask her to come over here tonight during visiting hours? They're trying to stick me in a foster home. I need to talk to her."

Kate decided this was her chance to play devil's advocate. "Russell, from what you've told us about your home life, maybe a foster home wouldn't be the worst thing in the world. I'm sure they'll try to find a family that fits your personality and your interests."

"Yeah, like Mr. and Mrs. Perfect want the friendly neighborhood pusher boy living with them. They'll stick me out in the boondocks with a bunch of toothless rednecks that are just doing it for the money."

He had a point. Sixteen-year-old drug dealers weren't at the top of anyone's Ten Most Desirable Foster Children list. "I'm sure Andrew's working hard on it. He seems like he really cares."

"Who'll take care of my mom while I'm gone?"

"I've got a feeling she's more of a survivor than you give her credit for."

"I'm the survivor! I'm the one who was paying the rent and buying the food. If they'd just leave me alone I'll be fine. I'll get a job and work until I can go back to school."

"You need to go back to school in September, Russell. Social services can look in on your mother. You shouldn't let her problems limit your options."

"How are they my options if other people pick them for me?"

"Good point," she conceded. "I'm just afraid if you stay where you are you'll never live up to your potential."

"Big deal. Who does?"

"Okay, end of lecture. Tell me how to find your mother."

"Let me see your pen." He scribbled the address on a napkin. "We live on Hull Street, over the Old Dominion Pawn Palace. It's a rat hole, so don't be surprised."

"Russell, this might be hard for you to believe, but when I leave here I actually have a life. I sing with a choral group on Thursday evenings. But I'll go by your place first and see if I can find her. Are you sure she'll be home?"

"If she's not, look in the bar across the street. She goes back and forth between Point A and Point B."

"Sounds like my life."

"If she can come, ask her to bring the backpack with my Nikon and lenses. I spent $500 on that stuff and I don't want her selling it when she gets hard up."

"Where on earth did you get $500?" As soon as the words left her mouth she held up her hand. "On second thought, don't answer that. The less your therapist knows about your financial activities the better off we'll both be."

"My lawyer said the same thing."

She pointed to his tray. "You haven't touched your lunch."

"Death Row kind of kills your appetite. Thanks, Kate. You're the only one in this place I trust."

"You're welcome, Russell. I'm looking forward to meeting your mother. I just hope it serves a purpose."

If he could get his hands on his camera, it would serve a purpose. It just wasn't one anybody was anticipating.

Chapter 3

Richmond philanthropist Edie Snellgrove had gone to the Great Charity Ball in the Sky without ever seeing the beautifully landscaped courtyard she'd given to the Riverside Center. Chris had noticed the benefactor's name on a bronze plaque and dubbed this little recreation yard the Garden of Edie. The staff liked the name, but his peers were too preoccupied with their own problems to worry about a shrubby mini-park with a koi pond and a gingerbread-trimmed gazebo. They especially failed to appreciate the twelve-foot serpentine brick wall that enclosed them, even though the architect had taken his inspiration from a similar wall Jefferson had designed at the University of Virginia.

It was early afternoon and the patients from Unit Three were enduring their mandatory dose of heat and humidity in the courtyard. Molly and Selena were sharing a bench by the pond. Russell and Roach were stretched out in the grass, catching some rays. Chris had maneuvered Sierra over to the gazebo for his long-awaited private moment with her. He'd heard that music soothed the savage beast, so he was playing his guitar and hoping it had a similar effect on the opposite sex.

"You're good, Chris," Sierra said. "Where'd you learn to play like that?"

"My folks used to send me to all kinds of lessons. Golf, tennis, violin, chess - you name it. Guitar was the only thing I liked, but the teacher wanted me to read music and play all this classical crap, so I quit. I started hanging around guys who played and I picked it up."

She watched his fingers picking the strings. "You're *really* good."

"I'm not that good. I'm approaching adequate."

"Why'd your folks send you to all those lessons?"

He stopped playing and looked in her green eyes. "Do you really want to hear about the boring life and times of Chris Dewberry?"

"Sure. You might be famous someday and I can tell people we used to be psychos together."

He let the guitar rest in his lap. "I've got a weird father, Sierra."

"But he teaches at William & Mary," she proved she'd been paying attention in their group therapy sessions. Her own father was a jobless alcoholic, so she didn't understand how anyone could find fault with a father who had a job.

"If you met him you'd understand. He lives in his own little universe. When he's home he holes up in his study and spends all his time reading and writing. He's written two books about the Civil War, but he can't figure out how to change the batteries in a flashlight. He can't even make normal conversation. When my friends try to talk to him he starts rambling on about whatever he's been reading. He goes on and on about all this weird shit, like the Twelve Tribes of Israel or the Peloponnesian War. It's majorly embarrassing. The only one he hasn't run off is my best friend Serge. He lives next door and he's used to him."

"At least you're rich," she saw his glass as mostly full.

"Professors aren't rich, Sierra."

"But he writes books, too."

"They aren't exactly bestsellers. Most people don't want to read 300 pages about the Battle of Drewry's Bluff. If you figured out what he made by the hour from his writing he'd be better off working part-time at Ben & Jerry's."

"But he had the money to send you to all those lessons."

"He'd mortgage the house to get me out of his hair. He's not the kind of guy who coaches Little League and goes hiking with the Boy Scouts. Every morning he sits in the kitchen and reads the *Washington Post*. The whole *Washington Post*. When he sees something he thinks I ought to know he reads it out loud. *Hmm, this is interesting,* he'll say. *The average American consumes 803,000 calories a year, but the average Mozambican only consumes 42,180.* I nod and grunt. That pretty much sums up our relationship."

"You haven't said anything about your mom. Are your folks divorced?"

"No, but they might as well be. Mom spends all her time doing charity work at St. Bede's Catholic Church so she doesn't have to deal with Dad. She's like the head of 18 different committees and she takes food to all the sick people. She's always telling me about poor Miss So-and-So and how she's got some dread disease so she's taking her a covered dish. We live on leftover tragedy food."

"That's sad," she commiserated.

"Yeah, poor me." He studied her shimmering blonde hair and the way the freckles on her nose and cheeks dappled across her face. Then there was the skimpy T-shirt that was struggling to contain her. If you had to be pitied by someone, Sierra McGuire was an excellent choice.

"Play something," she requested.

He'd been working on a song about his time at the hospital, but he hadn't shared it with anyone. He grabbed his guitar and played a blues progression in E.

> *Woke up this mornin'*
> *ate my French toast and my pills,*
> *helped myself to seconds,*
> *my insurance pays the bills.*
> *I'm under lock and key,*
> *they say I've blown my fuse.*
> *Got the loony bin blues.*
>
> *Got a roommate name of Russell,*
> *he's a local Richmond boy.*
> *He was dealin' at his high school,*
> *spreadin' that Jamaican joy,*
> *'til an officer named Sniffy*
> *went sniffin' round for clues,*
> *left him with the loony bin blues.*
>
> *Goin' back to Billyburg,*
> *the scene of my alleged crimes.*
> *I'm headin' to my hometown*
> *with my gee-tar and my rhymes.*
> *Can't seem to find the way,*
> *a home's a terrible thing to lose.*
> *Can't shake the loony bin blues.*

He stopped. "I'm working on another verse about how I go back home and discover it's the real loony bin."

"Do your folks realize they've got a talented son?"

He shrugged. "They think I'm going through a phase. I heard a story one time about John Lennon. When he was growing up his Aunt Mimi used to say, 'John, the guitar's a nice hobby, but you'll never make a living with it.' After he was rich and famous he gave her a plaque with her words on it. My folks are just like her. They want me to go to some Ivy League college and be a lawyer or a dentist. I just want to play music."

She remembered the story he'd related in one of their group sessions about running off to Washington. "Why did you run away?"

"I got this idea I could make a living playing at coffee houses and clubs, and busking on the street. Someone told me about this shelter where you could stay for free. Turned out the Catholics ran it and the director knew my mom. He called her and she came and picked me up. Game Over."

"And they put you here?"

"This place was my dad's idea. He wants me to have sanity lessons."

"Is it working?"

"It's working about as well as the golf and the chess did. Actually, it's been a nice break." Now that he'd let her give him the third degree, Chris felt he'd earned the right to ask a few questions of his own.

Roach lay on his back in the grass, staring at the clouds. "Man, this place sucks."

"We get the message, Roach," Russell said. "You don't have to keep saying it over and over."

"All they do is boss you around. They tell you when to get up, they tell you when to eat, they tell you when to go outside, they tell you when to go to bed. They're always in your face. I'm surprised they don't tell you when to take a shit."

"So what are you going to do when you're a free man?"

"Join the Marines."

Russell turned and stared at him. "Roach, you weren't standing at the front of the line when they issued brains, were you?"

"What's that spozed to mean?"

"I rest my case."

"I've been reading on the Internet about casting spells," Molly confided to Selena. "I've tried some, but so far they're not working."

"My Mambo Mama casts spells," Selena revealed.

"Your what?"

"That's what we call my great granny."

"You've got a great-grandmother who casts spells?"

"She thinks she's a voodoo priestess. She's half-crazy."

"Everybody around here's got an interesting family but me," Molly said dejectedly.

"She poisoned her first husban' but they couldn't prove it on her. She worked in a thermometer factory. Every day she'd bring home a little mercury and put it in his peanut butter."

"Wicca's better than voodoo," Molly felt sure the new black arts were an improvement over the old. "Like if I wanted to make Russell fall in love with me I could take a lock of his hair and put it under a rock and pray to the goddess Kore."

"You could try takin' off that black lipstick," Selena advised.

"What do you mean?"

"Girl, there's no kind of spell gonna make that boy fall in love with you."

"That was just an example, Selena. I don't care about him," she said unconvincingly. "I don't know how Wicca works. It just does."

"Girl, you can call on all the goddesses you want and drink all the chicken blood you want. I'm stickin' to Jesus and Dr. Pepper."

"Okay, you've heard my pathetic story," Chris said as he tuned his guitar. "Now tell me yours."

Sierra reacted with a pained expression. "If I told you about my family you'd think I'm trailer trash."

"You're the classiest trailer trash I've ever seen." He bit his lip. Somehow this hadn't come out sounding like the compliment he'd intended.

"At least your father has a good job and you live in a nice house. I'll bet you even take vacations."

"If you call tramping around Civil War battlefields vacations. How do you know we've got a nice house?"

"Your dad has a study. Shacks don't have studies."

He thought it was interesting she'd picked up on this little detail. "I've seen rich and we're definitely not it. They'll never feature the Dewberry house on *Extreme Homes.*"

"You're rich compared to us. We live out in the middle of nowhere, in a ratty old trailer next to the RonDayVoo Lounge. My mom works there."

"What's your dad do?"

"Drinks. My sister and I grew up hanging around the bar and watching the fights for entertainment. I bet you don't have stuff like that in your neighborhood."

"I live next door to 5000 college students. They get pretty rowdy."

"That's different, Chris. You just don't understand."

"Let's trade places," he proposed. "My folks can send you to Yale and I'll play music for the drunks at the RonDayVoo Lounge."

"No one goes there for the music," she assured him. "They go there to get trashed and cheat on each other."

"So why are you in this place, Sierra?" he dug deeper. "We've been here a month and I still don't know what you're doing here. They don't put people in treatment centers because they live in trailers." She didn't say anything, and he could see he'd hit on a touchy subject. He pressed ahead. "So what's your story?"

"Okay," she relented with a sigh. "I'll tell you. But you've got to promise not to tell anyone else, or give me a hard time or write a song about it. Okay?"

"No problem." He would have traded his left testicle for this information.

"I wanted to take the SAT test but my folks didn't have the money. I took a guy in the bushes behind the bar to get it."

This wasn't what Chris was expecting to hear, and it rendered him speechless. Was his golden goddess slightly tarnished or just hopelessly corroded?

"He turned out to be an undercover deputy," she continued her saga. "He arrested me for soliciting and they put me in detention. When I went to court the judge said he'd drop the charge if I came here. Then he pulled out his wallet gave me the money for the SAT test."

"How'd you do?"

"1430."

"Damn." He decided not to mention his 1120. "I mean, you're not Alberta Einstein or anything, but that's pretty good for a blonde."

"I'm glad you didn't say that's pretty good for a slut."

"You're not a slut, Sierra."

"Then what do you call what I did?"

He thought about it. "Improvising."

"Sierra's not even my name," she made another confession. "My real name's Jolene. My mom named me after some dumb Dolly Parton song they used to play on the jukebox. I hate it. I'm changing it to Sierra when I turn 18."

"Sierra's better," he agreed. "You're not a Jolene."

"I'm changing lots of other things, too."

From the way she said it he knew she meant it.

Chapter 4

Norman was working his way through a stack of mail when an envelope from Virginia Tech's Office of Alumni Affairs caught his eye. He hadn't heard from his alma mater in two decades. He opened the letter with curiosity and read it.

Dear Mr. Chase:

We recently learned of your work with troubled youth at the Riverside Adolescent Psychiatric Center in Richmond. We're always pleased to hear our graduates are doing well and making significant contributions to society. We're proud you're a Hokie, and we congratulate you on your life of service to the young people of Virginia. Somehow we've lost touch with you over the years. We'd love to renew our relationship. Successful graduates are a natural source of inspiration for our 28,000 current students. We'd like to profile your work in an upcoming issue of VT Magazine. We'd also like to extend an invitation to you to visit the campus and share your insights and experiences with our students – our psychology and counseling majors, for example.

Norman smiled. Back in his college days he'd been a nobody with a 2.2 GPA. Now he was an inspiration! He liked his new status. He especially liked the idea of free publicity for his hospital. He could take Meg and the kids along and let them bask in his reflected glory. He imagined watching the Virginia Tech – UVA football game from the president's skybox and waving to his classmates in the cheap seats. He returned to the letter eagerly.

We hope you'll also consider making a financial commitment to the university and its pursuit of excellence. We offer our major donors a wide range of opportunities, from sponsoring visiting lecturers to endowing academic chairs. As you're probably aware, endowed chairs traditionally bear the honoree's name. Your gift could be designated the Norman Chase Chair of Adolescent Psychology, for example. Endowed chairs are available at an entry level of $500,000, which we're sure you'll agree is –

He crumpled the letter angrily and hurled it in his trashcan. Obviously some idiot had tipped them off about his money. The only chairs he was going to endow were the ones he could put his own ass in.

The patients from Unit Three were at their computer stations in the basement classroom. They were supposed to be completing assignments from their schools back home, but Roach hadn't put any effort into academics since his kindergarten teacher had critiqued his hand turkey, and he didn't see any reason to start now. He was motivated to brouse porn sites, however, and several hundred Access Denied messages later he was still trying to beat the hospital's Internet filter program. In the carrel to his right Molly was having more success combing websites for love spells. The object of all this activity, Russell, was sitting in a carrel to her right, studying a map of Greater Richmond. Across the room Selena was composing a letter designed to reduce her mother to shame and guilt, and Chris was polishing a final verse for *The Loony Bin Blues*.

In the far corner Sierra had just finished taking a virtual tour of Georgetown University. She'd chosen this college only to discover it was breathtakingly expensive. She knew she was going to have to think outside the box. She'd friended Chris on Facebook before class. She wrote him a message.

sup dude? it was good talking 2 u @ the gazebo. sorry i gave u a hard x about being rich, but i guess i'm jealous. What i want most is college, but my folks can't afford it so I've been thinking about how 2 get the $. i've got an idea. i'll tell u, but promise u won't say anything, k?

She imagined her message winging through cyberspace and arriving on the other side of the room. She watched Chris read it. He turned and gave her a puzzled look. He tapped a reply and it appeared on her screen.

Okay, I'll do a benefit concert for you, but I don't have that many fans so you better plan on applying for financial aid.

Their teacher was circling the room, but for the most part she was ignoring what they were doing. Sierra knew she was taking a risk putting what she was going to say in writing, but Chris was leaving in the morning and it was now or never. *Go for it*, a little voice in her head whispered. She waited for the teacher to pass, and her fingers flew quickly over the keyboard.

Selena proofread her letter.

Dear Mama,

Three weeks down, five to go. Don't feel bad about them putting me in an insane asylum just cause you taught me to shoplift. Don't feel guilty cause people will think I'm crazy and I've got a criminal record. Lots of mental patients turn out to be big successes.

The other kids are here for felonies and bad families. My roommate Molly is a witch, but I think she's really a Baptist. We have work program every night. I get to scrub floors and clean toilets, so at least I'm picking up a useful trade. Like they say, "If you believe it, you can achieve it." Maybe if I work real hard someday I can scrub toilets in the White House.

Tell Juwayne, Denishia and Lashawn they better lose their sticky fingers or get better at it than their big sister.

Don't Worry About Your Loving Daughter,

Selena

Pleased with her effort, she smiled.

Molly scooted her chair back and stole another peek at Russell. He reminded her of the picture of the Roman emperor in her sixth grade history book. She imagined him in a laurel wreath and a toga. So far all the love spells she'd found on the Internet called for supplies she didn't have at the hospital, like jasmine incense and purple candles and peacock feathers. Frustrated, she'd composed her own spell.

All my love I send to you
Without incense, wax or feathers
Pretty soon you'll find that I'm not
Like the Brittanys and Heathers
Before we go our separate ways
I will hold you in my arms
The goddess Kore will convey
The mystick magick of my charms
Until you accept our love as fact
I will paint my face in black.

She realized the teacher was reading over her shoulder. "I finished my algebra," she said quickly. "I'm writing a poem."

"That's a very creative poem, Molly. Would you like share it with the class?"

"NO!" She highlighted it and pressed the Delete button. She glanced over and saw Russell's head still buried in his map of Richmond.

Norman retrieved the balled-up letter from his trashcan and smoothed it out on his desk. Maybe he was being rash. Maybe he needed to let the professional beggars at the university give him the celebrity treatment. As long as they saw him as a prospect he'd have them by the balls. They'd wine and dine him for months before they realized there was never going to be a Norman Chase Chair for some geriatric egghead to rest his withered buns in. In the meanwhile his hospital would reap the benefit of the free PR. It was exactly the kind of manipulative thinking that had gotten him where he was today.

He glanced at the name on the letter: *Edward Neill*, who'd signed it simply *Ed*. He took a piece of his personalized stationery and composed a handwritten reply.

Dear Ed,

Words can't describe how moved I was to read your letter about my work at the Riverside Center. I have many fond memories of Virginia Tech, and it's great to be back in touch.

My first reaction to your suggestion about honoring me was reluctance. My work here is its own reward, and I don't seek any applause or acclaim. As I mulled it over, however, I realized that those of us who have been successful in our endeavors have an obligation to inspire the next generation to pursue their own dreams. The more I thought about it, the more I realized I want to share the full range of my resources with your students. I'd like to try to make a difference in their lives, just as I've been trying to make a difference in young lives here in Richmond.

He congratulated himself on this inspired choice of words. When this flunky fundraiser read *I want to share the full range of my resources* he'd pee in his pants. He imagined him rushing into the president's office, excitedly waving his letter.

Please give me a call ASAP so we can schedule a time for your magazine folks to come. You mentioned visiting the campus. Weekdays are pretty hectic, but I could try to slip away on a Friday in September or October and spend a weekend. Maybe we could even check out a little Hokie football action?

Thanks again for your kind letter. I'm looking forward to returning to Blacksburg.

Always a Hokie,
Norman Chase

Sierra watched Chris's face as he read her follow-up message.

u know mr chase, the dude with the ferrari who owns this place? he's super rich. maurice the aide says the ferrari's a '98 f355. i googled it and it's worth $135,000! i've been cleaning his office every nite for my chore. i saw his coat hanging in the corner & the label said zegna. i looked up zegna suits & they're italian and cost $2000! he's a letch. he's been coming back to work every nite just to watch me. u mite think this is crazy, but I'm going to let him come on to me. he can get in a lot of trouble for trying to seduce a minor. This place could even get shut down. rich folks like to buy their way out of messes, so i'll let him buy his way out of this one with a scholarship to Georgetown. i need ur help. we'll talk later.

He looked at her and she could see he didn't know what to make of this, but she felt sure he'd come around. She needed a witness to walk in and catch them in the act and rescue her before things got out of hand. Chris was a perfect accomplice because he was leaving in the morning, and once he was gone he couldn't be intimidated by Chase. She sent him a reminder to delete the message. He complied and Operation Scholarship went to wherever deleted messages go.

Chapter 5

Zenia St. Clair was more than a licensed movement therapist. She was an interpreter of dreams, a crystal healer, a guided imagery specialist, a past-life tracker, a licensed numerologist, a holistic reflexologist and a certified aromatherapist. She facilitated channeling and read energy vibrations. She meditated at dawn and dusk. She painted mandalas in the sand. She had released her inner child. She practiced Tai Chi and Hatha Yoga. She was metaphysically aligned, and in tune with the music of the spheres and the Tao of the universe. She had clarity of purpose. She was a politically correct macro-vegan feminist who lived in harmony with nature. But at the moment she was royally pissed.

"Daniel, all I want you to do is take a deep breath and release it very slowly," she struggled to conceal her growing frustration with her client. "As you release it, I want you to feel all the negative energy leaving your body. Now is that too hard to do?"

Roach slouched against the wall and refused to cooperate. "Yeah, I don't know how to breathe. And don't call me fuckin' Daniel. Nobody calls me Daniel."

"I'd appreciate it if you wouldn't use language like that. If you'd rather be called Danny, I'll …"

"Call me Roach."

"Names are very important," she said in a voice that sounded like she was speaking at a kindergarten commencement. "They're outward signs of our inner essence. Our names are our energy signatures. Do you really want people to think of you as a disgusting household pest?"

"Who gives a shit? I'm puttin' my bandanna back on."

"Leave it off, Danny," she said sternly. "It distracts me from my work. And I refuse to call you Roach."

Roach retied his headgear.

Zenia hardly knew where to begin. She couldn't do body imaging work with an antagonistic 15-year-old who didn't mind if people saw him as a repulsive insect. She had friends named Wolf and Moonlight, and a friend named Heather who'd changed her name to Feather. It was important for people to feel comfortable with their energy signatures. She'd even considered changing her own to something that better captured her spiritual essence, like Dreamcloud. But Roach? She fortified herself with a cleansing breath. "Why don't we get back to work?" she suggested with a forced smile.

"Like this is your job? They pay you to run around in tights and tell people to breathe?"

Zenia felt the anger welling inside her. Her physical vessel was so finely tuned she could actually taste the anger as it traveled from her stomach to her throat. "Yes they do," she hissed. "And if you don't stop being such an obnoxious little turd, I'm going to smack that filthy mouth of yours."

"That's better," he congratulated her. Now they were speaking the same language.

Chris was propped on his pillow, staring forlornly out of his room's lone window. Little video clips had been playing and replaying in his head. Sierra in the bushes with a deputy sheriff. Sierra seducing the hospital administrator. Sierra skipping off to college with a Sugar Daddy scholarship. He'd been infatuated with this girl for weeks, but now he was having second, third and fourth thoughts.

"Earth to Captain Dewberry," Russell interrupted his meditation. "I'll let you in on something, but you've got to promise to keep it to yourself."

"I've got enough secrets, Russell."

"You're not the only one leaving here tomorrow," he informed him. "My social worker's taking me fishing and I'm running off. If I go to court they'll stick me in a foster home, but if I run off they'll forget about me. I'll get a job and send our landlord money to take care of Mom." He'd been thinking about it all afternoon, and now that he'd finally said it out loud, his plan sounded reasonable enough.

"What about school?"

"I'll get a GED."

"Where will you go?"

"Virginia Beach."

"Stay in touch," Chris requested. "I want to know how the story ends."

"Okay," Russell agreed. "I'll Facebook you."

"You're forgetting that when we get out of here they'll give our cell phones back," Chris reminded him. "You can text or call."

"You'll get yours," Russell said. "I'll have to leave mine behind and get a new one."

"Maybe you can get a better calling plan," Chris looked on the bright side.

"You don't have to worry about calling plans because you're rich, Dewberry."

"I'm not rich! Why does everyone around here think I'm rich?"

"Look at the way you dress, man."

Chris looked at his frayed shorts, threadbare T-shirt and worn Birkenstocks. "You call these nice clothes?"

"Only a rich guy can afford to dress that shitty."

"You'll eat those words when I'm on the cover of *Rolling Stone*."

"Sierra will make the cover of the *SI Swimsuit Issue* before you make page 82 of *Rolling Stone*."

Chris rolled his eyes. "Man, you don't want to know about that girl."

"What do I not want to know about her?"

He took a deep breath and gave his roommate an earful.

It was quitting time, and as Dr. Garcia made his way across the parking lot to the ancient Mercedes he'd purchased the week before, he saw Zenia St. Clair heading his way. Her black leotards hugged her skeletal figure and unfortunately left nothing to his imagination. She caught up to him. "Dr. Garcia!"

"Yes?"

"I just want you to know I'm glad you're here. If there's one thing this hospital needs it's more cultural diversity."

"Yes?" He had no idea what this strange woman was babbling about, but he'd discovered that if he said *yes* in the form of a question it seemed to satisfy these people.

"You have a natural healing energy. I can feel your aura."

"Yes?"

She slipped between the doctor and his car, blocking his escape route. "I know you probably don't have time to listen to my problems, but that little creep Danny Roach is driving me nuts. He's so resistant to therapy he makes me want to pull my hair out. Do these kids ever get to you?"

The doctor pointed at his balding pate. "I am having too leetle hair."

"You shouldn't feel self-conscious about hair loss," she counseled him. "A lot of bald men are very sexy. But if you're worried, I know a terrific holistic hair stylist."

He studied this odd creature, wiggling this way and that and talking about sex. It was obvious: she wanted a Latin lover. It was equally obvious a vow of celibacy would be preferable. He ducked around her and dove into the safety of his automobile.

The old clunker's diesel engine clattered to life and Zenia hovered at the window. "CAN YOU GIVE ME ANY IDEAS ABOUT HOW TO HANDLE MY FRUSTRATION WITH DANNY ROACH?"

"PEELS," the doctor prescribed, and he motored off.

Zenia thought about this advice. Peels were a departure from the essential oils she used in aromatherapy, but technically they would work the same way. She could steep some citrus peels in boiling water, drape a towel over her head and inhale the healing vapors. It was a refreshingly creative suggestion, one that gave her faith in this new psychiatrist, who obviously shared her holistic orientation. Pleased that she'd found a progressive ally, she headed home to treat herself to citrus therapy.

Chapter 6

Kate's yellow Mini Cooper crawled slowly up Hull Street, passing some young toughs idling on a corner with two pit bulls. Once she would have believed that beneath these hardened exteriors were wounded children who just needed some love and attention. Now, after two years of working with some of these young toughs, she knew that beneath their hardened exteriors were concealed weapons. She floored her Mini and shot quickly past them.

The Old Dominion Pawn Palace sparkled like a diamond in the urban rubble. She pulled into the weed-choked parking lot and made her way over shards of glass to the front door, where a stadium-type speaker was blaring a strange version of *Macarena*. Gold and black letters announced that the business was open from nine to six and the proprietor was Unkie Wilson. The door was locked, but she could see a dapper-looking black man at the cash register. She knocked and waved.

He came to the door and ushered her in. "Let me guess. You lost some valuables in a burglary?"

"Do I look distraught?"

"No, but you don't look like you're here to pawn the family jewels. I'm Unkie."

She shook his hand. "I'm Kate Oxley."

"Pleased to meet you, Ms. Oxley. Please forgive the music."

"It's hard to forgive."

"*Alvin and the Chipmunks' Dance Mixes*," he revealed. "Quite possibly the worst recording ever made. *Love Shack* is the album's only saving grace. The local hoodlums used to hang out in front of the shop and it was ruining my business. I didn't have any luck chasing them off until I put up that speaker and started playing show tunes and polkas. I hit gold with the Chipmunks." He smiled slyly. "Now they won't come within two blocks of the place."

"You're a creative man," she said.

"No, just a desperate one. I wrote a fan letter to the Chipmunks and suggested they record some operas. They sent me a nice letter back saying they felt there was 'a limited potential audience for such a release'." His brown old eyes danced merrily "Such a shame. Alvin will never sing at the Met."

"I won't take much of your time," she promised him. "I'm just looking for Grace Moss."

"Grace lives upstairs. I'm her landlord."

"I'm working with her son, Russell. I don't know if you're aware of his legal problems."

"I know they sent him away for selling drugs. Russell's a fine boy. He used to come in here all the time and look at my cameras. I gave him a good deal on a Nikon and some lenses. He takes wonderful pictures. Now how can a boy like that be a menace to society?"

"I don't think he is. If you're interested in his situation I'll bring you up to date."

"All right. Why don't we go to my office?" He led her past a jewelry display and a wall of stringed instruments to a small cubbyhole in the back of the store. A framed photograph of a younger Unkie caught her eye. He was standing at the entrance of Richmond's grandest hotel in a doorman's uniform. "I see you worked at The Jefferson."

"Yes, I was there twenty-eight years. I grew tired of being wallpaper in other people's lives. This little pawnshop isn't much, but at least I'm not wallpaper now."

She inspected the picture more closely. "You cut a dashing figure."

"I made a good living. I made enough in tips to buy this building and start my own business."

"That's quite a success story. Excuse me for being nosy. I'm curious by nature."

"And I'm talkative," he said with a smile, "so we're an excellent match."

"Let's talk about the Moss family."

"Let's do." He patted a chair. "Have a seat."

Richmond's Fan District was one of the South's historic neighborhoods. Named for the pattern of its streets, the Fan was an eternal work-in-progress, caught up in an endless cycle of urban decay and rebirth. Norman had purchased his Kensington Avenue townhouse with an eye to value. His wife had hired a small army of decorators and construction workers to transform the sorry structure into a tasteful palace, one that would obscure their lower middle class roots and hint that they were Southern aristocracy.

This evening the Chases were in their crystal-chandeliered dining room, polishing off a dinner Meg had taken lock, stock and curry powder from the Food Network. As the meal came to an end Norman had a surprise for his family. "How would you like to go to Blacksburg this fall and see the Hokies play?" he asked them.

"Awesome," thirteen-year-old Sean reacted.

Nine-year-old Drucilla wrinkled her nose. "What are Hokies?"

"The Virginia Tech football team, Brain Dead," her brother educated her.

"Sean called me Brain Dead!"

"Apologize to your sister," Meg ordered him.

"I'm sorry I called you Brain Dead. It's wrong to make fun of the mentally retarded."

"Mom, Sean called me mentally retarded!"

Meg turned wearily to Norman. Her husband's sudden interest in family activities had taken her by surprise. "That's a wonderful idea, Norman. You've been so wrapped up in your work lately we've hardly seen you."

"Someone's got to pay the bills," he liked to remind her. "I had a letter from Virginia Tech today. They want to do a story about me in their alumni magazine. I'm going to make them sweeten the pot with some football tickets."

"Dru doesn't like football," Sean said. "Can we take one of my friends in her place?"

"No!" Meg snapped.

"Are we going to the beach this summer?" Dru asked her parents.

"Yes, dear," Meg promised her. "We have a beach house we never use."

Norman knew where the conversation was heading and he pushed himself away from the table. "I'm not going to spend another evening bickering about that damned sand castle. I've got some business to take care of at the hospital."

His wife's eyes narrowed. "You act like you'd rather spend time with those little hellions than with your own children." She remembered an article she'd read recently in the *Gifted Child Quarterly* about parents undermining one another's authority, and she bit her lip. She didn't want to do anything to make her own offspring turn out like the hellions in question. "But if you really need to go, go."

"Thank you, Your Royal Majesty."

Her jaw tightened. "Tell me, Norman, are other women's husbands such condescending SOB's, or I am just lucky?"

"What's an SOB?" Dru asked as her father stormed out of the room with china and silver quaking.

"A son of a bitch," her brother educated her. "That's what Mom thinks Dad is."

"Sean!!!"

"You said it."

It was Meg's turn to leave the room.

Alone with his sister, Sean looked at her. "All the parents in the world and we get these guys."

Kate rapped on the flimsy door. She heard bare feet pad across a creaky floor, and a disheveled brunette with a cigarette hanging from her lips opened it and studied her warily. From his hospital records she knew Russell's mother was thirty-three, but she looked fifty. "Hi, Grace. I'm Kate Oxley. I'm the clinical director at the Riverside Center."

"Listen, honey, if you're here to try to talk me into going to a rehab program you're wasting your breath. Been there, done that, got the T-shirt. I've been Twelve Stepped to death. Never worked, never will."

"No, no," she said quickly. "I've got a message from Russell. He asked me to come by and see you."

"Come on in. Don't mind the mess. It's the maid's day off." She wheezed at her own joke and led her to the kitchen, where they sat at a Formica table scarred with cigarette burns. She lit another Salem from the one she was smoking. "I guess Russell's told you all about me."

"Russell's pretty private. He doesn't volunteer much about his home life."

"If I was your mother, you wouldn't either. You know the difference between a drunk and an alcoholic?"

"No, I'm afraid I don't."

"Drunks don't have to go to meetings."

"Mrs. Moss ..."

"Honey, I'm no Missus. Call me Grace."

"If you don't call me honey," she bargained. "Russell wants you to come by the hospital tonight. Visiting hours are between 6:30 and 7:30."

"He sent you here to cure me," she refused to accept her son's invitation at face value. "I know how that boy works. He's always got some plan to rescue me. You want a beer? You look like you can use one."

She felt like one, too, but she decided it wouldn't be very professional to toss back a beer with her client's alcoholic parent. "No, thanks. Russell has something he needs to talk to you about."

Grace's eyes narrowed. "The cops aren't pumping him for information about me, are they?"

"I'll let him explain it. Are you worried about being arrested?"

"Nah," she dismissed the idea with a wave of her cigarette. "I just smoke a little pot and drink a little beer. They don't throw you in jail for that."

Kate found the woman's candor refreshing, even if she wasn't making a very good case against foster care. She decided to bring up something she was curious about. "Russell never talks about his father."

"He doesn't know who he is."

"He must wonder."

"Oh, yeah. He used to pester the hell out of me."

"Don't you think he has a right to know?"

"Yeah. If I knew I'd tell him."

"Oh."

"Lady, I can tell you're a shrink. You've only been here five minutes and you're analyzing the hell out of me."

"It goes with the territory," Kate was unapologetic. She glanced at her watch. "Are you going to the hospital? Unkie said he'd take you."

"Yeah, I guess I better go play like a mother."

She remembered Russell's other request. "Oh, and he'd like you to bring his camera."

"Why's he need a camera in a hospital?"

"He doesn't, but he seems pretty attached to it."

Grace smiled mischievously. "Want to smoke a joint before you go?"

"Are you serious?"

"Honey, that was a joke," she said. "Boy, you should have seen the look on your face."

Kate made her way out to her car with the Chipmunks singing *Stayiin' Alive.* "Ah, ha, ha, ha, stayin' alive, stayin' alive," she harmonized with Alvin, Simon and Theodore.

Chapter 7

The six patients on Unit Three were in the recreation room when Sierra sidled up to Chris. "Let's talk now," she whispered. "We'll pretend like we're playing checkers." He followed her across the room with all the enthusiasm of a condemned prisoner walking his Final Mile. They sat down at the game board and arranged the checkers. On the other side of the room the two aides who were supposed to be watching them were engrossed in a movie.

Chris searched for an escape hatch. "I don't know about this, Sierra," he said.

She looked him deeply in the eyes. "Chris, I really need your help. If Mr. Chase comes on to me, isn't that his problem? And if he offers me something to keep quiet, isn't it just a private arrangement between the two of us? When he asks if there's anything I need, I'll tell him I need money for college."

"It sounds a lot like blackmail," he said uncomfortably.

"It's not blackmail if he makes us an offer and we accept it."

He couldn't help noticing he'd been promoted to partner status. "What's this *us* and *we* shit? I don't want this guy's money."

An aide glanced over and Sierra scooted a checker forward. "I hate my life, Chris," she said with obvious passion. "This is my best way out. Mr. Chase is filthy rich and he's got the hots for me. How often is something like this going to happen? Every night he comes back to his office and pretends like he's working at his desk. He stacks papers and scribbles notes and gives me these looks. I'm going to make him think his fantasy is coming true, and then he's going to make mine come true."

"What fantasy is that?"

"Going to Georgetown."

"Georgetown! Aren't you aiming kind of high?"

She smiled confidently. "If I can talk Mr. Chase into giving me $200,000 I can talk Georgetown University into letting me in."

Chris nearly fell off his chair. "You're going to ask him for *$200,000?*"

"No," she explained. "I'm going to ask him to send me to Georgetown and help him do the math. Think about it, Chris. Suppose you were super rich. What if something happened that could give your wife grounds for divorce and put you out of business and send you to prison? If you had a ton of money, wouldn't you be willing to spend some of it to make the mess go away?"

He saw her point. He also saw a babe in a halter-top and short-shorts begging for his help. His hormones were battling his brain cells. His brain threw in the towel. "So what do you want me to do?"

"Open a door."

"That's all?"

"Just open his office door and call my name, like you're looking for me. He'll think you accidentally walked in on us and you won't get in any trouble. That way you'll rescue me before anything happens and I'll have a witness so it won't be just my word against his."

Chris was relieved to learn that his role was so minor. "So all I have to do is walk in and act surprised?"

"Yeah. Think you can handle it?"

"I've been known to open doors."

"Okay, here's the plan," she got down to specifics. "I clean his office at eight. I usually ignore him, but tonight I'll act like I'm interested in him and lead him on. I'll make him undress and then I'll say I'm going to lock the door, but I'll leave it unlocked. At exactly 8:20 I'll have him down on the rug in front of his desk. That's when you walk in."

"You've been giving this a lot of thought, haven't you?"

"You would, too, if your whole future depended on it."

He wanted to ask if she would be naked, too, but he didn't have the nerve.

"When you open the door and call my name he'll freak out and start getting dressed. He'll know he can't lie his way out of it, so he'll have to buy his way out."

Chris marveled at this little scheme. However the drama played out, his parents were coming in the morning and his involvement would be short-lived. What could he lose? "Okay, I'm in."

"I'll pay you," she offered.

"I don't want any money."

"Really?"

He smiled. "I'm rich. Can't you tell by the way I dress?"

Andrew turned off Monument Avenue and into the driveway that led to his basement apartment. As he climbed out of his Jeep he saw his octogenarian landlady sitting on the porch in her wicker rocker, nursing her gin and tonic and staring with disgust at the statue at the intersection of Monument and Roseneath. "Admiring the city's public art, Miss Beauregard?" he baited her.

"It's the most ridiculous thing I've ever seen!" she launched into a tirade he'd heard before. "Monument Avenue is supposed to be a memorial to the Confederacy. So whose statues do we have? Robert E. Lee, Jeb Stuart, Jefferson Davis, Stonewall Jackson, Matthew Fontaine Maury - and Arthur Ashe! It ruins the whole historic context of the neighborhood." The War Between the States had never quite ended for some Virginians, and his landlady was one of them. When the Richmond City Council voted to place a statue honoring one of Richmond's most famous native sons in front of her home, Miss Beauregard had gained a neighbor she didn't appreciate.

Andrew climbed the steps to the porch where she held forth every evening, offering alcohol-fueled opinions to anyone who made the mistake of drawing within earshot. "I've been meaning to ask you this, Miss B. Are you any kin to General Beauregard? The guy at Fort Sumter?"

She sat up proudly. "Pierre Gustave Toutant Beauregard was my great-great grandfather. That's how I qualified for membership in the U.D.C."

"The U.D.C.?"

"The United Daughters of the Confederacy, dear. I can see you have some holes in your education."

"The fact that you're Confederate royalty doesn't have anything to do with your opinion of Mr. Ashe, does it?"

"It most certainly does! My father built this house on this very spot because he thought the city was going to put a statue of our ancestor here. He saved Richmond in the Battle of Drewry's Bluff, you know. They waited seventy-five years and then they put up a statue of a man in shorts with a tennis racquet! I don't know what this city's coming to."

Andrew was tempted to say that it was coming to terms with its racist past, but he held his tongue. "Was General Beauregard from Richmond?"

"No, dear, he was from New Orleans. That's why he had all those fancy French names. He was the superintendent of West Point for five days, and then he resigned to fight for the Cause. Would you like something to drink? I can talk about him for hours."

"That's a tempting offer, Miss B, but I'm going to grab a bite and get my tackle box in order. I'm taking one of my clients fishing in the morning."

"Fishing! Are they paying you to fish?"

He grinned. "Sort of. I've got to find this boy a new home. This is how I'm bonding with him."

"I see you coming and going with your rod and reel all the time. You're quite the nature lover, aren't you?"

"I'm not much of a city boy, if that's what you mean. I'm not planning to hang around Richmond forever."

"I don't blame you one bit. If I were younger I'd get out of here myself. God knows the future's not what it used to be." She hoisted herself from her chair. "I'm going to freshen my drink."

He watched Miss Beauregard dodder into her home's cavernous interior. He raised a clenched fist to the neighborhood's other misfit. "Give 'em hell, Arthur."

There's nothing sweet about these Adelines, Kate thought as she listened to her choral group bickering. The chorus had a jaded past. The members had broken away from the Greater Richmond Sweet Adelines when Penelope Swope had discovered she wasn't going to be promoted to director. When Penelope recruited Kate she hadn't bothered to tell her she was joining a renegade chorus, or that the city had a long-established, more harmonious chapter of the same organization.

Penelope peered at the singers over her half-frame glasses. "Do we all have our sheet music?"

The choristers examined their music with puzzled expressions. "*A Salute to the Captain and Tennille*?" Kate asked. "Is this the best we can do for the state competition?"

"I thought we needed something bouncy to set us apart from the other groups," Penelope explained.

She smelled a fiasco in the making. "This is going to set us apart, all right. All the others are singing patriotic medleys."

"I'm listing it in the program as *A Salute to the Captain*," Penelope said. "The judges will think it's another boring flag-waver, and then we'll get up there and knock 'em dead with *Muskrat Love*."

"The winners have to sing on the steps of the State Capitol, Penelope," Ruth Cohen reminded her. "If we win we'll look like idiots standing up there singing about Muskrat Suzie and Muskrat Sam doing the jitterbug in muskrat land. For heaven's sake, we're a chorus, not a comedy troop."

"You'll have to trust me on this," Penelope insisted.

"That's what General Custer said," Kate muttered. She'd joined the Adelines looking for something that would help her unwind from her work at Riverside Center. It hadn't taken her long to realize this activity was more stressful than her job. She made a mental note: *Quit the Adelines, get a life.*

Chapter 8

It seemed ironic to Russell that his mother was visiting him in a hospital since she was the one who needed treatment. Sometimes he doubted there was a God, because any halfway decent Supreme Being wouldn't let things turn out like this. He'd taken his mother and his landlord to the gazebo, where Grace had fired up a cigarette in violation of the hospital's No Smoking policy. He didn't call her on it; tobacco was the least she would need after she heard the news. Unkie was giving him knowing glances. He decided that Kate must have clued him in. "Listen, I've got something to tell you," he cut to the chase after they'd been talking for a few minutes. "They're planning to put me in a foster home until I turn eighteen."

"I knew it!" Grace said. "I smelled a rat when that social worker came over and gave me the third degree. They'll have to put up a hell of a fight to get you."

"Don't waste your time trying to fight it, Mom. The judge has already made up his mind. He thinks he's rescuing me."

"From what?"

He started to say "you", but he thought better of it. "Drugs."

"You'd think the authorities could overlook one little mistake," Unkie said softly.

"I've made more than one mistake, Unkie. I've been dealing since September and I didn't get busted until March. Where do you think the rent money's been coming from?"

Unkie winced and made a face. "Do they know that?"

He threw up his hands. "Who knows? Who cares? There's nothing left for them to take away. First they took my school and my friends. Now they're taking my home and my family. They'll probably stick me in some redneck place in the middle of nowhere."

"Maybe if I say I'll go to rehab they'll change their minds," Grace offered bravely.

"They know your history with rehab, Mom. Even if you went, it still wouldn't get me back in school. They're hung up on getting me back for my senior year."

"There must be something we can do," Grace said.

"There's nothing you can do, but there's something I can do. I'm running away tomorrow."

Unkie frowned. "Now how will that help things, Russell?"

"I'll get a job and send you the money to take care of Mom. I'll give you some now for the next couple of months." He grabbed his backpack, unzipped it and pulled out his Nikon. Turning his back to the building to avoid prying eyes, he popped the camera open and removed twelve $100 bills he'd tucked where the battery should have been. He unfolded them, handed four to his wide-eyed landlord and stuck the rest in his pocket. He fished the battery from his backpack and installed it in the camera. "Say cheese," he said.

If knowledge were power Raleigh Jones would have been the Riverside Center's Chief Executive Officer. A shadowy presence at the front gate, Raleigh sat perched on a stool in the security booth, chain-smoking Camels and gathering and dispensing rumor, gossip and innuendo. This still left him plenty of time for his other job, bookmaking. He was Richmond's only bookie with a drive-up window, and after fifteen years in the business he'd come to recognize the wisdom of the mantra *location, location, location*. Lately his business had been suffering from the growing popularity of online gambling. The surrounding states were opening casinos, but he wasn't worried about Virginia following their example. It seemed unlikely that the state that had spawned the ministries of Pat Robertson and Jerry Falwell would embrace casino gambling.

When he wasn't studying odds and accepting bets Raleigh spent his time thumbing through sports magazines. It was a perfect arrangement. In fact, the only thing he didn't like about his job was his boss, who had become wealthy doing even less than he did. An instinctive entrepreneur, Raleigh had been lying in wait for years hoping to come up with some dirt on Norman Chase that he could use to extract a level of compensation more in line with his talents. He had nothing to show for these eagle-eyed efforts, but recently he'd seen a light at the end of the tunnel. For the past three weeks his employer had been coming back to the hospital at the same time every evening. At first he'd assumed he was just trying to get away from his high-maintenance wife, but he didn't hang around long enough for that explanation to make sense. He'd brought his high-powered binoculars to work to look into the matter, but whenever he focused on the administrator's window, all he saw was Chase shuffling papers while a young patient cleaned his office. A half-hour would pass and then he would leave. He decided he was probably cooking the books. He needed to chat up Bernice in accounting and have her take a closer look at things.

Raleigh saw Norman's Ferrari streaking his way like a silver bullet, and he glanced at his watch. It was 7:50; exactly the same time he'd been showing up every night. The car glided to a smooth stop at the gated entrance. "Good evening, Mr. Chase," he tipped his cap. "Working late again?"

"Yes, I am, Raleigh. The secret to getting ahead in life is working twice as hard as the next fellow."

"You're so right," Raleigh endorsed this sentiment. As a security guard his first priority was guarding his own security, so he made a habit of agreeing with any ridiculous statement that issued from his employer's mouth.

Norman studied him fondly. "I like your attitude, Raleigh. How long have you been with us now?"

"Fifteen years," Raleigh said. He hoped this would somehow lead to his long-overdue raise.

"You're indispensable, Raleigh. Nobody does what you do better than you."

"That's probably true," Raleigh hadn't thought about it before.

"In fact, I've decided to start an Employee of the Year Award and give you the first one."

Raleigh suspected this award would take the form of a photocopied certificate in a cheap plastic frame, presented in lieu of his raise. "I really appreciate that, Mr. Chase," he lied through his teeth. He resented the fact that his job had reduced him to this level of ass kissing. He watched the Ferrari swoop up the hill and he fingered his binoculars.

When Norman entered his office he heard the phone ringing. One of the idiots on his staff had apparently failed to get the message they were supposed to leave him alone when he came back in the evenings. He pressed his speakerphone. "What do you want?" he growled.

"It's Rolina, Mr. Chase," the nurse in charge of the evening shift identified herself. "We've got a little situation I need to ask you about."

"You know I don't deal with behavior problems. Call Kate."

"This is more of an administrative question, sir."

"All right, make it quick."

"A mother came to visit her son tonight and she brought him a fancy camera," she reported. "He wants to keep it in his room, but I took it away and locked it up. Now he's throwing a fit and claiming we don't have a right to take it."

"Is he on a suicide watch? Is he going to hang himself with the strap?"

"Oh, no, sir. I wouldn't have called you in that case."

"So what's the big deal?"

"If he takes pictures of the other patients, wouldn't it be a violation of their right to privacy?"

"Their *right to privacy?*" Norman asked incredulously. "Where do you come up with this kind of crap, Rolina? These little bastards don't have any privacy. Give him the damn camera and tell him not to take any dirty pictures. Let 'em have their hobbies. It keeps 'em out of our hair."

"Yes, sir. Like I said before I hate to bother you, but I wasn't sure how to handle it. But if he's got your permission, that's all we need."

"He's got it. If anything else comes up, call Kate." He glanced at his watch. It was nearly time for his little hoochie mama to show up. He went in his bathroom, combed his hair and admired himself in the mirror.

Dr. Garcia was watching Elmer Fudd chasing Bugs Bunny with a double barrel shotgun when his phone rang. He grabbed it, expecting to hear one of the nice people who called him in the evenings to offer him fabulous gifts and prizes. Yesterday he had given them permission to put new aluminum siding on the house he was renting.

"This is Zenia St. Clair, Doctor," a familiar voice gushed. "I took your advice about the peels. They were fabulous! I used six different kinds, and I'm very centered now. I feel like I've been on a tropical cruise."

"You are taking six kinds of the peels?"

"Yes. It was your idea, remember?"

"You are doing what weeth the peels?"

"Inhaling them," she explained. "Breathing them up my nose."

There was a brief silence as Dr. Garcia considered this. "Where ees your casa, Zenia?" he asked nervously.

"My house? 2824 Bon Oaks Lane. Are you coming over? I'll run over to the grocery store and get some more fruit."

"No, no, no! You stay there!" He hung up and called 911 the way he'd seen people do on television. "I am Doctor Garcia of the psychiatry," he informed the dispatcher who answered. "A woman called Zenia puts the peels up her nose at 2824 Bon Oaks Lane."

"We prosecute prank callers," the dispatcher warned him.

"Overdosing of the *peels*."

"Oh, *pills*," she broke through the language barrier. "I didn't understand you, Doctor. Do you know what she took?"

"She ees taking six kinds. I am not knowing what."

"All right, we'll send the paramedics over. Is she one of your patients?"

"Si," he stretched the truth a bit.

"Is this woman dangerous? Do they need to take any precautions?"

"She ees loco in the head."

"Okay. They'll probably take her to Chippenham and pump her stomach and keep her for observation."

"Gracias." Pleased he'd been able to intervene in this crisis, he hung up. His coworker wouldn't appreciate what was about to happen to her, but she would thank him later. Feeling good about the way he'd handled the situation, he returned to his cartoon. These stories were childish and silly, but he was learning English by listening to the simple dialogue. He hadn't been able to find *wascally* or *wabbit* in his pocket dictionary. This could only mean one thing: he needed a bigger dictionary.

Rolina looked up from the nursing notes she'd been writing with the diligence of a Twelfth Century monk copying Holy Scripture. She saw Chris Dewberry dashing by the nurses' station. "We're having a little going away party for you, Chris," she called to him.

He screeched to a halt. "Now?"

"Right after chores. We're gathering in the courtyard."

"Great. Thanks." He started up the hall again and he saw Russell heading his way.

"Hang on, Dewberry, I want to show you something. I need to see Rolina first."

"Okay, hurry up." All these little delays were making him antsy; he'd synchronized watches with Sierra and she was expecting him to appear in Mr. Chase's office at precisely 8:20. He bounced nervously from foot to foot.

Russell popped his head in the nurse's station. "What 'd Chase say?"

"He said you can keep the camera," Rolina informed him.

He reached in and snagged his pack. He was prepared to sacrifice his camera for his freedom if necessary, but he hated the idea. The thought that this institution could confiscate his most valuable possession had only strengthened his resolve to leave.

Rolina wagged an admonishing finger at him. "No dirty pictures. Mr. Chase's orders. Are we clear?"

"Gee, I don't know, Rolina. I was hoping I could talk you into posing for some nude shots."

She gave him a stern look. "Just take it and get out of here and let me catch up on my notes."

As the boys took off up the hallway, Russell pulled his Nikon out of the backpack. "This is the camera I've been telling you about."

Suddenly Chris had one of the creative inspirations that had been his lifelong blessing and curse. "How'd you like to take a $200,000 picture?" he proposed to his friend.

Chapter 9

Sierra was irked that the hospital made her do chores. She didn't mind the work itself, but Medicaid was covering her bills at this place, so she didn't understand why she had to provide them with free maid service. On the other hand, her chores had given her access to her future benefactor and inspired Operation Scholarship, so she couldn't complain. This evening she reported to the work supervisor with no intention of accepting the vacuum, mop and broom he usually loaded her down with. They didn't strike her as the right tools for seduction. "Just give me some Windex and paper towels, Malcolm. I'm doing his picture window tonight."

Malcolm adjusted his Coke bottle lenses and eyed her. "That outfit's kind of skimpy, isn't it, Sierra? You should dress better when you're working in the big man's office."

"I couldn't find my evening gown," she brushed off his suggestion. "I like to feel comfortable when I'm working." She grabbed her supplies and sashayed off.

Malcolm watched her twitching butt retreating down the hallway. "Jesus, Mary and Joseph," he muttered.

Norman was at his desk when Sierra knocked on his office door at precisely eight o'clock. "Come in, Sierra," his voice rang out.

She entered his inner sanctum. "Hi, Mr. Chase. I'm just doing your window tonight. That's okay, isn't it?"

His eyes followed her progress across the room. "Oh, sure. Whatever."

She circled behind him and stood before the large expanse of plate glass that overlooked the front lawn, parking lot and the gatehouse. "I'm going to need some help getting up on this ledge. Can you give me a

45

boost?" Norman sprang from his chair and presented a gallant hand. She climbed up on the ledge and perched precariously. "This doesn't feel very safe. Can you prop me up so I can reach the high part? Then I can do the rest myself."

Norman drew closer. "What would you like me to do?"

She felt his breath on his bare legs. "Just grab my butt to keep me from falling," she requested. "Boy, I'm sure glad nobody's listening to this."

Norman planted two eager hands on her shapely bottom. He felt Little Norm stirring in his boxer shorts. He tried to calm himself down by thinking about his wife, but Little Norm had a mind of his own. Sierra took her time cleaning the upper part of the window, rubbing with little circular motions and swaying gently to and fro. Norman's hands remained glued in place. He followed her movements like he was taking hula lessons.

She kept this up for several minutes. "Are you getting tired, Mr. Chase? Am I keeping you from your work?"

"Oh, God, no," he gasped. "Take your time, Sierra. Safety first. Here, let me get a better grip." He placed a helpful hand on one of her thighs.

She gave him a smile. "Thanks. If I'd grown up around nice guys like you, I probably wouldn't even need to be in this place."

Norman had scant interest in his patients' backgrounds, but he was suddenly very interested in this one. "Why *are* you here, Sierra?"

She continued rubbing and swaying. "Didn't you read my records?"

"No. I don't get involved with treatment end of things. I stick to the finances."

"I have low self-esteem," she reported.

"*You* have low self-esteem?" He could feel his own esteem for her growing by the second.

"Can you help me down? Oops!" She lost her balance and tumbled into his arms with the grace of a ballerina. She lingered a moment before extracting herself. "Thanks, Mr. Chase. Boy, it's a good thing you were there."

"Uh, you were saying something about, uh, low, uh, self-esteem?"

She turned her attention to the lower part of the window. "Sometimes I just feel so worthless."

"Worthless?"

"If you met my family and saw where I live you'd understand. My real name is Jolene. My father's name is Blackjack. That says just about everything you need to know."

"How could you possibly feel worthless, Sierra? You've got so much going for you! You're bright, you're a hard worker and you're an attractive young lady. Very attractive."

Sierra stole a peek at her watch; it was time to maneuver him into position. She turned and faced her benefactor, who didn't know yet that he was her benefactor. "I don't know why I feel that way. I just do."

"Has being here helped you?"

"I've figured out how to solve some of my problems, if that's what you mean." She thought about the most traumatic thing that had ever happened to her, the time one of her father's drinking buddies had backed his pickup over her Cocker Spaniel, Ginger. Her green eyes welled with tears as she thought about poor little Ginger, lifeless on the gravel in front of the bar.

"Why, Sierra, you're crying!" Norman hurried to his desk and grabbed a tissue. By now her tears were flowing like miniature waterfalls. He took the young woman in his arms to comfort her. "It's okay," he patted her head. Before he knew what was happening he was running his fingers through her long blonde tresses.

"Life is just so unfair," she said. She slipped her hands around her comforter. "I guess I just needed a good cry. I feel better now."

"Sierra, how can I convince you you're really a very, uh, worthwhile young woman?" he bleated. "I mean, is there anything in the world I can *possibly* do? You're one of the most, uh, the best, actually..." Their faces were inches apart and he read the invitation in her eyes. He gave up on words and he planted a kiss on her lips.

If there was a Richter scale for grossness, Sierra would have given this a 10, but she reminded herself that she was doing it for a higher purpose. When they made full body contact she knew she could start packing for Georgetown. "I think I've got special feelings for you, Mr. Chase," she whispered.

"I have special feelings for you, too, Sierra," he panted. "But we can't tell anyone about these feelings, can we?" He studied her questioningly.

She gave him an innocent look. "Why would we want to?"

Suddenly Norman realized the blinds were up. "I think we'd better kill the lights." He dashed over to the wall switch and turned off the light. He looked out of the window and saw Raleigh sitting faithfully at his post by the front gate.

Chris and Russell were hunkered in a little used stairwell between the hospital's first and second floors. "Let's take off our shoes," Chris said as he slipped out of his Birkenstocks. "That way Chase won't hear us coming. We'll take the picture and we'll run like hell."

Russell pulled off his Nikes. "What if we open the door and she's dusting his bookcase?"

"We'll look at the crack at the bottom. If the lights are off it means it's a go. If they're on it means something went wrong and we'll scratch."

"I still think you're nuts," Russell wanted his reservations on record in case this thing blew up. "Does she really need money this badly?"

"She's not going on a shopping spree at Aeropostale," Chris countered. "She wants an education."

"Hasn't she ever heard of financial aid?"

"It's too late to apply for the fall."

Russell played a hunch. "You're a virgin, aren't you, Dewberry?"

Chris was caught off-guard by this question. "That's kind of personal, isn't it?"

"Yeah, but you just answered it."

"And the reason you're bringing this up now?"

"We don't know what we're going to see when we open that door. If they're doing the dirty deed, don't go postal, okay?"

"Jesus, Russell."

"My mom used to whore around," Russell shared a part of his background he didn't usually talk about. "She'd pick up drunks in bars and bring them home. We lived in these dumps with paper-thin walls and I could hear everything. It drove me nuts. She finally lost her looks and had to change her ways and that's when we started running out of money. I know from experience that seeing someone you care about making it with an asshole can drive you crazy. So just be ready for it, okay? Don't rush in and try to save her. Sierra can take care of herself."

"Okay," he said quietly. "So did that whole scene like turn you off to sex?"

"No, I just don't have your level of desperation."

"I prefer to think of it as enthusiasm."

Russell returned to the business at hand. "I figure I can get off two or three shots before Chase realizes what's happening. He'll be blinded by the flashes and he won't see who took the pictures."

"This plan is better than Sierra's," Chris felt confident. "This way we're anonymous."

"He won't even know you're in on it," Russell agreed. "But he knows I've got a camera, so he'll figure out it was me. He'll try to get the picture away from me, so we'll have to stay a step ahead of him."

"How?"

"I'll switch the memory chips. If he confiscates the camera he'll get a chip with nothing on it."

Chris looked at his watch. "X minus two minutes. Let's boogie."

They left the stairwell and crept up the corridor to the office. The hall was deserted; all the activity was going on upstairs, where the other patients were finishing their chores, and in the courtyard, where the staff members were setting up for the Chris's farewell party. They reached the office and looked under the door. The light was off. Russell readied his camera and nodded to Chris.

Chris looked at his watch and slipped his hand quietly on the doorknob. "*On three*," he whispered. "*One, two, three.*" He opened the door in a swift motion.

Russell fired three shots in rapid succession, illuminating a startling tableau. Norman Chase was naked on his back on the Oriental rug in front of his desk. Sierra was topless and straddling him. He was reaching for her breasts, which she'd carefully positioned just beyond his reach. The first flash caught Norman looking at the door with a deer-in-the-headlights expression. The second and third captured a blur of activity as he scrambled to extract himself from his compromising position.

They slammed the door and sprinted up the hall. "He's not coming after us," Russell felt sure. "First he's got to get dressed, then he's got to be pissed at Sierra. That could take a while."

"God, did you see her, Russell?"

"I was busy taking pictures."

"She's awesome."

"You only saw her for a hundredth of a second, three times."

"Yeah, but I'll spend the rest of my life thinking about it."

"Get a life, Dewberry."

"I want copies of those pictures."

They reached the stairwell and put on their footwear. "We can look at the pictures later, man." He popped the memory chip out of his camera and gave it to Chris. "Stash this someplace safe."

"She's unbelievable."

Russell smiled. "Mr. Chase is probably thinking the same thing."

Chapter 10

"What the hell is going on?" Norman demanded as he grabbed his boxers. He knew exactly what was going on. The little hussy who was standing there cool as a cucumber, wiggling into her halter-top, had set him up. "What are you trying to pull, Sierra?"

Sierra arranged herself and went over to the wall switch and flicked on the light. She picked up her Windex and paper towels and headed for the door.

A half-naked Norman blocked her path. "You're not leaving here until you tell me what's going on, young lady! You seem to have forgotten you're a patient in this hospital and I'm the administrator!"

She looked him in the eyes. "I think you're the one who forgot that, Mr. Chase." She squirted him in the face with the window cleaner and left him hopping around the office, rubbing his eyes and cursing furiously.

Rolina was exiting the nurse's station when her phone rang. "Rolina!" Norman's voice had a breathless urgency she'd never heard before. "I've been thinking about what you said about that boy with the camera."

"I gave it back to him, just like you said," she reported.

"Get it back! You were absolutely right – we can't have kids running around here taking pictures of each other! Some lawyer could sue our pants off! What did you say his name is?"

"Russell Moss. He's out in the courtyard. We're having a little going away party for his roommate."

Norman scribbled the culprit's name on a scrap of paper and shoved it under his desk blotter. "Listen to me, Rolina, and listen very carefully. I want you to go out there right now, confiscate that camera and bring it to me. We can't afford to take this kind of risk. Check his pockets and if he has another memory card get it, too."

Rolina wasn't used to receiving direct marching orders from her employer, but she was a dutiful lieutenant. "I'll take care of it right away, Mr. Chase," she promised. She hung up and headed for the courtyard.

Chris was surrounded by well-wishers. He wanted to crawl off in a quiet corner with Sierra and compare notes on Operation Scholarship, but at the moment there weren't any quiet corners.

An aide named Maurice was slicing a cake that said *Good Luck, Chris.* "Is this party therapy?" Chris asked him.

"Say what?"

"You guys stick the word therapy after everything we do. When we're sleeping you probably call it slumber therapy and bill our parents for it."

"Give us some credit, man," Maurice said dryly. "We call it nocturnal behavior management."

Roach and Russell approached. "Hey, Dewberry," Roach said. "Moss is gonna take a picture of you and me and Selena. Selena, get your fat booty over here."

"You're smooth with the ladies, Roach," Maurice said.

"Yeah, I know," he missed the irony. He slung his tattooed arms around his ward mates. "Okay, man, take it."

As Russell focused his camera he sensed someone standing behind him. "No more pictures," a stern voice said. He turned and saw Rolina looking like she was ready to pounce on him. "Mr. Chase changed his mind. He wants your camera." She stuck out a hand.

"He's takin' a picture," Roach complained. "If Chase don't like it, he can kiss my ass. Go on, Russell."

Rolina glared at him. "You would like to leave here someday, wouldn't you, Roach?"

"Yeah, so I won't have to put up with bitches like you."

The nurse started to reply, but she decided she couldn't afford to get distracted from the task at hand. "Give the camera, Russell. We'll put it someplace safe until you're ready to leave."

Russell backed away. "I won't take any more pictures. Honest."

Her hand remained outstretched.

"Give it to her, man," Chris urged him. "If you don't she'll get the goon squad to wrestle it away from you and it'll get busted up."

"We have a goon squad?" Maurice asked.

Russell opened the camera and removed the one-gig memory card.

Rolina's eyes narrowed. "What are you doing?"

"Saving my pictures. You can have the camera."

"Mr. Chase wants the card, too."

"I'll bet he does."

"Just give it to her, Russell," Chris said. "It's not worth it."

"But these are *my* pictures."

"We'll take good care of them," Rolina promised as she relieved him of the camera and card. *Mission accomplished*, she congratulated herself. "Do you have any more cards?"

Russell turned his pants pockets inside out. "Nope. You can strip search me if you want."

"I'll take your word for it." Rolina wheeled and hurried off with her trophies.

Norman heard clip clopping in the hallway. He poked his head out and saw Rolina heading his way with the camera. This big, horse-faced woman reminded him of a Clydesdale, but he liked Clydesdales; they were sturdy and reliable. "Did you get it?"

She reached in one of the kangaroo pockets of her nurse's jacket and waved the card. "It's right here."

Norman snatched the incriminating evidence. "You're a model of efficiency, Rolina. What did he say when you took it?"

"He wasn't happy."

"Lock up the camera," he ordered her. "If he complains, tell him to come see me."

Rolina watched with wide eyes as her boss pulled a hammer from his desk and smashed the memory card to smithereens. "Boy, you really mean business."

He gave it a few more whacks for good measure. "Good work, Rolina."

"I take my job very seriously, Mr. Chase."

Norman slipped an arm around the nurse's broad shoulders and steered her to the door. "I know you do, Rolina. As a matter of fact I've decided to start an Employee of the Year Award and give you the first one."

She blushed. "Why, thank you, Mr. Chase."

"Don't mention it. In fact, don't mention it to anyone. I'll let you know when I'm ready to make the announcement."

As his Employee of the Year left, Norman collapsed wearily in his leather chair and stared at the pieces of metal and plastic on his desk.

Chapter 11

Kate was lounging on the deck of her bungalow, sipping a glass of Pinot Noir and gazing at the stars. Her Golden Retriever, Gilda, was at her feet and Grieg's Concerto was drifting from the sound system in the living room, drowning the city's insistent hum. She loved her comfortable little house, filled with books, old furniture, contemporary art and her baby grand. She wished she had more time to enjoy it.

With each sip of wine her life was coming into clearer focus. The main issue, of course, was her job. She'd gone into psychology because she wanted to make a difference in the world. Riverside Center had seemed like a natural place to do this, but she'd discovered that working with kids who were there one day and gone the next didn't give her enough time to make much difference to anyone. Her young patients viewed their hospital stays as prison terms, and they were preoccupied with their release dates.

She'd always had a creative bent. She played the piano, she sang, she dabbled in watercolors. The patients she enjoyed most were the ones who had the same impulse to express themselves creatively. She'd tried to persuade Norman Chase to let her start some programs that tapped into her young charges' artistic sides, but her pleas had fallen on tone-deaf ears. It hadn't taken her long to realize that the day this man had opened a treatment facility he'd Peter Principled himself up to his level of incompetence and remained there happily ever after.

She took another sip of wine. And then there was her personal life. She'd put so much effort into becoming a competent professional that she'd neglected to have one. She realized now that she should have spent less time in libraries and more at parties. She hadn't let herself get serious about any of the young men who were interested in her, and now here she was on the doorstep of thirty, an old maid in her cozy little cottage, shuffling off to a workplace that was less fulfilling every day.

She needed to work up the nerve to do the same thing about her job she'd done about the Sweet Adelines. Since she never had time to spend her money she'd socked away enough to be able to survive a year or so without working. She could stay home and paint. She could play the piano for a community theatre. She could build houses for Habitat. She could travel.

"We need a vacation, Gilda. How does the beach sound?" Gilda cocked her head and seemed to be considering the proposal. "We'll take long walks at sunrise. We'll meet a nice jogger. He'll have a dog, of course. You'd like that, wouldn't you, girl?" Gilda wagged her tail and sealed the deal.

Raleigh glanced up from his racing form in time to see Norman's Ferrari streak past him and hang a ninety-degree turn onto Riverside Road. He reached for the phone and punched the boss's cell phone number. "You're in a hurry tonight, Mr. Chase," he said as he watched his taillights grow smaller in the distance.

"I'm running late, Raleigh. I've got to get home."

"Could you spare a few minutes for me tomorrow? I need to see you about a personal matter."

Any other time this request would have piqued Norman's curiosity. This man hadn't sought him out for a private conversation in a decade-and-a-half of employment. At the moment, however, he was too preoccupied to think about it. "Yeah, sure, Raleigh. Come see me before your shift."

"Thanks. You have a good night now, Mr. Chase. Give the missus my best."

As Norman rocketed up Riverside Drive the wind whipped his hair into a frenzy that resembled his thoughts. This sports car was one of the many things he stood to lose if he didn't play his cards right with little Lolita. In the morning he'd summon Sierra and the Moss boy to his office and get to the bottom of things. If they needed favors, he was in an excellent position to trade them. He was also in an excellent position to make their lives hell if necessary.

Unfortunately they were in an even better position to reciprocate.

Zenia opened her eyes and saw a woman in a surgical mask, silhouetted by a circle of light. Surely this angel of mercy would rescue her from the paramedics who'd strong-armed her into an ambulance and sped her off to the Emergency Room. "Ms. St. Clair, I'm Dr. Tyler-Jones," the angel addressed her. "We're going to perform lavage on you."

"Whatever it is, I don't need it!" Zenia insisted as she wiggled to free herself from the straps immobilizing her. "Someone made a big mistake, Doctor! The ambulance must have gone to the wrong house!"

"Just relax, Ms. St. Clair. All we're going to do is flush out your system with a harmless saline solution."

"But my system is perfectly …" The doctor threaded a thumb-size tube up one of her nostrils, and her protests became gurgles. A team of assistants materialized and hovered over her. She felt like a frog pinned to a dissection board, with the sophomore class preparing to slice her open.

The doctor studied her chart. "Apparently you took quite a mixture of pills, so we're going to have to treat you pretty aggressively. When we're finished we'll give you a charcoal drink to absorb anything left in your stomach lining, and a diuretic and a laxative, just to make sure we've got everything. You'll feel like a new woman tomorrow. You're lucky Dr. Garcia called 911."

Zenia's eyes grew as big as ping-pong balls. She realized what had happened and she tried to signal the doctor to explain the mistake, but she was busy feeding the tube deeper inside her. She heard a click and a whir, and a clear liquid started flowing up her nose. She decided to use astral projection to take leave of her physical body, like she did when she went to the dentist. She closed her eyes, but she was immediately summoned back to reality. Her stomach was doing the Mexican hat dance.

Kate poured another glass of wine and studied the letter she'd composed. "Okay, Gilda, listen to this."

Dear Mr. Chase:

After giving the matter much thought, I've decided to tender my resignation as clinical director. This was a difficult decision because I've enjoyed my work and I've grown quite attached to many of the young people I've worked with during my time at Riverside. At the same time, for reasons both personal and professional, I feel it's time to move on.

Rest assured that your failure to implement most of my suggestions had nothing to do with this decision. It's simply a matter of personal growth. I plan to take the summer off and then open a private practice. I'd like to be able to work with clients for longer periods than I can in a hospital setting, and I'd also like to do some work with adults.

Thank you for giving me the first job of my career and for placing trust in my clinical judgment. I'll always have fond memories of Riverside. I hope my contributions will prove to be lasting ones.

Our personnel policy requires a two-week notice, so please consider my resignation effective two weeks from today.

> *Sincerely,*
> *Kate Oxley*

She looked at Gilda. "So what do you think, girl? Should I give it to him?"

Gilda walked over to her favorite spot in front of the refrigerator, circled six times and curled up on the floor.

"You're right, I'd better sleep on it."

Chapter 12

There was chaos in the Garden of Edie. A catfight had broken out between two of the girls on Unit Four, and they were wrestling in the fishpond. The other patients were enjoying this cross between a wet T-shirt contest and a mud-wrestling match. Things became even more entertaining when three aides sloshed to the rescue, only to discover the garden's water feature was a slippery slope that wouldn't support foot traffic. Others had joined into the spirit of the fray by starting a food fight with what was left of the *Good Luck, Chris* cake.

Russell was missing the excitement. He'd gone back to his room to sort through his things and prepare for his escape. Chris and Sierra had taken advantage of the chaos and slipped off to a corner to compare notes on Operation Scholarship. Chris expected Sierra to be in high spirits after her triumph, but she looked upset. "Is something wrong?" he asked when the others couldn't hear them.

"Why did you take pictures, Chris?" she asked angrily. "Now Mr. Chase knows it was a setup! If you'd just done what I told you and opened the door and acted surprised it would have been perfect! Now he's blaming me instead of himself! You've ruined everything!"

He was surprised she couldn't see the advantages of having pictures. "This is better," he insisted. "Now you've got proof it happened. It's not just your word against his."

"Rolina's got the pictures!"

"Russell gave her a decoy. The real card is duct-taped inside my guitar. I'll give it to you."

"Why did you drag Russell into this? I thought we said it was between us?"

He shrugged. "He had a camera."

"I can't believe you did this, Chris. I trusted you. I had a perfect plan and you screwed it up. Now I look like some kind of extortionist."

"It'll still work out. Chase is up the creek without a paddle."

"I'm the one up the creek."

"I'm sorry, okay? Just calm down and think about it. Now you're in a perfect position to pull this thing off."

Six aides had used passive restraint to subdue the two wrestlers, and they were removing them bodily from the courtyard. "The party's over, kids," Maurice announced loudly. "Go back to your wards."

Sierra turned to go, but Chris grabbed her arm. "Wait. I'll give you the pictures."

"Take them to Williamsburg with you tomorrow," she said. "They'll be safer there."

"What am I supposed to do with them? Take them to Wal-Mart and order prints? They don't give you pictures of people having sex."

"We *weren't* having sex," she resented this accusation. "I can't stand that creep."

Maurice herded them in the direction of the building. "Let's go, you two."

"I'll Facebook you when you get home tomorrow," Sierra promised.

Chris considered his situation. Things hadn't really gone so badly. He had topless pictures of Sierra McGuire and she had a $200,000 reason to keep in touch.

When Norman got home he found his family watching a movie in their home theatre. The actors on the giant screen seemed more lifelike than the three people immobilized in front of it. He sank wearily into a chair and kicked off his loafers. "I've been thinking about what you said at dinner, Meg. You're 100% right. I'm spending too much time at the office. From now on I'm devoting my evenings to the family. But we need to find something better to do than watch the boob tube. We need some wholesome family activities."

Meg did a slow take. "Exactly what kind of wholesome family activities do you have in mind, Norman?"

He thought of the things he'd done during his last wholesome period, when he was eleven at Camp Minnehaha. "Archery," he remembered his favorite.

"Archery?" his wife asked incredulously. After all the effort she'd put into finding the *right* friends, the *right* church, the *right* schools and the *right* clubs, she wasn't about to let her husband choose some bizarre social activity. "In case you haven't noticed, we don't live in a wigwam, Norman. I'm not your squaw and Sean and Dru aren't your papooses."

"Forget it."

"I already have."

Sean was listening to this exchange. "If my friends ever saw me with a bow and arrow they'd call me Geronimo Chase for the rest of my life."

Norman turned his attention to the movie. "What are we watching?"

"*Your Cheatin' Heart*," Sean said. "It's some chick flick Mom picked. The lady in the red scarf just killed her husband for cheating on her, and now she's driving around with his body in the trunk, looking for someplace to ditch him."

Norman sprang from his chair like it was an ejection seat and padded into the kitchen in his sock feet. He rummaged around in the freezer, grabbed a pint of Hershey's Moose Tracks and retreated to his den. Surrounded by four reassuring walls filled with laudatory plaques and ennobling portraits of himself, he dug into his favorite comfort food and tried to convince himself that everything was going to be fine.

Chris looked at his mountain of belongings, then at his roommate's molehill. Even with all the stuff he'd brought to the hospital he'd found himself wanting things he'd left behind - his harmonica, his chord book, his eggplant-colored long sleeve T. Russell had a seaman's knack for light travel; he'd stuffed three changes of clothes in his backpack and saved room for his camera in case he managed to rescue it. Chris admired his friend's portability. About the only thing he didn't like about Russell Moss was his opinion of Sierra McGuire, which he was tired of hearing.

"You're making a mistake taking those pictures with you, Dewberry," he offered some unsolicited advice. "She's manipulating you."

Chris flopped down on his bed. "She's not manipulating me if I'm letting her."

"She's got you by the balls."

"I wish. Look, Russell, you don't have to tell me there's something weird about a 17-year-old girl getting naked with a forty-year-old guy so she can blackmail him for $200,000. Believe it or not I figured that out myself. But you can't blame Sierra for wanting a better life. I know this whole thing seems nuts, but I'm going to let it play out."

"You're not as dumb as I thought," Russell said. "You're dumber."

"All right, Einstein, what would you do?"

"Trash the pictures, give her the number for Georgetown's financial aid office and take a cold shower," he prescribed.

"That's easy for you to say. She's not interested in you."

"Breaking news, Dewberry - she's not interested in you either. You're interested in her. There's a big difference."

"Ouch. Why don't you stick the knife in a few more inches and twist it?" True, this girl hadn't paid any attention to him until this morning, but he detected a flicker of interest and he intended to fan it into a flame. "Worry about your own problems, Russell. It's not like you don't have any."

"This is my problem. Chase knows I took those pictures. If he goes to the cops I'm the one who's screwed, not you."

"He's not going to the cops! What would he say – this guy took pictures of me trying to screw one of my patients? Sierra's got a decent chance of getting something out of this."

Russell saw he was getting nowhere, so he dropped the subject. "If you don't mind, take the rest of my stuff to Billyburg with you and I'll come by and get it. If I leave anything here Roach'll steal it."

"No problem. My mom's always turning my favorite shirts into dust rags, so I'll just give her yours instead."

"You're nuts, Dewberry."

Chris smiled. "If you can't act nuts in a psycho ward, where can you?"

Chapter 13

Norman leaned back in his chair and studied his clinical director. "All right, how much do you want?"

"What do you mean?" Kate didn't understand the question.

"I read your letter of resignation. I agree you're overworked and underpaid, but you run this place and I can't afford to lose you. How much more do you need?"

"Mr. Chase, I didn't say anything about being underpaid."

"But you are, aren't you?" He knew this was a safe bet since he underpaid everyone.

"I could probably make more somewhere else."

"You're making forty-two now. I'll give you forty-five."

"My salary's beside the point," Kate tried to convey what her letter apparently hadn't. "I need a life, Mr. Chase. I spend most of my waking hours here. I'm the one who's institutionalized. I can't even get away from it when I go home. Last night two of the girls got in a fight and they had to be restrained. Rolina called and wanted me to calm them down over the phone. I'd had a couple of glasses of wine and I'm not sure what I said, but it wasn't one of my shining moments as a clinician. I'm at work or on call 24/7. I realize that what we do here is important, but I don't intend to sacrifice my life for it."

"Fifty," he sweetened the pot.

"Mr. Chase..."

"What the hell - fifty-two," he upped the ante. "That's a $10,000 raise." He knew that even this was a bargain since it would take two people to replace her. "You take a big weight off my shoulders, Kate. I can't afford to lose you."

"I appreciate that, Mr. Chase, but..."

He stood up and paced the room like a trial lawyer pleading his case before a jury of one. "It would take months to find someone of your caliber.

Meanwhile I'll have to run the place myself. In case you haven't noticed, teenagers aren't my forte. I don't know what to do with these damned kids! I don't even know what to do with my own! You're not going to leave me in a lurch like this, are you?"

"Mr. Chase, I'm afraid my mind is ..."

"I'll give you the ten grand up front as a re-enlistment bonus."

"That's very generous of you, but I can't put a price tag on my happiness," she surprised herself with the strength of her resolve. "This is something I need to do. I've given it a lot of thought and I'm sure it's the right decision."

Norman wasn't used to people who couldn't be bought. He gave it another try. "Kate, before you came here we went from one crisis to the next. I was ready to sell the place and bail out of this business. You're worth your weight in gold, and you'll never have another employer who says that to you. So let's figure out how much gold it's going to take and I'll see about raiding Fort Knox."

"Mr. Chase, I've made up my mind. If you'll excuse me, I've got some parents waiting to pick up their son." As she stood to leave she noticed what was left of the flash memory card on his desk.

"We had a young man taking unauthorized pictures," explained. "I confiscated his camera and destroyed the memory card."

"Are you talking about Russell Moss?"

"Yes."

"I said he could have that camera. I'm hoping to use his interest in photography as a treatment tool."

"There won't be any cameras here. It violates the other patients' right to privacy."

"Mr. Chase, every time one of these kids tells their mother their roommate's name it violates someone's privacy. Frankly, I think we'd do better if we treated them more like normal teenagers. You can take this liability business too far."

Norman decided to make one last effort. "You know it's funny, Kate. Just yesterday I decided to start an Employee of the Year Award and give you the first one."

"Yes, it is funny," she agreed. "Raleigh and Rolina said you told them the same thing. It must be nice to have so many outstanding employees."

Martin Sykes was a very busy man. Despite his hectic schedule as Chief of Psychiatry and Addiction Services at Chippenham Medical Center, he always made it a point to spend time with his patients. He'd heard the woman in Room 305 was a handful, so he was prepared to give her up to five minutes if necessary. He strode confidently into the room and took a seat on the foot of her bed. This violated a tenet he'd learned in medical school, but he believed this informal approach helped him establish rapport with more difficult patients. He gave the woman a look that conveyed strength, compassion and expertise. He'd practiced this look for hours in a mirror until he'd gotten it down pat. "Are we feeling better today, Ms. St. Clair?"

"There should be a law against that hideous procedure," Zenia complained. "I threw up so much I felt like the girl in *The Exorcist.*"

"That procedure may have saved your life. Maybe the next time you'll have second thoughts before you take an overdose."

"I didn't take an overdose!" she said adamantly. "One minute I was leaning over my stove doing aromatherapy and the next minute three EMT's were strapping me to a gurney!"

"Aromatherapy?"

"I belong to the American Association of Aromatherapists," she thought this credential would impress him. "I use essential oils, but last night I was trying citrus peels. I was leaning over my stove, enjoying the experience, when paramedics barged in and dragged me out of my own house."

He flipped through her chart. "This you took six kinds of pills."

"I was using six kinds of *peels*, not six kinds of *pills*," she said in frustration. "Lemon, lime, orange, grapefruit, tangerine and tangelo."

Dr. Sykes considered this. "Tell me more about this Dr. Garcia."

"He's a brilliant psychiatrist from Mexico. We're colleagues at the Riverside Center. We have similar views of the mind-body-spirit nexus, and I feel a strong spiritual connection with him. Actually, I remember him from one of my previous lives. I'm the vice-president of the Past Life Reenactors Society too, by the way."

"I see."

"I can tell he's a natural healer from his aura."

"You don't say." The doctor glanced at his watch and remembered he had 17 other patients who needed attention before his twelve-thirty tee time at Willow Oaks. "It's been very interesting talking with you, Ms. St. Clair."

Zenia watched him scribble what she imagined was a favorable note about her mental status. "Are you discharging me?"

"Yes, I called Dr Garcia. He's on his way over to pick you up. He seems very concerned about you."

"So what's your specialty, Doctor?"

"Reality Therapy."

She made a face. "I've never tried that one."

"Unfortunately, Ms. St. Clair, it doesn't work for everyone."

Kate was heading to her office to meet Chris and his parents when she heard a heated exchange going on in the nurse's station. She popped her head in and saw Russell arguing with Jon Sawyer, the retired Army medic who covered the day shift. "What's going on?"

"My social worker's taking me fishing and Jon won't let me have my camera," Russell complained. "He's being a dickhead."

"I'm just following Chase's orders," Sawyer said. "Get out of my face, Russell. I can't write up my notes with you yapping at me."

"Yes, for God's sake, Jon, don't let the patients get in the way of the paperwork," Kate said pointedly. "We wouldn't want that to happen."

"What the hell's that supposed to mean?"

"Give him the camera. I'll take responsibility."

"Chase says it's an invasion of the other patients' privacy."

"Russell's going fishing. You can't invade a fish's privacy."

Grumbling, Sawyer retrieved the camera and thrust it at Russell, who snatched it wordlessly and accompanied his rescuer up the hall. "Thanks, Kate."

"I spent some time with your mother last night, Russell. Personally I don't think a change of address would hurt you for a while. I hope you'll listen to what Mr. Boone has to say about foster care."

"I'll move in with you," he volunteered. "You can be my foster mom."

"To quote one of my esteemed colleagues, get out of my face, Russell."

"As you wish," he quoted a line he'd seen in *The Princess Bride*. Before the morning was over he'd be out of all their faces.

Andrew balanced his tackle box on the hood of his Jeep, flipped it open and inspected the contents. Some men collected cars and some collected wives; he collected fishing gear, which was considerably less expensive. Everything was in place, so he latched the box and turned to fetch his ice chest. His landlady was sitting on her porch, eying him with interest.

"Good morning, Andrew," she called. "I see you're ready for another hard day of social work. If they're paying you to fish you're a much smarter boy than I thought."

"You should take up fishing, Miss B. It might get your mind off Arthur Ashe."

She regarded him with amusement. "You didn't invite me to come along."

"I can't today. Technically, I'm working."

"Technically."

"Tell you what. When I get back this evening I'll join you for Happy Hour."

"I'd be honored. What's your pleasure?"

"Rolling Rock."

She made a face. "What on earth is that?"

"A fermented beverage flavored with hops. You'll find it in the beer section. I'll sit on the porch with you and you can teach me about life."

"Thank you, dear. Now I have something to live for."

"See you later, Miss B." He went downstairs and returned with his ice chest. Under his landlady's vigilant gaze he climbed in his Jeep and took off. It was nine-thirty and the sun was shining. It was a perfect day for fieldwork.

Chapter 14

Why do professors have to look so much like professors? Kate wondered as she took stock of the man sitting in her office. *Do they issue the seersucker suits and bow ties when they grant them tenure?* David Dewberry could have been from central casting, with his rumpled suit, flyaway hair, and translucent skin that looked like it only saw the light of day when he strolled between the lecture hall and the library. His wife Debbie made a more contemporary statement with her bobbed hair, earth tones and scarf. Kate noticed that Chris had parked himself on his mother's left, as far away from his father as he could maneuver.

"We've enjoyed having Chris with us," she opened the meeting. "He's a very bright and talented young man."

"We think so," the professor agreed. "If Chris would just apply himself, he could do anything he wants."

"If I'd just apply myself," Chris repeated. "You make me sound like some kind of pathetic slacker. I apply myself, just not to what you want."

His father gave him a look of irritation. "Dr. Oxley said you're bright and talented and I agreed with her. Do you really find that so insulting?"

"Oh, cut it out, you two," Debbie stepped in. "We're not here to argue, we're here to make a fresh start." She reached down and retrieved an item wrapped in foil and tied with a festive ribbon. She handed it to Kate. "I made you a loaf of English muffin bread. We appreciate your work with Chris."

Kate accepted the gift. "Thanks, Debbie. That's very thoughtful of you. Let's go back to what you were saying, David. What makes you think Chris doesn't apply himself?"

The professor issued a strangulated sigh that suggested he hardly knew where to start. "Oh, he applies himself, but very selectively. If he spent half as much time on his studies as he does on the guitar he could go to Princeton."

Kate turned to Chris. "Do you want to go to Princeton?"

"Nope. I don't want to go to college, period."

It was his mother's turn to get upset. "Now Chris, how can you say something like that? Sometimes I think you say these things just to get us stirred up."

"It's the truth, Mom. I keep telling you I want to be a musician."

"You've gotten totally carried away with this music thing and you're going to regret it," his father predicted. "We're only trying to keep you from making a foolish mistake. We want the best for you. We've tried to expose you to a wide variety of experiences so you can become a well-rounded person. A Renaissance Man."

Kate suppressed a smile. "I'm not sure becoming a Renaissance Man is at the top of Chris's To Do list."

"No, but it would make a great song title," Chris filed it away. "*I Just Want to be a Renaissance Man.*

His father wasn't amused. "We're trying to have a serious discussion and you're making jokes."

Kate stepped in. "One of the things Chris has been telling us is that he feels his life is too programmed. He says that's why he ran away to Washington."

"Too programmed?" his father asked incredulously. "How programmed is someone who sits around strumming a guitar?"

"Are you saying we shouldn't provide structure and guidance?" Debbie asked.

"No, I'm not even saying it's true. I'm just trying to make sense of his recent behavior."

The professor snorted. "There's no sense to be made of it."

"You guys have been worried about where I'm going to college since I was in diapers," Chris complained. "When I was six we went to Shiloh and you detoured through Nashville to show me Vanderbilt. How many parents take their six-year-olds on college tours? You're always saying stuff like 'maybe you should consider Emory' or 'maybe you should take a look at Duke'. I don't want to consider anywhere. I want to see more of the world before I make any big decisions."

"We've hardly raised you in a hermitage, Chris," his father countered. "You've seen lots of places."

"Sure – Manassas, Gettysburg, Antietem. I want to see places that don't have battlefields. I want to bum around with my guitar. Maybe I'm a crappy musician, but I want to find out."

"Can't you play music and go to school at the same time?" his father proposed. "Do you have to be some kind of vagabond to strum a guitar?"

He grinned. "No, but it helps."

"A lot of young people would love to have your opportunities, Chris," his mother said. "Think of all the students who want to go to college and can't afford it. We're fortunate to be able to send you wherever you want to go."

"Now you'll have a lot of extra money."

The professor turned to Kate. "Let me get this straight. Our son thinks his life is too programmed, so we're supposed to abandon our hopes and aspirations for him and let him go off in the hills and become a wandering minstrel?"

She started to reply, but Chris cut in. "Dad, I'm as interested in the blues as you are in the Civil War. I know Washington Irving coined the term. I know how it developed from slavery and church music. I can tell you all about W. C. Handy and Howlin' Wolf and Muddy Waters. I can tell you about the Crossroads in Clarksdale, Mississippi. I could write a research paper on this stuff without having to look anything up. I didn't learn any of it in a classroom. I learned about it because I'm interested in it. Think of all the students you've had who were clueless about what they wanted to do. At least I've got a clue. You're supposed to do something that makes you happy, aren't you?"

His mother sighed. "Chris, when I think of the blues I think of African Americans. Having a white son who wants to be a blues musician is like having one who wants to be an Indian medicine man. It's just – well, it's just *odd*."

"Plenty of white guys play the blues."

"Play the damn blues then," his father threw in the towel. "But don't expect us to support you."

Chris sensed a delicate truce in the offing. "I won't."

"And when you get tired of it and want an education, I reserve the right to say I told you so." He looked at Kate. "You can't win with young people, can you? They wear you down like water on a rock."

"If we didn't have differences with our parents we'd all still be living at home," Kate shared a bit of her own philosophy. She had some observations she wanted to talk about privately with his parents, but she decided to call them later. She stood up, signaling that the session was over. "I expect to hear wonderful things about you, Chris. Let me know when I can download your songs on iTunes."

"I'll send you tickets to my first concert."

Debbie gave Kate's hand a little squeeze. "We appreciate your help. Do you mind if we call when we need a shoulder to cry on?"

Kate gave her a card. "I'm leaving Riverside in two weeks, but you can reach me at home."

"Why are you leaving?" Chris was curious.

"Let's just say I'm expanding my horizons."

He smiled. "You've got the Loony Bin Blues."

Chapter 15

Norman buzzed the classroom in the center's basement. "Send Sierra McGuire and Russell Moss up to my office right away," he ordered the teacher who answered.

"Russell's not here, Mr. Chase," she reported. "He went fishing with his social worker."

"Fishing!"

"He took him down to the Pony Pasture to talk with him about foster care. He'll be back this afternoon."

Norman was livid. "We let these kids out for appendectomies, not fishing trips! This is a hospital, not a damned summer camp. The patients are supposed to have treatment regimens. Who said he could go fishing?"

"Kate did," the teacher said.

Norman decided it was probably better to interrogate his culprits separately. "Send the McGuire girl up."

"Yes, sir."

He looked up and saw his psychiatrist standing in the doorway. "Jesus, Garcia! You scared the piss out of me! What are you doing in here?"

The little man hung his head. "I am doing the bad thing, Señor Chase."

"What the hell are you talking about? What bad thing?"

"The one called Zenia? The one who is having the movements?"

"St. Clair? The movement therapist?"

"Si. She ees smelling the leemons and I am calling the 911."

"What the hell's that supposed to mean?"

"I am confusing the leemons weeth the peels."

"You're confusing the hell out of me, too. Vamoose, Garcia. Go write prescriptions."

Frustrated by his inability to communicate, the doctor decided to act out his message. He held his stomach, stuck his tongue out and made a sick face.

"St. Clair's got an upset stomach?" Norman gathered.

"Si!" He made a vigorous pumping motion, like he was fixing a flat on a bicycle.

"And she blew up?"

"Si! Ees my fault."

"St. Clair blew up and it's your fault?" He decided there had to be more to the story, but he didn't have time to pursue it. He put his arm around the little man and steered him into the hallway. "You win some and you lose some, Garcia. Don't beat yourself up over this."

"I am not to be beaten?"

"No, you're doing a helluva job. You've got a great future here."

"I am having the good future?"

"I guarantee it." He made a mental note to call Ernesto and order a new shrink. "As a matter of fact, I'm starting an Employee of the Year Award and giving you the first one."

The Mexican's face lit up. "I am being the Employee of the Year?"

"You're Numero Uno, Garcia. Congratulations."

He grabbed Norman's hand and pumped it. "Gracias, Señor Chase."

"No problemo." He saw Sierra McGuire heading to his office. *The criminal always returns to the scene of the crime,* he reminded himself. "Come in, Sierra."

Sierra followed him and made herself at home in one of the chairs facing his desk. "Mr. Chase, before you say anything, I want to apologize for what happened last night."

This caught Norman off-guard. His eyes narrowed suspiciously. "You do?"

"Yes, I'm sorry. I guess I got a little carried away. "

"A little carried away! I'd hate to see what you're like when you're out of control! Would you mind telling me what that little stunt was all about? I intend to get to the bottom of this one way or the other."

"I thought if I had something I could hold over your head you'd let me go home early," she explained. "I'm graduating from Buckingham County High School next week. I'm supposed to go home Thursday, but I'm afraid something will go wrong and you'll decide to keep me here and I'll end up missing graduation. I want to see my friends next week and go to the rehearsal. I know it probably doesn't seem very important to you, but it's a big deal to me."

Norman picked up her file and waved it. "I read your records, young lady. You're here for soliciting! Apparently you have a pattern of this kind of behavior. What are you, some kind of nymphomaniac?"

"No. It just seemed like a way to get what I wanted."

"According to these test scores you're a intelligent young woman, but you certainly couldn't prove it by me."

"I said I'm sorry."

"Sorry doesn't cut it." He was pleased to find her in such a remorseful frame of mind. "Come over here to the window. I want to show you something. And don't pull any monkey business." Obediently, Sierra left her chair and joined him at the window. "Look out there and tell me what you see."

"Grass. Trees. A parking lot. Cars. A little gatehouse thingy."

"I see twelve acres of the most valuable real estate in Richmond," he shared his own perspective. "I see proof that a person can start out with very little in life and end up successful. They tell me this property is worth 4 million dollars! I have 109 people working for me! My wife wears dresses worth more than some of those cars! I own three homes! I didn't start out with anything Sierra. My father worked in a shoe store and my mother worked at Dairy Queen. Do you think I got where I am today by dumb luck?"

"No."

"Apparently you must or you wouldn't have pulled that crazy business last night. You must think I'm a complete idiot." He returned to his chair. She took her cue and sat down. "What's the Moss boy got to do with this?"

"Russell had a camera, so I asked him to help me."

"I suppose the two of you went back and blabbed to all your friends?"

"No. I made him promise not to say anything. I figured I couldn't trade my silence for my freedom if I didn't have any silence to trade."

Her words fell on his ears like music. He moved to the edge of his chair. "No one else knows what happened in here last night?"

"Why would we tell anyone? People around here run their mouths."

"In that case, Sierra, we've got some possibilities."

"What kind of possibilities?"

"I'm sure you're aware that you could be in hot water for what you did last night. The court sent you here for soliciting and you're already back at it. Any reasonable judge would conclude that you need a much longer course of treatment."

"Longer!"

"I think you can see it's in your best interest to keep this unfortunate little incident to yourself. If you agree, I'll send you home this afternoon."

Sierra's mouth fell open. "This afternoon? Really?"

"I'll call your parents myself. But if you violate our little agreement I can arrange for other consequences. You won't find them very pleasant. Are we clear?"

"So if I don't tell anyone what happened you'll let me go home today?" she wanted to make sure she understood their agreement.

"That's what you want, isn't it?"

"Yes."

"We still need to consider what to do about your friend Moss. Is there something he wants? Something I can arrange that would help him forget about last night?"

"They're trying to put Russell in foster care. He wants to live with his mother." She was unaware that even as she spoke her friend was releasing himself on his own recognizance.

"I think I can arrange that, too." His position gave him some leverage with the courts, and in this case he didn't mind using it. He'd chat with the boy, make a couple of calls to the right people and put the situation behind him. Everything was falling into place nicely. He studied the young femme fatale who had cost him a night's sleep. "What are you planning to do after you graduate, Sierra?"

"I'm not sure," she said. "I'll get back to you on that."

"It looks like we're all set. I'll call your parents right now. Tell Kate you're being discharged. If she has any problem with it, tell her to come see me. I think this little meeting has been very productive for both of us, don't you?"

"Yes, I do. Thank you for letting me go home, Mr. Chase."

"You're very welcome."

As he watched her leave Norman congratulated himself on the way he'd handled things. He'd always been good at these little games of Cat and Mouse.

He didn't realize he was the mouse.

Chapter 16

Russell was bouncing along in the passenger seat of his social worker's Wrangler. They were passing under a canopy of oaks, following the gentle bends in the James River. He couldn't believe these lush woods were part of the city where he'd lived for seventeen years. "Are you sure we're in Richmond?" he asked Andrew.

"Yep," Andrew replied. "A few hundred thousand people live up there, but when you're down here on the river it feels like you're in the Shenandoah Valley."

"Why's this place called the Pony Pasture?" Russell asked. He didn't see ponies or a pasture.

"Beats me. I'm not looking for ponies. I'm looking for smallies."

"Smallies?"

"Smallmouth bass."

"I'm not into this fishing stuff," he repeated what he'd told him the day before. "I'll just walk around and take pictures while you fish."

"Russell, as long as we can spend some time talking about foster care I don't care what you do. But I really wish you'd throw your line in the water a couple of times. You might discover you like it. I'm supposed to be taking you fishing. At least give it a try."

Russell decided he needed to pretend to be more cooperative. "Okay. Thanks for getting me out of that place. You don't know what it's like being trapped in the same building day after day."

"I know exactly what it's like. You've only got two more weeks and then you're out."

"After that I get to go to your jail."

"For a guy who's never seen a foster home you sure have strong opinions about them. The folks who take kids in their homes are usually pretty decent."

"They want a cute little 3-year-olds, not 16-year-old dudes with attitudes."

"What about a group home?" Andrew proposed an alternative. "There's a decent one in Charlottesville. It's kind of like a junior frat house. Six or eight guys live in a house in a regular neighborhood and they go to the public schools and hold jobs. A houseparent couple lives with them to keep them out of trouble. The kids at this place even get in free to the concerts and ball games at UVA. And at least you'd be living with guys in the same boat as yourself. We can drive over to C-ville next week and check it out."

"That sounds a lot better," he agreed, even though he didn't have any intention of taking him up on it. He studied the hilly terrain on the right. He could see the rooftops of expensive-looking homes poking up through the trees. According to his map if he made his way to the top of the hill he could cut through this neighborhood, hang a right on Huguenot and eventually hook up with the interstate. With a little luck he could make it to Virginia Beach in two or three hours. Thousands of high school and college students descended on the beach in the summertime, and he planned to descend with them and blend into the crowd.

He sized up his social worker; he looked like the Mayor of Margaritaville in his shades, backwards Orioles cap, shorts and T-shirt. He read the logo on his shirt. "Sun Dried Opossum? Is that a band or something?"

"No, it's my favorite snack food," Andrew replied.

"Are you kidding?"

"You city boys sure are gullible."

"We've got street smarts," Russell came back at him.

"If you say so."

They pulled into a gravel lot overlooking the river. The area was heavily wooded, perfect for his getaway. He hopped out of the Jeep and shouldered his backpack. Andrew noticed its heft for the first time. "Why'd you bring so much stuff? We're not hiking the Appalachian Trail."

"I've got my camera gear, and I brought some extra clothes in case I fall in," he explained. Andrew handed him a rod and reel. He read the name on it: Expedition, which seemed fitting. Andrew rummaged through his tackle box, selected two lures and went to work rigging their lines. Russell examined his. "What's this?"

"It's called a Slug-Go. Smallmouth bass are predators. They go after slender fish that move erratically, like they're injured or dying. A Slug-Go mimics that kind of action."

"What are you, like a fish psychologist?"

"Something like that."

They gathered their gear and followed a footpath to the river. The James was dotted with gray boulders and marshy islands. Russell estimated it was a quarter mile wide at where they were standing. A small flock of Canada geese were floating in an eddy. He dug out his camera, attached his telephoto lens and fired two shots. He'd discovered that if he paid attention to the four corners of his pictures his subjects usually fell into place. His photography teacher had praised his eye for composition, but he knew it had everything to do with this little four-corner trick. He squatted and took a third shot, catching the sunlight playing on the underside of a boulder. His only other trick was deleting most of his efforts. He probably ditched 19 out of every 20 shots he took. As a result people only saw his best work and thought he had a magic touch. The only magic was getting rid of the crap. Now that he thought about it, that's what he was about to do with his life, too.

Andrew came over. "Nice place, huh?"

"It's all right."

"It's the best damn place in Richmond. Leave your backpack and follow me. I'll teach you the art of casting."

After a brief lesson, Russell practiced what he'd learned, trying to keep the action in his wrist. It didn't take long for this to get old. He couldn't feel any bites, and twenty minutes dragged by like a minor eternity. He looked over and saw his social worker trolling contentedly. Apparently fishermen were born, not made. "Any strikes?" Russell asked.

"I've had a few nibbles. They're out there. Try reeling slower."

Russell set his rod on the boulder. "I've got to take a leak."

"Don't go far."

It depends on your definition of far, he thought. He returned to the bank, grabbed his pack and hurried back to the parking lot. When he was out of his social worker's line of vision, he sprinted across Riverside Drive and plunged headlong into the dark woods. He slashed his way uphill through briers and brambles, heading for the Promised Land.

A few minutes later he heard his name echo off the hillside. There was a pause, followed by, "Answer me, you little shit!"

He smiled. He imagined Andrew Boone slinging his gear in his Jeep and cursing. He'd scout the area and eventually give up and go back to the hospital to give them the bad news. *You won't believe what that little shit did to me! One minute he was standing right there and the next minute he was gone!* They'd play the blame game, and someone would call the police and report him as a runaway. The hospital folks would make a few token drive-bys around the Pony Pasture, then they'd promptly forget about him and go back to the impossible task of reforming Danny Roach. He'd become a statistic in some agency's computer, another runaway teen who wasn't worth wasting their bloodhounds and choppers on. In a week's time only his mother would remember he was gone.

He thrashed through the underbrush, thankful the river was drowning the noise he was making. As he climbed higher the sky grew lighter. Suddenly he was in the backyard of a two-story Colonial house with a swimming pool. He hurried around it in time to spy a tan Jeep cruising slowly up the street. Andrew was at the wheel, rubbernecking and looking pissed. He ducked behind some garbage cans until the coast was clear, then he headed in the same direction.

Twenty minutes later he reached Huguenot Road and the old Huguenot Bridge. The concrete-and-steel structure spanned the river and a train track and connected with Cary Street Road, the city's most exclusive neighborhood. He knew from his map that Cary would take him to an expressway that connected with I-64, and this interstate would take him to Virginia Beach. He adjusted his pack and started across the bridge. With each passing vehicle the old span shook, and he could feel the vibrations in his legs. When he reached the middle he stopped and looked down on the boulder-strewn ribbon of water. He pulled out his Nikon, turned it vertically and brought the scene into focus. He checked the four corners and took a shot.

Dr. Garcia stared at the emaciated creature in the hospital bed. Then he remembered she'd looked like this before she went the hospital. "You are feeling better, Zenia?"

"I was perfectly fine before they hauled me off to this place."

"I am being sorry."

"It wasn't your fault," she forgave him. "Actually the peels worked beautifully. I'm thinking about starting an aromatherapy service where I go around to people's houses and give them the same treatment. I thought of the perfect name – Peels on Wheels."

"Señor Chase says I am not to be beaten," the doctor was pleased to report. He pulled two Goo Goo Clusters from his coat pocket and offered her one. "You are liking the Goo Goos?"

She waved the candy away. "I don't eat refined sugars. I follow a strict macro-vegan diet."

The doctor unwrapped the candy and took a bite. "In Chihuahua we are having no Goo Goos," he said through a sticky mouthful.

Zenia picked up the other patty and read the label. "Chocolate, caramel, pecans and marshmallow - yuck." But her mouth was watering and she remembered she hadn't eaten in 24 hours. Violating her nutritional principles she removed the wrapper and took a tentative nibble. She felt the goo rushing into her sugar-starved cavities and restoring her physical and spiritual balance. "If you think about it, these things are mostly nuts," she rationalized. "You're such a creative healer, Dr. Garcia. I'm impressed with you use of non-traditional therapies. We think so much alike. We need to work together to address some of Riverside's problems."

"Problemos?"

"If we made a few changes we could turn the place into a model facility." Energized by this vision, or possibly the candy, she sat up in bed. "We could be the first New Age hospital," she imagined a holistic Camelot on a hill. "I don't think it's a coincidence that you and I ended up working together. It's karma."

"You are ready to go, Zenia?"

Reinvigorated, Zenia hit the floor. "Yes, I am." She undid the neck of her hospital gown and let it drop to the floor. The doctor averted his eyes too slowly to miss what looked like a flesh-draped skeleton. "I don't mind if you stay in the room while I dress. I don't have anything to hide. We shouldn't be ashamed of our bodies, we should celebrate them. I'm sure Mexicans aren't as puritanical as Americans."

Dr. Garcia bolted for the door, only to find his path blocked by an orderly who gave him a knowing wink. "Sorry, man, I'll give you guys some privacy." He shut the door, trapping him in the room with Zenia.

He turned and caught a rear view of his coworker. "*Ai yi yi*," he crossed himself. He reached in his pocket and fortified himself with another Goo Goo.

Russell was walking up Cary Street Road. Houses had given way to mansions so big they needed their own zip codes. He knew he wasn't born to breathe this rarified air, but he wasn't born to breathe the stale smoke in his mother's apartment either. He imagined himself in a loft decorated with his own photographs. As he walked along with his backpack, a

Bob Dylan song he'd heard on the classic rock station his mother always listened to played in his head.

> *How does it feel*
> *To be on your own*
> *With no direction home*
> *Like a complete unknown*
> *Like a rolling stone?*

He didn't like Dylan, but the guy had obviously hit the road a time or two. How else could he have come up with such a perfect description of what he was feeling? The problem with Dylan was that when his songs got stuck in your head they were stuck in his nasal, croaky voice.

> *Hooow does it feeeel*
> *To be ooon your ooown*
> *With no direeection hooome?*

It felt pretty damn good. Better than being locked up in a nuthouse. Better than living with some foster family in the boondocks. Maybe even better than going home.

He reached I-195 and he saw a sign for I-64 halfway down the entrance ramp. He readjusted his pack, stuck out his thumb and started down the hill. A dozen vehicles whizzed by before a furniture delivery truck squealed to a stop. A man with long white hair and a bushy beard stuck his head out the window. He looked like God the Father. It seemed like an omen.

"Where you headed?" the driver called to him.

"Virginia Beach."

"I'm going to Norfolk. Hop in."

Russell jogged around to the passenger door, tossed his pack up and climbed into the seat. As they merged with the traffic he saw downtown Richmond's skyline looming in the distance. He'd lived in the shadow of this skyline his entire life. He'd always known the day would come when he'd emerge from it; he just hadn't expected it to happen so soon.

Chapter 17

Runaways at Riverside weren't exactly news of the Man Bites Dog variety. Anyone who could make it out the door and over the fence had a shot at freedom, however short-lived. The lucky ones enjoyed two or three days of liberty before they were collared, usually at home. The unlucky were back in minutes. Dealing with the center's rabbits was one of Kate's many duties, and when Andrew returned and reported that Russell was missing she swung into action, calling the police, then marching him to Norman Chase's office to explain the situation.

Norman eyed the social worker's outstretched hand like it was a dead carp. "Are you the lamebrain who took this boy fishing?"

"Lamebrains 'R Us," Andrew said sheepishly. "I was trying to build a relationship with him so we could talk about foster care. I guess it wasn't such a great idea."

Norman appreciated having someone to blame who wasn't connected with his facility. "I'm holding you personally responsible for this," he informed him.

Kate spoke up. "Mr. Chase, this whole thing was really my fault."

He shot her a dirty look. "No it wasn't."

"Yes it was. I should have seen it coming when Russell was resisting the idea of foster care. I authorized the fishing trip. I don't think he'll go far. He lives here in the city."

"I don't care if he lives in the damn basement, this should never have happened." He turned back to his whipping boy. "Does your supervisor know you're running around dressed like a bum, fishing on company time?"

"Not exactly," Andrew squirmed like a night crawler on a hook. "He knew I was meeting with Russell to talk about foster care, but I didn't explain my methodology."

"Your 'methodology' sucks. You might as well drive him to the airport and buy him a plane ticket."

"Mr. Chase, Russell is the fourteenth runaway since I've been here," Kate had been keeping count. "There's no need to treat this situation any differently than the others. Andrew was trying to connect with this young man. We should be praising him, not condemning him. Russell should be easy enough to find. He's not armed and dangerous."

"Why don't we move his discharge date up to today?" Andrew offered a solution. "I'll take his things with me now. If he shows up at home I'll let him stay there until his court date. You can close his case and forget about him."

This was the last thing Norman wanted, since he needed to have words with the young man who'd witnessed the scene in his office. "The court sent him here for six weeks of treatment and I'm going to see that he gets it," he said adamantly. "He's coming back here and he's finishing the program."

"Mr. Chase, there's no therapeutic reason to bring Russell back," Kate sided with Andrew. "If we let him go home at least he'll be able to spend time with his mother before he goes to foster care."

He gave her a look of irritation. "I'm taking charge of this case."

Kate's mouth fell open. "You don't even know this boy! I'm not sticking around for two more weeks if you're going to be making the treatment decisions. Sierra McGuire told me you're sending her home today! Since when did we stop having team meetings about these things?"

"Since you submitted your resignation."

"I'm not putting up with this kind of petty vindictiveness. I'm making my resignation effective today."

"I'm holding you to two weeks."

"You can hold me to whatever you want. I'm cleaning out my office and leaving." She wheeled and made her exit with Andrew on her heels.

"Jeez, what a charming guy," he said. "Do you think he'll call my supervisor?"

"He won't even remember your name," she assured him. "I've given him more pressing matters to worry about."

"That was gutsy."

"I lost a job reference, but I'm going to open my own practice so it won't matter. The only thing that worries me about all this is Russell. I don't like the idea of him drifting around out there. If you find him, please give me a call. I have a thing about closure."

"I'll look for him some more before I go back to the office," he told her. "You're welcome to come along."

She smiled. "If you'll help me carry my things out to the car, I'll take you up on it."

The truck driver was a compulsive radio sing-a-longer, his delivery truck a rolling Karaoke parlor. For the first forty minutes on his road to freedom Russell listened to the man perform agonizing duets with Kenny Chesney, Beyonce, Willie Nelson, Kid Rock, Norah Jones, Wu Tang Clan and Nine Inch Nails. His duet with John Mayer on *Your Body Is a Wonderland* was more than he could handle. "I'll get out here," he decided when he saw an exit sign for Williamsburg.

"I thought you were going to Virginia Beach?"

"I've decided to visit a friend here first."

"Suit yourself." He pulled onto the shoulder.

His escape was well timed. As the truck rolled away Russell heard the opening strains of *Bohemian Rhapsody*.

PART II
Williamsburg

Chapter 18

Chris surveyed Duke of Gloucester Street from the back seat of his parents' Subaru Forester. It was hard to ignore the fact that he lived in a theme park - there were relatively few communities in America where you saw grown men walking down the street in powdered wigs and knee britches, and children in tricorn hats tooting pennywhistles. Every year a few hundred thousand tourists passed through this little town, and some days they all seemed to be there at once. The Subaru made its way through the 18th Century and along the edge of the William and Mary campus, turned off Jamestown Road and pulled into their Powell Street driveway.

"We're dropping you off, Chris," his father told him. "I'm going back to the campus and your mother has a church meeting. Do you need help with your things?"

"Nope." He jumped out and pulled his belongings out of the hatchback. He walked around to the passenger side and gave his mother a peck on the cheek.

"I made you a blueberry pie," she said. "It's on the kitchen counter."

"Sweet." He appreciated this thoughtfulness after six weeks of institutional indifference. He heard his dog inside the house, going berserk. "Mosby knows I'm home."

His parents left, and when he entered the house through the garage the little Scottie was trembling with excitement. He picked him up. "Did you miss your big brother, you little Gray Ghost, you?" He swung him back down to the floor and the dog trotted behind him to his bedroom. His things were exactly the way he'd left them. His CD towers were standing sentinel in the corner, his harmonica collection was gathering dust on the windowsill, and the mandolin he'd never learned to learn to play was hanging between a Blues Traveler poster and a picture of his old Boy Scout troop at Philmont Ranch. He tossed his guitar and duffel on the bed and booted up his laptop.

When he went to Facebook he saw an urgent message. CHRIS!!! PLEASE READ THIS NOW!!!

everything's perfect. russell's gone & mr chase is sending me home so i can't blab. i'm calling him next week to negotiate so please make prints of the pix. i'll call u tomorrow at noon so please be there. if u can come to Buckingham i'd liketo2 c u. i'm counting on u chris! ttfn, sierra

He went over to his guitar case, loosened the strings of his Martin and carefully extracted the memory chip taped inside. He was thinking about what to do with it when the front door opened and Mosby streaked down the hall, barking. His neighbor Serge Tabanov bounded into the room and threw him a high five. "It's my favorite Russkie," Chris welcomed him.

Serge sized him up. "Damn, you've gotten skinnier, Dewbie. What'd they feed you in that place?"

"Gruel and unusual punishment," he used a line he'd been saving for the last verse of *The Loony Bin Blues*.

The Tabanovs had moved to Williamsburg from Russia when Chris and Serge were in the fourth grade. Over the years he'd had logged enough hours with this family to pick up bits and pieces of their story. Serge's father, Gregor, had apparently worked undercover for the Central Intelligence Agency in his homeland. Since coming to Williamsburg the handsome, multilingual Russian had been working as an instructor at Camp Peary, a sprawling military base on the other side of the interstate. All the locals and every Tom Clancy reader knew the compound was a school for spies, known in CIA circles as The Farm. Chris assumed the family's fast track citizenship and Gregor's teaching job were rewards for whatever chores he'd performed for the Agency. He'd always been impressed by this athletic man, who was willing to accompany their Scout troop on the outdoor activities his own father avoided like the plague. His line of work fascinated him, and he'd peppered Serge with questions for years without getting any satisfactory answers.

"So what did they do to you in that hospital?" Serge wanted to know. "Hook you up to machines and shock you?"

"You're confusing psychiatric care with your dad's interrogation methods," he said. "They drugged us and made us talk."

"No one has to drug you to get you to talk, Dewberry. They were probably trying to shut you up."

"Good point. So why aren't you in school today?"

"Finals. My next one's Monday."

"Oh, yeah." Chris had forgotten his classmates were taking exams; he had already taken his at the hospital. "So what's happening in Billyburg? What have I missed?"

"The AP history class took a trip to Monticello," Serge related. "As soon as we got there Mr. Cody had a heart attack. They put him in Jefferson's bed and sent us outside until the ambulance came. He's okay. He's proud of the Jefferson's bed thing. When he talks about it he sounds like he wishes he'd died in it."

Chris imagined his history teacher laid out at Monticello. "Sorry I missed it."

"A bunch of college students had a protest march in front of Staples. Something about the rain forest. Three of them were dressed up like trees. Oh, yeah - the Callisons' house burned down. They think he torched it for the insurance. And the school choir had their spring concert."

"Yeah, I know. Ms. Baylor sent me a CD."

"Tell me about this Riverside place."

Chris thought about the events of the last four weeks, and especially the previous night, and he hardly knew where to start. He fingered the memory card and took a deep breath. "It's a long story."

The McGuires' trailer and the RonDayVoo Lounge sat side-by-side on the crest of a hill, sad derelicts sharing a park bench in the middle of nowhere. A gravel lot served as their front yard, and dense underbrush grew up behind them. "Well, Jolene," her mother said as their '77 Gremlin kicked up a cloud of dust in the lot, "I'll bet the old home place looks pretty good to you now."

"Fabulous. Is this the month we're on the cover of *Southern Living?*"

"Honey, I don't know what you're talking about."

Sierra's 14-year-old sister, Viola May, helped carry her matching luggage inside. They deposited the three plastic garbage bags on the living room floor. VM collapsed in front of the TV, grabbed the remote and flipped to a *Saved By the Bell* rerun.

Sierra didn't see any sign of her father. There were lots of words that described Blackjack McGuire, and they all ended in *less*: jobless, shiftless, worthless. Her father was the King of Less. There was no doubt in her mind this man had sired her sister, but she liked to think that in her own case some attractive, ambitious traveling sales rep had stopped for a drink 18 years earlier and hit it off with her mother. "Where's Dad?"

"Helpin' Tater pull his engine block," her mother reported.

"I don't know what makes him think he's a mechanic. Oh, wait a minute, yes I do. Colt 45."

"Don't you talk about your daddy like that, Jolene," her mother scolded her.

"Please call me Sierra," she requested for the umpteenth time. She turned to her sister. "VM, have you ever thought about turning off the TV and getting a life?"

"Shhh!"

She'd been home less than a minute, and she already remembered why she didn't want to be there. "I'm going over to Tina's."

"I can't take you," her mother said. "I'm already late for my shift."

"I'll walk." After four weeks of confinement a walk sounded good. Besides, Tina had a computer and she needed to see if Chris had gotten her message. Only her whole future depended on it.

Serge stared at the memory card in Chris's hand. "That's one hell of a story, Dewbie. So when can I see what this babe looks like?"

"When I can find a camera to stick this in," Chris promised him. "I can't take it in a store and print it, so I've got to transfer it to my computer and print it myself. I need to find a Nikon like Russell's and a cord to connect it to my computer."

"Where's Buckingham County? I feel a road trip coming on."

Mosby jumped up and bounded for the front door, barking. Chris cracked his blinds, expecting to see the mailman. "Speak of the devil. It's Russell."

Serge sprang to the window. "Your fugitive roommate? Do we get a reward for capturing him?"

"Yeah, seventy-five cents dead or fifty cents alive. I'm glad my folks aren't here." He opened his window. "Come on in, man. Watch out for the attack dog."

Serge looked at Chris. "Your dorky life is finally getting interesting, Dewbie."

Chapter 19

There were few things Norman hated worse than empty beds. Empty beds equaled empty coffers, and he had three of them getting colder by the minute. He let himself into Kate's vacant office took a seat behind the desk and rifled through a small mountain of paper, searching for a waiting list. He heard a noise at the door and he looked up and saw his psychiatrist standing there.

"You are wanting to see me, Señor Chase?"

"Yeah, I've been looking all over the place for you, Garcia. Kate walked out on me and I need you to run the therapy groups. You do that kind of thing, don't you?"

The doctor shook his head vigorously. "No, no."

"No! What the hell kind of psychiatrist are you? I expect a little something in return for that thirty-five grand a year I'm giving you."

"Kate ees taking the walk?"

"She hit the road, Garcia. She left me high and dry. I started to cancel the therapy groups, but then I realized we could charge more if we had a psychiatrist running them. You can help me out on this, can't you?"

"She heets the road?"

"Forget it. I'll run the damn groups myself." He shooed him away like a pesky fly, but his security guard Raleigh announced his presence with a cough. "What's up, Raleigh?"

"We have an appointment, Mr. Chase. Remember?" Without waiting for a reply he closed the office door removed his cap and helped himself to a chair.

"Make it snappy, Raleigh. I'm going to keep looking through this stuff while you're talking." He disappeared behind a stack of files.

"I need a raise, Mr. Chase."

Norman's scowling face peered from behind the stack. "Raleigh, every month a dozen employees come to me and plead wretched poverty. If I gave raises to all the people who wanted them I would have gone broke years ago."

"But I've been here fifteen years, Mr. Chase."

"True, but you spend your time sitting on a stool, smoking and reading magazines. I could put a chimp in a uniform and train him to do what you do."

"That's a creative thought, sir, but I still think I'm worth more than the minimum wage."

"The minimum wage has gone up a lot over the years," Norman reminded him.

"My position requires good judgment and I think my judgment makes me a valuable employee."

"Yeah, you're a real valuable guy, Raleigh, but - "

"Sometimes I see things," the security guard hinted mysteriously. "I work late and when the lights are on and the blinds are up I can see what's going on in the offices and wards. Occasionally I see things others might find – well, let's just say embarrassing. Maybe even illegal. A man in my position needs to know what to report and what to keep to himself." He gave his employer a knowing wink.

Beads of sweat appeared on Norman's brow. "Uh, exactly how much more do you figure you're worth, Raleigh?"

"Four times my current salary," the guard said coolly.

"Four times your salary!" Norman sputtered. "That's outrageous! You've got other sources of income. I'm well aware of your activities down at that booth."

"Yes, I've taken the initiative to supplement my income. But I have expenses."

"Expenses! Don't tell me about expenses! I've got 109 people on my payroll! Do you think I can afford to shell out that kind of money for one person?"

Raleigh shrugged. "You'll have to be the judge of that."

Norman shifted uncomfortably. But in view of your many years of faithful service I suppose we could consider doubling it."

"I want sixty grand a year."

"Sixty grand! Raleigh, no one here makes that kind of money."

"You do," Raleigh reminded him.

"Yes, but that's a little different. I own the place."

"Over the years I've developed a special relationship with the advisory board," Raleigh played his ace. "I park their cars when they come to meetings. They give me nice tips. They call me by name. They ask me how things are going."

"Forty."

"Sixty."

"All right, sixty, damn it." He couldn't believe his own ears. "We'll make it effective in January."

"That's very generous of you, sir, but I need it sooner than that."

"September."

"Sooner than that."

"July."

"I'm thinking more along the lines of today."

"Okay, okay," Norman admitted defeat. "Now give me a little privacy, Raleigh. If I don't fill these beds we'll all be in the poorhouse."

"No problem." Raleigh stood up and replaced his cap. "Thanks for your time, Mr. Chase." And with that he vanished.

Norman slumped in his chair. This conniving weasel had gotten the better of him. Now he was going to have to find some naïve idiot to take the clinical director's job for squat so he could afford to pay his security guard. This turn of events had completely blindsided him. He consoled himself with the thought that it could have been worse. The only witness to his indiscretion was a greedy bastard. He understood greedy bastards. He was one himself.

The three young patients who were left on Unit Three didn't know what to make of the sudden disappearance of their therapist and half their group members. Like shell-shocked survivors of a bombed-out platoon, they weren't sure who was in charge or what lay ahead. They were speculating on their future in the therapy room. "Maybe they'll split us up and put us in the other units," Molly said.

"Maybe they'll send us home," Selena hoped.

Roach still couldn't get over it. "Man, can you believe this shit? Yesterday Russell sits right there and tells me I'd be stupid to run off. Then he runs off! You can't trust nobody in this damn place."

Suddenly the door opened. The three young teens watched silently as Norman claimed a seat in their midst, loosened his tie and rolled up his sleeves. "I'm running your group today," he informed them. "What do we do first?"

"You ask about our issues," Selena explained the drill.

"Your *issues?*" Norman scoffed. "You people think you've got issues? Wait until you've got mortgages and screaming brats. Wait until you're footing the bills for your kids' private schools and your parents' nursing homes. Wait until you've got the IRS breathing down your neck. Wait until your hair's falling out and you need a triple bypass and a lung transplant. Then you can tell me about issues."

"Man, life sucks," Roach was thoroughly convinced.

"You think fifteen sucks? Try forty-three! Don't be so naive. These are the best years of your lives. All you've got to do is go to school and bitch."

"Why do I gotta spend the best years of my life in this dump?" Roach wanted to know.

Norman turned to the young troublemaker. "What's your name, son? Why are you here?"

"Roach. Me and my brothers got drunk and stole a Hummer from the National Guard."

"And you can't figure out why you're here? What did you expect them to do – pin a medal on you? You screwed up, kid. You were stupid. That's why you're here."

"Man, that's bullshit."

Norman turned his attention to the girls. "Next."

"Why did you let Sierra go home?" Selena wondered.

"She had a family emergency."

"I've got a family emergency, too," Molly said. "My stepfather's an asshole."

"That's not an emergency," Norman corrected her. "It's an opinion."

"It's my issue. It's why I'm here."

"Let me give you a hot tip, young lady. The world is full of assholes. Someday you'll have one for a boss, so get used to it." He studied her black lipstick, purple mascara and studded dog collar. "Who said you could run around here in that ridiculous getup? It's not Halloween."

Molly stiffened. "It's not ridiculous."

"Have you looked in a mirror lately?"

She folded her arms and glowered at him.

Selena spoke up. "I'm here for shopliftin'. I learnt my lesson, so when can I go home?"

"When your insurance runs out."

"What if I've got good insurance?"

"Then you'll have a long lesson."

"Why can't we smoke in this place?" Roach filed another grievance. "My folks let me."

"Lighters and matches make me uncomfortable," Norman replied. "That's why we don't admit anyone with a history of fire setting. I don't even let the staff smoke."

Roach was expecting the standard lecture on health. This safety angle caught him off-guard. "Raleigh smokes." He'd seen the clouds billowing from the gatehouse.

"Raleigh doesn't work in the building."

"I'll go down and smoke with him."

"You don't know when to shut up, do you, Roach?"

"Yeah. When I get my way."

"You're not getting your way, so shut up."

Molly had been doing a slow burn. "You're not a therapist. You don't care about us. Kate cared about us."

"Yeah, she probably did. I'll try to replace her by Monday. Then you can feel loved again." He stood up and left the room.

Molly looked at the others. "Can you believe that man? He's worse than my stepfather."

"I'm leavin' tomorrow," Roach decided. "I got it all figured out."

Selena rolled her eyes. "Roach, you've been sayin' that every day since you got here."

"Yeah, but this time I got a plan."

Norman was congratulating himself on the masterful way he'd handled his first therapy session when his phone rang. "Hold my calls," he instructed the receptionist.

"It's Ernesto, Mr. Chase. He's calling from Mexico. He says it's important."

"I'll take it." He intended to give his man in Chihuahua an earful. In their younger days Ernie had been his sales partner at Abbott Labs. When their supervisor had asked some uncomfortable questions about missing drug samples he'd fled the country. He didn't know if his expatriate amigo ran his employment agency from a penthouse or a broom closet, but he always seemed to be able to come up with doctors and spirit them across the Rio. He punched the line. "Ernie?"

"Buenos dias, big guy. How's life in the good ol' US of A?"

"Skip the bullshit, Ernie. What's the story on this wetback you sent me? He doesn't know a taco from a turd. I want a new shrink and I want one pronto."

"That's why I'm calling," Ernie said. "Seems like we made a little mistake on this one."

"A little mistake? What kind of mistake are we talking about?"

"He not a psychiatrist," his friend gave him the bad news.

"What the hell is he - a proctologist?"

"He's not exactly what you'd call a doctor," Ernie continued.

"Not a doctor! What is he?"

"A short order cook. I swear I didn't know it. You wouldn't believe how many palms I've had to grease to save my ass on this one."

"A cook! This man's writing prescriptions! How fast can you get me a new shrink?"

"These guys aren't exactly sitting around waiting for your calls, Norm. Finding docs who want to move to the States for what you pay them takes time."

"Don't give me any of your flimsy excuses. I want a new shrink in two weeks or you're going to be doing a swan dive off the cliffs at Acapulco. Are we clear?"

"There's no reason to get bent out of shape. I'll do what I can."

"It's called liability, you asshole. I've got to keep using this quack until you send a replacement because I don't have anyone who can write prescriptions or sign off on treatment plans. If something happens, I'll have to plead ignorance, so you need to forget we had this conversation."

"What conversation?" Ernie aimed to please. "We haven't talked in months."

"Call me next week and let me know where we stand."

"You got it, big guy."

"You'd better come through on this, Ernie. If you don't, someone just might whisper your name to the Immigration Service."

"Always the big threats, huh, Norm?"

Norman banged the phone down. Strangely, the Mexican cook had managed to pass himself off as a psychiatrist for a month. His clinical director was the only one who'd picked up on his incompetence. He'd given him the Spanish language editions of the Physicians Desk Reference and the Diagnostic and Statistical Manual of the American Psychiatric Association. They were the cookbooks of the mental health trade, and the cook apparently knew how to follow recipes. He just needed to keep following them until his replacement showed up.

Chapter 20

Chris and Russell were polishing off slices of blueberry pie in the kitchen while they were reliving their hospital experiences for Serge. Chris was describing Sierra. "She's got long, ash-blonde hair with natural highlights, and the kind of skin you only see in soap commercials. Her eyes are like green lasers, and when she smiles the corners of her mouth do this little curly thing." He noticed his two friends giving him funny looks. "What's wrong?"

"Keep going," Russell said.

"As we head south we notice ..."

"Her big tits?" Russell asked.

"Please, Russell," Chris said. "Sierra has breasts, not tits. They're not like water balloons stuffed in spandex. They're perky. She doesn't need a hydraulic lift to hold them up. Her stomach is toned, and she's got this cute bubble butt and legs that go... " He tried to think of the right description.

"All the way to the ground?" Russell asked. "Are you done, or do you have any observations about her toes?"

Serge shook his head. "Romeo didn't have it this bad for Juliet."

"Don't hassle me, man." He turned to Russell and changed the subject. "So are you on your way to Virginia Beach?"

"Yep."

"Why don't you stay here?"

"You mean like with your family?"

"Are you kidding? My folks wouldn't take in the world's cutest stray puppy. I mean stay in Billyburg. We've got tons of jobs. There's all the Colonial crap, Busch Gardens, Water Country, and all the restaurants and outlet stores."

Russell thought about it. "Where would I live? No one's going to rent a place to a 17-year-old. At least at the beach I can find someone to crash with."

"You can camp in the woods by Lake Matoaka," Chris suggested. "I can give you a tent and a sleeping bag."

"Where's Lake Matoaka?"

"Behind the college," Serge said. "Campus security patrols it, but they won't see you with all the foliage. I've got a bike you can use to get around."

"I've never camped before," Russell felt foolish admitting. "Isn't there like poison ivy and stuff?"

"Yeah, but just don't wipe your butt with it," Chris said.

"What about snakes?"

"They're harmless," Serge told him. "Except for the copperheads and rattlers and moccasins. You can tell the poison ones by their slanted eyes."

"Great. So all I've got to do is get down on my hands and knees and look them in the eye to make proper identification. Thanks but no thanks. I'm going to the beach."

"You can work in the Colonial village," Chris refused to give up. "You can bike there in five minutes."

"So what would I put on the job application for my address? Russell Moss, The Woods?"

"Use ours."

"Wouldn't it make your folks kind of suspicious if a homeless stranger started getting his mail here?"

"I'll tell them you're living in the woods for a school project," Chris was on a roll. "I'll tell them you're writing your senior research paper on Thoreau and you're trying to have a *Walden*-type experience. The worst you'll have to put up with is my dad quizzing you about your paper."

Russell gave him a blank look. "Who's Thoreau?"

"Didn't you have to read *Walden* for English?" Serge asked him.

"Nope."

"He was this dude who built a little shack in the woods in the 1800's and lived there and wrote a book about it," Chris educated him. "Walden was name of the pond he lived by."

"Let me get this straight," Russell went over their proposal. "You want me to live in a tent with no running water, no electricity and no toilet. I've got to hide from security patrols. Every morning I've got to put on a ruffled shirt, knickers, buckled shoes and a three-cornered hat, bike into the village and spend the day making soap and candles. In my spare time I have to read the classics so I can take pop quizzes from your dad. This is the life you envision for me? This is what I ran away for?"

Chris shrugged. "I like it."

"Sounds good to me," Serge voted.

"And you think I'd be better off doing this than renting beach chairs and boogie boards to babes in bikinis?"

"We've got babes here," Chris said. "They just wear different outfits."

"Yeah, like full-length dresses and Pillsbury Dough Boy hats. They could be 40-year-old transvestites and you'd never know the difference. You guys really think I'm falling for this crap?"

"No, but we need your camera so we can look at the pictures," Chris revealed an ulterior motive.

Things were clearer to Russell. "So you're proposing this ridiculous scheme just to satisfy your lustful desires?"

Chris grinned sheepishly. "Yeah, basically."

"Why the hell didn't you say so?"

Tina Lester was sitting in front of her computer with Sierra. Tina, who was morbidly obese, had never understood what Sierra saw in her, except someone who would give her money and computer access. Over the years she'd watched with envy as her friend had turned into a ravishing beauty and she'd blimped into a bad joke. She'd stopped telling people she lived in a doublewide so they wouldn't make wisecracks. But her gorgeous, brainy friend always seemed so unhappy. Right now she was staring glumly at her Facebook page. "I was expecting to hear from this guy I met in the hospital, but he hasn't written."

"Guys are like that," Tina spoke less from experience than what she'd gleaned from magazine advice columns.

"Do you mind if I use your computer to apply to a college?" Sierra requested. "A businessman in Richmond wants to give me a scholarship, so I need to apply."

Tina was surprised by this news. "I didn't know you were going to college. Are you going to the community college? We can ride together." She watched as Sierra clicked on to the Georgetown University website, followed the link for Prospective Students and navigated to the Office of Undergraduate Admissions. "Georgetown?"

"I want to study Foreign Service so I can live as far away from here as I can," she explained. "Tina, do you still have all that money you saved from babysitting?"

Tina knew what was coming next. "You still owe me thirteen dollars for the class T-shirt."

"I have to buy a cell phone. I like this guy I met at the hospital. You know how that kind of thing goes."

Tina didn't know how that kind of thing went, but she could imagine. "How much do you need?"

"A hundred dollars."

"A hundred dollars! You must *really* like him."

"I'll pay you back the week after next," she promised.

"Are you getting a summer job?"

"No, that's when I get my scholarship money. I swear I'll pay you back, Tina. I really need to talk to this guy."

"Okay, but if you end up marrying him I want to be your maid of honor," Tina negotiated as she pawed through her dresser for the money. "What's his name?"

"Chris Dewberry. If I marry him you can definitely be my maid of honor," she felt safe promising. "But you've got to buy your own gown."

"Okay," she agreed, aware that 330-pound beggars couldn't be 330-pound choosers.

Chris and Serge were hovering over Russell's Nikon, examining the small picture on the display screen. A stark naked Norman Chase was flat on his back, reaching for a topless Sierra, who was astride him. She was wearing a look of disgust. The effect was more comedic than pornographic, a reluctant Beauty with an eager Beast.

"This picture isn't worth two hundred grand," Chris decided. "It's worth five hundred."

"If I was that dude I sure wouldn't want anybody to see it," Serge agreed.

Russell advanced to the next picture, which showed a blurred Norman scrambling. The third shot was even blurrier. "One masterpiece, two deletes," he decided.

"Sierra wants an 8x10," Chris informed Russell. "And I want one without Chase in it."

"It's called cropping," Russell educated him. "We can do it on your laptop after we import it."

Serge scrutinized the picture. "I think we need to visit this girl and make sure she's okay. She looks traumatized. She looks like she needs our help."

"*Our* help?" Chris had no intention of introducing Sierra to his best friend, whose chiseled features and blond hair made him a babe magnet. "For your information she's calling me tomorrow, Serge, not you. That's spelled m-o-i."

"Sierra's more interested in getting her hands on this picture than she is in getting her hands on you," Russell gave him a reality check.

"We'll see about that," Chris said.

Serge was still examining the picture. "I can't believe a girl like her would do something like this. She must be really desperate."

"Or crazy," Russell opined.

Chris shot him a dirty look.

"We've got to consider all the possibilities," Russell reminded him.

Chapter 21

Andrew and Kate were parked in the alley behind the Old Dominion Pawn Palace, staking out the Mosses' apartment, when Andrew suddenly remembered he had a date with his landlady. They hastened back to Monument Avenue, where they found Miss Beauregard waiting patiently on her porch. "Miss B, I'd like you to meet someone," Andrew introduced his guest. "This is Kate Oxley."

She stood and extended a blue-veined hand regally. "It's lovely to meet you, dear. Do you drink Rolling Rock, too?"

"I will today," Kate said. "I just quit my job and I feel like celebrating."

"You two youngsters make yourselves at home and I'll get the drinks." She headed inside.

"I am at home," one of the youngsters reminded her.

They claimed the porch swing and watched a pigeon make a deposit on Arthur Ashe's head. "I'll bet she trained that bird," Andrew said. "Miss B's a Daughter of the Confederacy. She hates that statue. She's into ancestor worship."

"Richmond's full of little old ladies just like her," Kate spoke from experience. "They think they run things, but the only things they run are the historical societies."

"She needs a hobby besides drinking and keeping track of me. You don't know some nice old geezer we can fix her up with, do you?"

"Yes, but I'd like to get to know her better before I introduce her to my father."

"She's got money."

"That makes her more attractive," Kate agreed.

Their hostess reappeared and doddered their way with a silver tray filled with bottles, glasses and a bowl of pretzels. Kate rushed over. "Let me help you with that, Miss Beauregard."

"Oh, pish posh. I'm perfectly capable of serving people in my own home." As the words left her mouth everything went sliding precariously to the tray's edge. Kate latched on and steered her to a nearby table.

Andrew saw she was planning to pour the beer into glasses, so he helped himself to a bottle and took a swig. This earned him a scowl of disapproval from his landlady. "I'm impressed by your bartending skills, Miss B," he said. "You make a mean beer."

Miss Beauregard ignored him and turned to Kate. "You sound pleased that you're leaving your job."

"I've been working with teenagers for the past two years," Kate explained. "I didn't realize how much of my life the Riverside Center was eating up."

Miss Beauregard's mouth fell open. "Please don't get me started on that place. My late sister gave them a lovely courtyard."

Kate remembered the name on the plaque. "Was Edie Snellgrove your sister?"

"Yes. Edie passed away three years ago," Miss B reported sadly. "She lived with me after her husband died. That horrid man who runs the place heard about our money and he started pestering us for donations. Our father was the man who air-conditioned Richmond, you know."

"Wow, now there's the guy who deserves a statue," Andrew had new respect for her lineage. "On second thought, make it a holy shrine."

"I saw right through him from the start," Miss Beauregard continued. "But Edie was a soft touch. He sat right there in that very swing and he went on and on all the poor children he was helping. Edie promised him $500,000 dollars! I nearly fell off my rocker! She died before he could get his hands on it. I thought that was that, but then he turned around and sued the estate for the money! I was afraid he'd keep things tied up in court for years, so I settled for a $250,000 to get rid of him. He had the gall to invite me to the dedication! Needless to say, I didn't go." She drowned this bad memory with a swig of gin.

"If it makes you feel any better, the courtyard's beautiful, Miss Beauregard," Kate said.

"It should be for $250,000."

"They use it all the time. One of the patients called it the Garden of Edie, and now everyone calls it that."

"Oh, that's a hoot," she loved the name. "Edie would have gotten a kick out of it." She turned to her tenant. "How was your day, Andrew?"

"I'd rather not talk about it, Miss B," he said. "The young man I took fishing ran off and we're still looking for him. The cops aren't any help. Runaway teenagers are like missing purses – it all depends on who loses them. Russell's family doesn't have any connections, so he's not exactly a top priority. They put him in their computer and if he ever gets stopped for something and they run a check on him they'll discover he's missing."

"We'll hire a private investigator to find him," Miss Beauregard proposed.

"This isn't a case for Lieutenant Colombo," Andrew declined her offer. "If Russell doesn't turn up by this weekend Kate's going to scout around for him next week. I'd do it myself, but I've got 18 others on my caseload she's got some time on her hands now."

"Suit yourself, dear. We can always hire a private eye."

"I wouldn't want you to have to cut back on your alcohol budget, Miss B." He raised his empty bottle. "You wouldn't happen to have another one of these in your fridge, would you?"

"Help yourself. While you're gone Kate and I can have a little girl talk."

"She's a nice person, Miss B. Don't corrupt her."

"I'll leave that to you, dear," she said sweetly.

A few blocks away on Kensington Avenue, Sean Chase was making a face at his braised salmon steak with mango salsa. "Mom, why do we always have to eat this kind of weird stuff?" he complained. "Other families have meat loaf and fried chicken. And why do we eat by candlelight? We have electricity."

"I think meals should be interesting," Meg defended her menus.

"They're *too* interesting. And when we have pizza, why can't we have pepperoni and sausage? We always have seven-grain crust with artichokes and sun dried tomatoes and pesto. I don't even know what pesto is, and I've been eating it for years."

"All right, Mr. Know It All, what's pepperoni?"

He eyed his salmon sullenly.

"This recipe came from the Richmond Symphony cookbook. You're lucky you can sit down to a nice meal like this, Sean. Children are starving all over the world."

"Name one country where they're starving," he challenged her, knowing geography wasn't his mother's strong suit.

Meg remembered the pictures of her church's mission trip. "Central America."

"Central America's not a country."

"Well I know it's a continent, Sean," she qualified her answer. "I'm talking about all those Third World countries down there." She was pleased she'd come up with this, even though she'd never figured out where the First and Second Worlds were, much less the Third.

"Even if everyone else is starving, how does it help if we eat braised salmon steaks with mango salsa?" Sean failed to see his contribution to mankind.

"Oh, honestly, Sean." She turned to her husband for support, but his cell phone chirped on cue. "Norman, would you mind turning that damn thing off so we can enjoy a pleasant family meal?" she snapped. She resented the little electronic device that tethered him to his business affairs, even though she considered her identical device a dire necessity.

Norman ignored her. "Chase here," he answered it. His face turned crimson, then purple, and he brought his fist down on the table. "Son of a bitch!" China leapt and drinks sloshed, and the other family members paused with their forks in mid-air. "How much damage is there? Where'd the little shit get matches? Since when did we start letting parents smoke? Why do we even bother to have a security guard? Don't say a word to the press. I'll be right there."

After fifteen years of crisis calls, Meg viewed them as minor irritations. "Norman, I really wish you'd exercise some self-control. How can we eat with you pounding on the table and cursing? How do you expect Sean and Dru to learn proper etiquette?"

"For your information, Miss Manners," he said acidly, "a little bastard set his mattress on fire and they had to evacuate the building. Everyone's outside with the fire department, the police department, two ambulances and the Channel Twelve News."

"Are the children all right?"

"Yes, but I know one who's not going to be feeling so hot after I get through with him."

Sean pictured the chaos. "Wow. Is the building burning up?"

"No, they took the mattress out and its smoldering on the front lawn." He speared a last piece of salmon and got up. "The only damage is smoke and water."

"So where'd the little bastard get matches?" Sean asked him. He saw his mother giving him The Look. "That's what Dad called him."

"Please don't ever quote your father."

"He bummed a cigarette and a lighter from a parent who was visiting last night," Norman shared what he knew. "I've got a staff of incompetents. I might as well hire the deaf and the blind and get a tax break."

"You can always sell the hospital and get a normal business," Meg offered a suggestion she'd made before. "Then maybe we could have a normal life."

"That hospital happens to be a gold mine, Meg. We're worth ten million dollars. You tell me another business where we can make that kind of money and I'll unload the place tomorrow."

"You could be a drug lord," Sean suggested.

"I *am* a drug lord," his father replied. "And the drugs are legal."

Meg filed this net worth away for future reference. "It's a strange way make a living, Norman. How many of our friends get phone calls in the middle of dinner saying someone's trying to burn down their business? Other people have sensible jobs with sensible hours. You never know what those little hellions are going to do next."

"Tell me about it. The clinical director quit today. Now I've got to supervise all these bumbling incompetents myself until I can replace her." He headed for the door.

"Don't be late," she requested. "I made Death by Chocolate, Norman. It took me two days."

"We'll have it when I get back."

"No fair!" Sean objected. "I want Death by Chocolate Norman now."

Norman glanced at him. "You're going to have Death by Strangulation if you don't stop being such a little wisenheimer."

Dru made a face. "What's a wisenheimer?"

"You," her brother said.

"Mom, Sean called me a wisenheimer!"

"Later," Norman left his loved ones to work out their differences.

Meg listened to her husband's Ferrari roar to life in the garage and she stared at his empty place at the table. The new and improved Norman Chase, the one who was going to spend evenings with his family, had lasted less than twenty-four hours. It was vintage Norman, and it was a lousy vintage. There was really only one solution. She'd been putting it off for years, hoping this man would evolve into the sensitive, loving, attentive partner she deserved. She'd just heard a very intriguing figure. Five million dollars could buy a woman a lot of sensitivity, love and attention.

By nine o'clock the fire-related chaos at Riverside Center had subsided and the regular chaos was back in full swing. Norman bid Richmond's Finest farewell and gave Channel Twelve's bush league reporter an interview designed to elicit a heartfelt response from the community. He retreated to his office with his culprit in tow. The boy slouched in his chair and cracked his knuckles. "Mr. Roach, it would be the understatement of the century to say I'm pissed," Norman let him know where he stood. "You're nothing but a damn punk."

"Don't call me Mister," this part bothered Roach more than the damn punk part.

"I'll call you Asswipe if I want to."

Roach sat up in his chair. "You're not supposed to talk to kids that way."

"You're not supposed to set the place on fire either," he shot back. "I realize the teenage years are a period of temporary insanity. I make a good living from it. But this time you picked the wrong adult to mess with. I happen to be the one who's going to decide if and when you ever leave this hospital."

"You can't keep me here! You don't keep fire setters!"

Norman remembered his comment in the group session. "Are you stupid enough to think that I'm going to send you home for torching your bed?"

"You ain't kickin' me out? Oh, maaan … "

"Don't you oh man me, you little turd. I'm hiring a crew to come in and clean up your mess and you're going to work with them."

Roach folded his arms defiantly. "I ain't cleanin' shit."

"If I say you're cleaning shit, you're cleaning shit. If you do a good job I might consider letting you out of here someday. You're here for a psychological evaluation. Unfortunately we lost our psychologist today and I just might take my sweet time getting another one. You could be getting your Christmas stocking from Jolly Old Saint Norman."

"Christmas!"

"You can't beat the system, Roach. Especially when I'm the system. I've had years of practice dealing with little jerks like you."

"I'll run off, like Russell."

"Your friend Russell went on a fishing trip and I can guarantee you there won't be any more of those. I don't care if I've got to hire two armed thugs to watch you day and night. You're staying here until I say you can leave. Are we clear?"

"Fuck you!"

"Ah, the dying gasp of the powerless," Norman said. "I wish I had a thousand dollars for every time some incorrigible little bastard has said that to me. Well, actually, I suppose I do. Do you have any idea what this little episode's going to cost me? Do you know how much it takes to clean walls, repaint rooms and replace ceiling tiles, furniture and carpets?"

"It ain't costin' you shit. The staff says insurance'll pay for it."

"Oh, really? That sounds just like the ignoramuses who work here. For your information and theirs, we have a hundred thousand dollar deductible."

Roach didn't know a deductible from a duck. "So?"

"By the time I finish with you, you're going to enlist in the Army just so you can go to boot camp and get some rest. Get out of my sight. I'm sick of looking at you."

Roach started to leave, and he turned back. "Everyone says you're a big prick," he made a parting shot.

"They're absolutely right. And you're about to find out exactly how much of a prick I can be."

Chapter 22

Russell was staring at the ceiling of Chris's North Face dome tent. When they'd finished printing the pictures it was too late to set out for the beach. His fate was sealed when Professor Dewberry had come home and Chris had introduced him as the fictitious Thoreau scholar. Fortunately the professor hadn't asked him any questions, or he would have looked as foolish as he felt.

Chris and Serge had set up an encampment for him in the woods. He'd crawled into the goose down sleeping bag at midnight, but he hadn't been able to sleep. He was used to tuning out the urban symphony outside his bedroom window, but these woods seemed even noisier than screeching tires, wailing sirens and alleyway voices. For all he knew ravenous wolves were circling the tent, looking for a midnight snack. He unzipped the flap and poked his head out. The lake was bathed in a silver monochrome; it reminded him of an Ansel Adams picture. He remembered his photography teacher talking about how the famous photographer had tooled around the West with a tripod on the roof of his Cadillac. He climbed on top of the car to take his romanticized pictures of the wilderness, erasing the power lines and graffiti in his darkroom.

He zipped up the tent and rearranged himself in the sleeping bag. He'd been a runaway less than a day and he already knew he wasn't cut out for the life of a drifter. Unfocused pictures bothered him, especially when he was the subject matter. But what were his choices? He could go home and wait for the law to pick him up. He could turn himself in and go to foster care. He could hang around Billyburg and make apple butter. He could go to Virginia Beach. It was a no-brainer; come Monday he'd stick out his thumb and head to the beach.

With the picture finally in focus, he drifted off to sleep.

Sierra was listening through the flimsy wall of the bedroom she shared with her sister as her mother berated her father for staggering in drunk at three in the morning. She covered her ears with her pillow.

She was turning eighteen in and month and so far her life was more noteworthy for what she hadn't done than what she had. She hadn't learned to drive, she hadn't been more than a hundred miles away from her home, and she hadn't ever held a job, except when she was pressed into service to wait on tables at the RonDayVoo. She'd never had a checking account or a credit card or a computer. She'd never been in love either, but that was the least of her concerns. She'd thought about marrying her way out of her plight, but what promising young man would be interested in her after he met the future in-laws?

Her mother accused her of being uppity, but what did she expect her to do – embrace their wretched existence? The stork had accidentally left her on the wrong doorstep, and the solution was getting a new address. She hadn't been able to figure out how to do it without money or a car until Norman Chase had come along. Her hospitalization had been a blessing in disguise. She had her benefactor exactly where she wanted him and things were falling neatly into place.

But she needed Chris's help to carry out her plan. Would he forget about her now that he was home? Maybe if she invited him to visit and let him witness her horror show of a life firsthand, he'd realize the urgency. She usually tried to hide her circumstances from her friends, but seeing this squalor would surely renew his interest in helping her.

She removed her pillow and heard her mother still harping. She banged on the flimsy wall. "WOULD YOU TWO PLEASE KEEP IT DOWN?" She'd slept better at the treatment center than she could in her own home. Then again, it might have had something to do with the pills they'd given her. Where was Doctor Garcia now that she really needed him?

Chris was sitting on his bed, strumming his guitar and making notes on the pad he kept handy in case inspiration struck. He'd discovered the only way to rhyme her name was in fake Italian – *Sierra, Sierra, fairest of the fair-a, let-a down-a your golden hair-a*. It was so bad it was almost good. He put his guitar back in its case and snapped off his reading light. He wondered if the people called her Jolene at home. He could rhyme with Jolene. For some reason girl was much more intriguing than the ones at his high school who cheered teams to victory, danced across the stage in school musicals and warbled the Star Spangled Banner at assemblies. Of all the reasons to blackmail somebody, attending Georgetown was probably the strangest one anyone had ever come up with. There was something noble about her desire to get a credential that would prove to the world she was okay. She hadn't figured out that academic credentials only went so far. His father was living proof.

The girl from Buckingham County wasn't just coloring outside the lines; she was finger-painting in the stratosphere. He clicked his light back on, reached for his notepad and scribbled *finger-painting in the heavens*. He snapped off the light and flipped over. He imagined Sierra filling the starry sky with streaks of color, and he fell asleep.

Kate awoke with a start. In her dream a psychologist and a social worker were skinny-dipping in the James River. She'd looked for runaways before, but it had never turned into drinks and dinner and a dream where she was cavorting in the nude.

After two years of thinking about teenagers she realized she needed to start giving more thought to adults, especially the opposite sex. She'd learned what little she knew about men from her three brothers, who were only passionate about four things: food, sex, cars and sports, and not necessarily in that order. She could handle the food and the sex part, but she was going to have to start paying more attention to teams and vehicles.

She felt foolish. Grown women with Doctor before their names weren't supposed to lie awake at three-thirty in the morning, thinking schoolgirl thoughts. It was silly to lose sleep over a man. Women didn't need men to feel happy or fulfilled.

She wondered if Andrew Boone felt the same way.

Andrew awoke in a sweat. In his dream he'd been tooling along the Blue Ridge Parkway in a Jeep Rubicon instead of a Jeep Sahara. He wondered if this meant he should have gotten the Rubicon, with its heavy-duty drive shaft and disc brakes, instead of his Sahara. He decided it would have been too gnarly and over-the-top. Reassured, he peeled off his soaked T-shirt and went back to sleep.

Chapter 23

It was Saturday morning at The Farm, and sixteen agents-in-training were attending the first day of a covert operations school that covered subjects they hadn't studied in their previous lives, subjects like surveillance, infiltration and clandestine communications. Gregor Tabanov could have lectured comfortably on any of these topics, but he'd been assigned to teach surveillance. He trained his steely blue eyes on his students, who were posed with pens over their notepads. *I've got to turn stenographers into spies,* he thought. He saw them sneaking glances at the shelves behind him, where an array of rearview sunglasses, night vision goggles and miniature cameras disguised as clocks and toasters were on display.

"I know you're all dying to play with the goodies," he addressed them, "but it's going to be another month before you get acquainted with these little wonders of modern technology. Contrary to what you may think, your most valuable surveillance tools aren't any of these gadgets. Your most valuable tools are your powers of observation." He paused to let this to sink in. "For example, I can tell you that sometime this past week a man named Jake has been in this room." He pointed to the Presidential portrait on the wall. "That picture wasn't here last week. People hang pictures at their own eye level, and that one 's too high for most of us. One of our maintenance men is a gentleman named Jake who's six-foot-five. I'll wager $20 that Jake hung that picture. Now where do you suppose I picked up that odd little tidbit about picture height?"

A hand went up. "Yes, Fisher?"

"Didn't Sherlock Holmes solve a murder that way?"

"Very impressive, Fisher," he congratulated her. "As a result of your reading you're able to answer a question in thirty seconds that the rest of your classmates would have tried to answer by watching a week's worth of surveillance tapes."

"I'm not that brilliant, sir."

"Time will tell, Fisher, time will tell. The point I'm making is that while technology is helpful, common sense is even more so. An inquisitive mind is a spy's greatest asset."

A hand shot up in the back of the room.

"Yes, Branigan?"

"Agent Hopkins said we shouldn't call ourselves spies."

"Yes, the word spy is out of fashion, but I happen to like it. Spy is a simple, straightforward explanation of who we are and what we do. There aren't many occupations with three-letter job descriptions. Feel free to call yourselves an espionage agent or whatever fancy name you prefer. You won't be handing out business cards."

"Excuse me, sir," Branigan followed up. "How did you know my name?"

It was time for the elaborate joke Gregor played on every class. He'd studied their pictures and memorized their names in advance, and then he used this knowledge to create a little mystique. "Your class roster only lists one person with an Irish surname. Your hair is reddish-brown. You have a light complexion and your skin looks like it freckles in the sun. You have an outgoing personality. Those are typically Irish traits, so I deduced that you must be Branigan. It would have been embarrassing if you weren't, so I appreciate your cooperation."

"You're entirely welcome, sir."

He strolled around the room. "Ms. White, Mr. Adams," he nodded at the students on his right. "As I was saying, the bad news is you can't play with these nice toys yet. The good news is you're not going to have to listen to your instructor drone on endlessly, Saturday after Saturday. This morning I'm going to teach you how to observe people. Next Saturday you're going to Colonial Williamsburg to observe them in the field. I have an associate who will be pretending to be a drug courier en route to a drop. Your challenge will be to identify this person and bring them back here. You'll be divided into two-person teams, and I'll have a prize for the winning team."

White's hand went up. "What if we nab the wrong person?" she asked with a worried look.

"That would be most unfortunate, wouldn't it?"

Heads bobbed.

"You certainly wouldn't want to haul some poor, unsuspecting tourist back here. That's why you're going to pay close attention to what I'm going to tell you this morning. That's also why you're going to follow any suspect for at least an hour. It might comfort you to know that in all the years I've been playing this little game with my students no one has ever apprehended an innocent bystander. You'll make some initial mistakes, but you'll find that an hour's worth of observation is more than enough to clear things up. You'll also discover that when you know what to look for, it isn't hard to tell when someone's up to something."

"What if our suspect denies being your associate?" Fisher asked.

"Are you expecting a full confession on the spot, Fisher?"

"Well – no, I guess not."

"That only happens in the movies. In real life villains deny their villainy. Bad guys don't have a code of ethics that precludes lying." He saw Branigan's hand waving like a flag and he nodded wearily. There was one in every class. "Yes, Branigan?"

"Why are we looking for a drug courier? We're not going to be do drug busts in real life, are we? Isn't that a job for the Feds or the county mounties?"

"It's just a game, Branigan," Gregor informed him. "It has nothing to do with drugs. I'm really teaching you how to avoid being obvious when you're carrying something of value. If it makes you feel better, you can think of this little lesson as Smuggling 101." He saw sixteen Ah Ha looks. He knew he had them.

Serge surveyed Buckingham's main street from the driver's seat of his Toyota Tacoma. "You said she lives in a dump, but this place looks okay."

Chris looked up from his roadmap. "She doesn't live in town, she lives out in the boonies. If we get to the turnoff for Appomattox, we've gone too far."

"Hurry up, I feel like a sardine," Russell complained from the jump seat behind them.

Chris was pleased that Sierra had invited him to come, but she'd asked him to do a small favor on the way: deliver the incriminating photograph to Norman Chase's house. After agonizing over it, he'd put the 8x10 in a manila envelope and printed *Norman Chase* and *Confidential* on it, and underlined the word *Confidential* three times. His parents had turned down his request to use the family Subaru, so he'd enlisted Serge's help. They'd picked up Russell and set off for Buckingham. When they stopped at the Chase home in the Fan District, Chris had gotten cold feet. Serge snatched the envelope, marched up to the door and gave the brass knocker a few bold raps. When Norman answered, he'd given him the envelope and a brief message: "This is from Sierra. She'll call tomorrow afternoon." Serge returned to his idling truck, where his friends were ducking out of sight. They sped off, leaving Norman standing on his doorstep, puzzling over the envelope.

They crested a hill and saw the RonDayVoo Lounge and the McGuire trailer. They pulled into the gravel lot. "Check that out," Russell pointed to the trailer's stoop, where Blackjack had fashioned an awning from a car hood and two metal poles.

The door opened. "Hey, guys," Sierra welcomed them. "Mi casa, su casa."

"God I hope not," Serge said in a low voice.

Chris navigated around a stack of wooden skids, kicked a stray tire iron out of the way, climbed the sagging front steps and gave her a hug. "This is my friend Serge," he introduced the third Musketeer.

She gave them a smile. "Thanks for coming."

"I delivered your package to Mr. Chase," Serge took credit where credit was due.

"I took the picture and printed it," Russell one-upped him.

"I licked the envelope," Chris offered weakly.

Sierra led them inside. She let the warped paneling, threadbare carpet, grease-stained furniture and noise from the bar speak their usual volumes. "My dad has a deal with the guy who owns the bar. He keeps an eye on it when it's closed, and we get free rent and all he can drink."

"That's like putting the shark in charge of the aquarium," Chris observed.

"Where do people work around here?" Serge wondered. "There's like nothing here."

"We've got two prisons at Dillwyn," she said. "A lot of people work there."

"I'll never complain about Billyburg again," Chris vowed. "So what kind of excitement do you have lined up for us this evening?"

"I'll get some drinks and munchies and you can help me figure out how to work out the exchange with Mr. Chase," she laid out the agenda.

Russell gave her an accusatory look. "Is that why you wanted us to come here?"

"I can't pull this off by myself, Russell. I don't even have a car. Did you bring the picture?"

"Chase has the only print," Chris lied. Technically it was true, since the print he'd stashed in his bedroom had half of the subject matter cropped out. "I wish we could have seen the look on his face when he saw it."

"I can show you the original on my camera, but I didn't bring it," Russell said. "Sorry."

"Is it good?" she asked.

"It's perfect," Chris assured her. "There's no way Chase would ever want anyone to see that picture."

Sierra went next door to get their snacks from the bar. While she was gone her accomplices studied the family photos on the fridge. "Her sister's a babe, too," Serge noticed.

"How could these two parents have these two kids?" Chris puzzled. "They must have been adopted."

Russell examined Blackjack's picture. "No adoption agency would give a kid to this guy."

Chris glanced around nervously. "I hope he's not listening in the bedroom."

"This is the crappiest place I've ever seen," Russell said. "And I'm a lifelong veteran of substandard housing."

Sierra returned, and they brainstormed about how they could exchange the camera's memory card for $200,000. Chris came up with the plan they eventually adopted, but Serge emerged as the master strategist, finessing the details until it seemed foolproof. They set their rendezvous with Norman Chase in Colonial Williamsburg on the following Saturday, the day after Sierra's graduation. If all went well she would be the first independently wealthy member of her graduating class.

Russell had his reservations; he'd been listening and saying little. He decided to try to inject some sanity into the proceedings. "Have you guys ever considered that we might get arrested for this?"

Sierra faced him calmly. "Russell, if we went around telling everyone what happened in Mr. Chase's office, would it be a crime?"

He shrugged. "No."

"If I asked Mr. Chase to give me a college scholarship, would that be a crime?"

"No. People probably hit up for money all the time."

"Okay," she connected the dots. "If you take two things that aren't crimes and put them together, what makes it a crime?"

"Extortion's illegal, isn't it?"

"So's selling pot to your friends," Chris said pointedly. "Pressuring a rich guy to send you to college isn't any worse than what you were doing, Russell. You're the one who's wanted by the law."

"All right, all right," he admitted defeat. "But if this thing blows up in our faces, just remember I warned you."

"It's not going to blow up as long as we have all our bases covered," Serge said.

"I didn't ask you to take that picture," Sierra reminded her troops. "But now that we've got it we need to use it to make this thing work." They heard footsteps in the gravel. She cracked the blinds and looked outside. A drunk from the bar was urinating on the side of her trailer. She turned back to her friends. "You really don't know how much this means to me."

Chapter 24

On Sunday mornings the Chases attended Reveille United Methodist Church on Cary Street Road. There were closer churches, even closer Methodist ones, but Meg preferred Reveille because she aspired to live in this lovely, upscale section of the city. If the family went to church here, she reasoned, they would get to know the people in the neighborhood. When she was ready to spring the idea of moving on Norman she could point out how many of their friends lived in this area. Of course they were really *her* friends since he didn't have any, but there was no sense bringing that up.

This morning Norman and Sean were warming the pew while the Chase women were ringing out *Jesu, Joy of Man's Desiring* with the hand bell choir. Norman saw his house of worship as a religious country club, a place where he could make business contacts over potluck suppers instead of the expensive restaurants where people expected him to pick up the tab. His church affiliation had paid off handsomely. He'd hospitalized several youngsters from the congregation, and the church's outreach ministry had adopted Riverside as a project, not realizing it was a for-profit corporation. He only saw two downsides to church attendance: he had to roll out of bed on Sunday mornings and listen to preachers yammer about virtue and vice, and they wanted his money. He solved the first problem by napping through the sermons and the second by making in-kind donations of castoffs from his hospital, which he deducted on his tax returns for exorbitant sums. When it came to virtue and vice Norman was a contrarian; he saw many of the alleged virtues as vices, and many of the traditional vices as virtues.

Despite the soothing tones of the hand bells he was having trouble catching his usual nap. The photograph had come as a shock. He'd sequestered himself in his den for the rest of the day, contemplating his next move. He was forced to face the grim reality that the next move wasn't his to make. *She'll call you tomorrow afternoon*, her messenger boy had promised him. She could send him to the state pen, and he was supposed to sit by the phone, twiddle his thumbs and wait.

He decided to focus on his other problems, which seemed like minor annoyances by comparison. Tomorrow he'd whip things back into shape at the hospital. He'd find a cut-rate outfit to clean up the smoke and water damage. He'd appoint an acting clinical director to fill the empty beds. He'd have everything back on cruise control and he could turn his attention to teaching Miss McGuire the lesson she needed to learn.

He closed his eyes and listened to his wife and daughter ringing their hearts out in the sanctuary. He'd never understood the Methodist obsession with hand bells, but over the years he'd come to enjoy the ringing and the dinging of the bells, bells, bells, of the bells, bells, bells, bells, bells, bells. The tintinnabulation of the...

He awoke with a start. The congregation was standing for the closing hymn and Meg was giving him a dirty look.

On Sunday mornings the Dewberrys strolled across the William & Mary campus and attended Mass at St. Bede's. A few months earlier Chris had broken his mother's heart by turning in his cassock and dropping out of the acolyte corps. No self-respecting bluesman wanted *altar boy* in his resume, but she didn't get it. She took a dim view of his lack of enthusiasm for church, but if God wanted him to be a more enthusiastic churchgoer He should have given him a greater appreciation for liturgical music. He'd reached the point where he could daydream through sermons of any length on any topic. This morning as Father Reynolds took to the pulpit, he slouched down in his pew and made himself comfortable.

"In case any of you are wondering what God's phone number is," the priest said to his congregants, "it's not 911." He paused to let this little message sink in. "You don't have to wait for an emergency to call God. In fact, you've got a toll-free, wireless connection all the time, and it works even better than a Blackberry or an iPhone. It's called your conscience."

Chris looked up.

"In this morning's lesson from First Kings we heard the story of Elijah. Instead of communicating with Elijah by earthquake, wind or fire like the prophet was expecting, the Lord spoke to him in a 'still small voice'. Interesting, isn't it? Instead of thundering to get our attention, God speaks in whispers. Alluding to this passage, the poet John Greenleaf Whittier wrote, 'through earthquake, wind and fire, the still, small voice of calm.'

Often our most memorable spiritual experiences, our most transcendent moments, don't take place in churches, with choirs and pipe organs. They take place when we're alone, listening to that still, small voice."

Chris rearranged himself in the pew and tried to focus on the money drop this coming Saturday.

"Mahatma Gandhi once observed, 'the only tyrant I accept in the world is the still, small voice within me.' God's voice, which secular humanists call a conscience and Freudians call a super-ego, is indeed tyrannical because it's the enemy of impulsive, self-centered, immoral behavior. That little voice can be our worst enemy or our best friend. Who would ever dream that a Creator who could get our attention with thunderclaps and lightning bolts prefers to tap us on the shoulder and whisper? Who would ever think that a quiet voice could convey a message more compellingly than a roaring one? Ah, but it's true, my friends, it's true."

"A member of this congregation once told me that the only sermons he ever remembers are the short ones. I believe he was giving me a hint. So I'm going to do you a favor this morning and quit while I'm ahead. I'm going to leave you with the still, small voice within you, and let you reflect for a minute or two about any personal struggles you may be having. So instead of listening to a man in fancy vestments standing up here telling you what to do, you can listen to God. I have it on good faith that He knows quite a bit more about most subjects than your pastor does."

And with that the priest left the pulpit, sat down for three minutes, and then continued with the service.

Later Chris would reflect that in all his years of churchgoing it was the only sermon he ever remembered.

On Sunday mornings, while her father slept off his Saturday nights, Sierra accompanied her mother and sister to the Timber Ridge Assembly of Divine Revelation. She'd noticed that Brother Hancock didn't think much of the activities other people found enjoyable. The preacher viewed his flock as naughty children who needed to be scolded and threatened and put back in line. He talked about a God who sounded like a state trooper in the sky, waiting to nab sinners in the speed trap of life. Interestingly, this God held the same deeply conservative political views as the preacher. He hated gun control, abortion, homosexuality, MTV and the United Nations. He liked the death penalty.

Brother Bart and Sister Hattie led the singing with guitars. Their music worked best with a captive audience, and Sierra usually found herself feeling extremely captive. This morning, however, they were singing her favorite hymn. She sang along with gusto.

> When the shadows of this life have grown,
> I'll fly away.
> Like a bird from prison bars have flown,
> I'll fly away.

She'd been waiting all her life to fly away. Many of her classmates had similar desires, but they lacked her sense of urgency. While they were resting their eyes on at the surrounding hillsides she intended to take wing and see what was on the other side.

> Just a few more weary days and then,
> I'll fly away.
> To a land where joy will never end,
> I'll fly away.

Just a few more weary days, she told herself.

On Sunday mornings Zenia practiced Tai Chi with Richmond's Chinese community in Maymont Park. The graceful, dance-like movements restored her balance and prepared her for the coming week. The slow tempo and smooth transitions made her feel more alive. This morning as she went through the Wind Rolls the Lotus Leaves form she could feel her Chi circulating. Now that she'd decided to take on the task of reforming her workplace, she imagined herself a New Age Joan of Arc, girding for battle. She'd been fortunate to attain enlightenment at a relatively young age so she could devote herself to sharing her insights with others and leading them along the shining path. Under her gentle prodding the treatment center's staff would become a cohesive unit, a team she would root, balance, connect, center, focus and enable.

The only thing that bothered her about these sessions was the leader's stubborn insistence that they do the Tai Chi exercises in unison. Often she felt moved to improvise, and this seemed to threaten the others. They'd tried to kick her out of the group, but she'd pointed out that they didn't own the park. They pretended to ignore her, but every now and then when she finished a particularly inspired set of forms she would catch them sneaking admiring glances.

This morning as they moved on to White Crane Spreads Wings she closed her eyes and imagined that she was a giant whooping crane with an eight-foot wingspan, a snow-white bird with black wingtips. She flapped her wings gently from side to side, then over her head, removing the hospital's negative energy and hurling it over the nearby rock outcroppings and into the James River. She imagined all this negativity flowing downstream and washing into a vast ocean of positivity. She flapped her wings and took off, soaring above the park and gliding on the wind. She spiraled higher, and then swept lower, following the river on its journey to the Chesapeake Bay, then the Atlantic. She touched down elegantly on the beach. She watched the hospital's negative energy dissipate in the ocean and she did a joyous dance of celebration.

She opened her eyes and saw her Asian friends giving her inscrutable smiles.

Andrew came out of his apartment to check the weather. He saw his landlady parking her Studebaker in the one-car garage behind the house. Apparently no one had bothered to tell her it was the 21st Century. She headed for her back door wearing a look of irritation. "How was church, Miss B?" he called to her.

"Terrible. The Episcopal Church certainly isn't what it used to be. All they talk about is tolerance and inclusiveness. This morning they were talking about the miracle of the loaves and the fishes, and guess what the moral of the story was?"

"Be tolerant and inclusive?"

"Of course! It's the meaning of every passage and the moral of every parable! You show me one place in the Bible where it says anything about being inclusive and I'll eat my hat."

"You can always go back to ancestor worship," he offered helpfully.

"Leave me alone, Andrew," she said.

But from the look on her face he thought he seemed to be considering it.

Chapter 25

Norman pulled the offending photo out the file cabinet in his den and took another look at it. Every time he laid eyes on this testament to his stupidity he knew that if this photograph ever circulated he was dead meat. Overnight he would go from being a respected member of the community to being a dirty old man preying on the young innocents in his care. He'd never be able to convince anyone that the girl was the predator and he was the prey.

He studied the family portrait over his mantel. His wife had paid a society photographer a small fortune for this picture of familial harmony. He'd posed them in front of the Virginia House on Sulgrave Road, a 16th century manor imported stone-by-stone from England. They looked like a royal family standing on the lawn of their castle. He knew this backdrop was a not-so-subtle hint from Meg that she wanted a similar castle. He remembered the afternoon well. They'd bickered up to the moment the photographer was ready to snap the shutter, faked smiles, then gone back to bickering.

The phone rang and he sprinted for it. "Hello?"

"Are you having a nice weekend, Mr. Chase?"

"Cut the crap, Sierra. I was trying to take care of your concerns when I sent you home Friday, but apparently you've got another agenda. Why don't you tell me what the hell is going on?"

"How do you think our picture turned out?"

"Don't play games with me, young lady. What do you want?"

"A college education," she laid her cards on the table. "I need a benefactor to give me a scholarship."

"That's very interesting. And what will this benefactor get in return?"

"The satisfaction of knowing he's helping a deserving student."

"As deeply satisfying as that would be, somehow I don't find it enough."

"Plus the memory card from the camera and my word that I'll forget what happened in your office."

"Your word?" he scoffed. "Am I supposed to believe that you're such an honorable young lady that your word is worth something? I think we're well beyond that point. How do I know you haven't made a hundred copies of this thing and that you're going to keep pulling them out of your dresser drawer for the next 30 years?"

"If I have a degree I can take care of myself."

"You already seem to be doing a good job of that."

"Mr. Chase, we don't have any reason to trust each other, but we're going to have to anyway. What's our alternative?"

"Let's talk about our alternatives. Suppose I refuse to bite?"

"Then I'll mail copies of the picture to the members of your Advisory Board and let them decide what to do."

Norman gasped. How on earth did she know about this meddlesome group of community members the health care bureaucracy had foisted upon him? He'd filled his board's ranks with clueless patsies who rubber stamped his every decision and served as human decorations at official functions. But even these featherbrains weren't going to ignore a picture of him frolicking in the nude with one of his young patients. "How do you know about the Advisory Board?"

"I cleaned the conference room after your last meeting. I found a list with their names and addresses."

He had to give her points for doing her homework. "Let's talk about college, Sierra," he changed his tune. "I gather we're not talking about a semester at the Happy Valley Beauty College?"

"No, we're talking about four years at Georgetown University."

"Georgetown?" he asked incredulously.

"Yes, but it's expensive."

"How about Virginia Tech?" he proposed. "I've got some connections there. I can arrange a full ride." It was perfect. He could buy off the girl, get the professional beggars from his alma mater off his back and claim a tax deduction in the process.

"I want to be a Hoya, not a Hokie," she turned down his offer. "I want to study Foreign Service. Georgetown's the best school."

"What does it cost?"

"Two hundred thousand dollars."

"Two hundred thousand dollars!"

"I have to cover my tuition and living expenses for four years."

"What makes you think I have that kind of money?"

"You," she refreshed his memory. "You told me your property was worth 4 million, and you have three houses and your wife owns dresses that cost more than some people's cars."

Norman cursed himself for opening his big mouth. "Before we make any hasty decisions I'd like you to give some more thought to Virginia Tech. That's my offer – a full scholarship at the state's largest university. I'll arrange for you to be the first Chase Scholar. Think about it and call me back at eight o'clock tonight."

Sierra realized he'd bought the basic concept and now they were just dickering over the price. "All right, I'll think about it."

"I think we're making progress on this, Sierra."

"I think so too," she agreed.

Russell was stretched out in William & Mary's Sunken Garden, flipping through the *Walden* Cliff's Notes Chris had given him. He'd never been much of a reader, and it seemed ironic that now that he was a free man he was being forced to engage in this activity. When he opened the booklet the first thing he saw was a disclaimer: THESE NOTES ARE NOT A SUBSTITUTE FOR THE TEXT ITSELF. Yeah, right. Did this Cliff guy really think that the slackers who bought his cheat sheets actually read the books, too? He reviewed what he'd learned. Henry David Thoreau was a pencil maker's son in Concord, Massachusetts, in the early 1800's. Henry had devoted his short life to living up to his own advice about marching to the beat of a different drummer. He'd flitted from one occupation to the next, working in the family business, surveying, doing carpentry, teaching and writing. He eventually retreated to Walden Pond on the outskirts of town, and he built a one-room shack. He lived there for two years, gardening, fishing, playing his flute and keeping a journal. His only love interest was Mother Nature, and this was one of his two big themes. Grumbling about society was the other one. Despite his ties to the pencil industry, Henry wasn't much of a capitalist. He considered working for bigger and better things a waste of time. He believed most people "led lives of quiet desperation" and the solution was to "simplify, simplify". He published these insights when he moved back to town, and they were received with a giant yawn. He died a failed writer, but somewhere down the line history decided the odd duck on the pond was a brilliant social critic who'd penned a classic and fathered the environmental movement.

He stretched out in the grass and stared at the passing clouds. According to Cliff the pond was a metaphor, but he'd never understood what the metaphor thing was about. He must have missed that day in English class. The only part he could relate to was Thoreau's interest in nature. If he'd discovered anything the past few days it was the outdoors. He realized he'd been wasting his time taking snapshots of basketball teams and cheerleading squads for the school yearbook. He needed better subjects. He needed a Mac laptop like Chris's, and a decent printer so he could make bigger enlargements. He needed a job, he needed a roof over his head, he needed a set of wheels and he needed a plan for pulling it all together. So much for simplifying.

He'd spent the morning riding around Williamsburg on Serge's bike, scoping things out and taking pictures. It seemed like a decent place. He'd gotten a shot of the past colliding with the future when he photographed a guy riding past some people in Colonial costumes on a Segway. It wasn't hard to imagine living in this place. He could apprentice to some photographer and sell his pictures in the shops. He could use the town as a home base and make forays into the natural world, like Ansel Adams did. At the end of *Walden* Thoreau had urged readers to go confidently in the direction of their dreams and live the lives they imagined. Maybe this was the dream he was supposed to have and the life he was supposed to imagine: Russell Moss, Nature Photographer. He wouldn't even need to go back to school to make it happen.

He grabbed the Cliff's Notes and rocked to his feet. It was the flimsiest of plans, but more of one than he'd ever had before. Feeling optimistic, he hopped on his bike and pedaled out of the Sunken Garden.

At eight o'clock Sierra called Norman Chase on her new cell phone. He picked up on the first ring. "Hi, Mr. Chase."

"I hope you've been giving my offer to send you to Virginia Tech serious consideration, Sierra," Norman resumed his sales pitch. "It's not every day an opportunity like this comes along. I looked at Tech's website and they've got an international studies program. They even have a villa in Switzerland. They send students over there every year. College doesn't get much better than that, does it?"

"I still want to go to Georgetown," she stuck to her guns. "I don't like the way you want to do this. You want to give the money to the school instead of me, and stretch it out over four years. Suppose you get hit by a car? Or suppose you get mad and decide to stop paying my tuition? We need a simple arrangement."

Norman knew where this was heading. "Let me guess. I'll bet this so-called simple arrangement involves giving you a big fat wad of cash. Am I right?"

"If you give me the money, I'll give you the picture. We'll never have to deal with each other again."

"Well I've got a problem with that, young lady. A big problem. In the first place I don't keep $200,000 in a cookie jar. My money's tied up investments. In the second place, if I gave it to you instead of your school I wouldn't be able to take a tax deduction."

"Mr. Chase, I'm not worried about your tax problems. Maybe the money's not in a cookie jar, but you seem like the kind of man who can do anything he wants, so I'm sure you can come up with it. I'll tell you what you need to do. You'd better write this down." She reached in her pocket and pulled out the napkin that contained the list of instructions she and her friends had developed. "Meet me on Saturday morning in Colonial Williamsburg at ten o'clock. Bring your family along. You'll be taking a tour, and we'll make our exchange after that."

"My family! Don't be absurd! Even if I cooperate with this ridiculous scheme, I'm not involving my family. This is entirely between the two of us."

"No family, no picture," she explained the ground rules. "If you follow my instructions they'll never know what's going on." Making him bring his wife and children was Serge's suggestion, a way to keep him from bringing along some thug to try to intimidate them. Sending him on an exhaustive tour of the Colonial village was Chris's inspiration, designed to wear him down mentally and physically until he was dying to fork over the cash and leave. "Are you writing this down?"

Norman considered his alternatives. He didn't have any. As painful as this was, it paled in comparison to the hell his life would be if his Advisory Board ever saw the incriminating photograph. "Go on."

"Bring $150,000 in hundreds and $50,000 in twenties," she read from the napkin. "Put the money in a backpack and cover it up with a sweatshirt or a sweater."

"I don't own a backpack," he objected. "If I start carrying one my family's going to be suspicious."

"I'm sure you can think of something to tell your darlings about your new accessory." She gave him the parking and ticket information. "And bring your cell phone," she added. "I'll be calling you during the day and giving you more instructions."

"You've put a lot of thought into this, haven't you?"

"I had help from my associates." She wanted him to know she wouldn't be alone.

"Your associates? Are you a corporation now?"

"Something like that."

"Don't you think you're getting a little carried away with all this foolishness, Sierra? We don't need to turn this into some silly game. Why do we have to meet in Williamsburg?"

"It's more convenient for my associates."

"I don't like the sound of this associates business. You and your confederates aren't planning to double cross me, are you?"

"If you follow my instructions you'll end up with what you want and you'll never hear from me again." She asked for his cell phone number. He gave it to her and she said goodbye and hung up.

She felt sure he would show up. He might try to give her counterfeit bills with a few real ones on top, but this would mean spending hours over a copy machine, and he probably didn't even know how to work one. He was the kind of man who was used to having other people do things for him.

The more she thought about it, the more she was convinced the plan was foolproof.

Chapter 26

Zenia had never been summoned to employer's office before, but she felt sure she knew what he wanted. She'd missed work on Friday and she hadn't called in. She was pleased he'd noticed her absence, but apprehensive about how she was going to explain it. She knocked on his door. "Mr. Chase? It's Zenia."

"Come in, St. Clair."

She entered the office and noticed the furnishings, which had an elegance that wasn't evident anywhere else in the institution. "Wow, you've got a nice office."

"Have a seat, St. Clair." Norman watched curiously as she folded her birdlike legs in a modified lotus in one of his chairs. "I'm sure you've heard that Kate's no longer with us."

"Yes, I couldn't believe it! What happened?"

"She took a wild notion she could make more money somewhere else. She upped and left. She didn't even give us notice."

"That doesn't sound like Kate. She has such positive energy."

"Yeah, whatever. Anyway, I've had my eye on you, St. Clair."

"If you're wondering why I missed work Friday, I've got a good explanation."

"I'm promoting you to acting clinical director."

It took a few seconds for this to register. "But I'm a movement therapist, Mr. Chase. Do you really think I can supervise medical people?"

"Absolutely. But work on admissions first. I want a warm body in every bed by the end of the week. Don't be too picky. Quantity is Job One."

"I – I don't know what to say. This is just so unexpected."

"I'll give you a $2000 raise in January. That'll bring you up to twenty thousand."

Zenia considered it. "Please don't take this the wrong way, but isn't that a little low for a clinical director? Not that I'm here for material reasons. I embrace the Buddhist concept of Right Livelihood and I view my work as a calling. I just wish I were being called to make a little more."

"Let's see what kind of job you do, and we'll revisit the salary issue later," he kept it vague. "We won't hire a movement therapist in your place, so your old job will still be available if things don't work out." He did the math. He'd been shelling out $42,000 for Kate Oxley. By shuffling St. Clair to this job, underpaying her and not filling her old position, he'd be 40K ahead. Another 5K and he'd have Raleigh's raise covered. He made a mental note to look for a lower grade of institutional food.

"I'll do my best, Mr. Chase," Zenia promised him. "I think you'll be pleased with some of my ideas."

"Save the ideas for later, St. Clair. Work on the intakes. Now get to work."

She hopped to her feet. "We're going to make a great team."

"Leave me off the team for now. I've got to get this mess from the fire cleaned up, and then I've got some personal business."

She gave him a mock salute. "Aye, aye, Captain."

"I appreciate your dedication to the chain of command, St. Clair, but you can dispense with the salutes."

Zenia drifted out the door. She saw her elevation to clinical director as karma, her reward for personal excellence, a sign she was meant to lead the hospital into a New Age. She needed to find Doctor Garcia and give the good news.

Norman was even more pleased. He'd given the clinical director's job to a harmless flake who didn't seem to have any personal life. This meant she was available 24/7, so the staff could pester the hell out of her instead of him. They would resent her promotion, and he'd eventually agree and replace her with someone qualified, giving his staff the false impression he cared about their concerns. It was a perfect strategy. Now he could turn his attention to more serious problems.

Sierra had two Facebook messages. She read Chris's first.

Another mundane Monday. Serge loaned Russell a kayak and even as I write our boy is communing with turtles and ducks. He's succumbing to the charms of our fair village. At least he's hanging around until Saturday to assist with Operation Scholarship.

Dad's getting on my nerves. He thinks I'm treading water in the Pool of Life when I should be swimming vigorous laps. He thinks I need a job. I told him I was putting a band together, but he doesn't see this as work because I enjoy it. We ate at Olive Garden after church yesterday and when he heard the waiters singing Happy Birthday in Italian he tried to convince me that I could get paid for singing if I worked there. I don't think he gets the basic idea of music.

I'm taking Russell and Serge to the Blues Shack. It's a place in Newport News where the players jam. The News ain't exactly the Delta, but music's wherever you find it, except Olive Garden.

How are the negotiations going with Chase?

Your man in Billyburg, Chris

Sierra clicked on her other message and saw it was from Georgetown University.

Dear Ms. McGuire:

I'm contacting you on behalf of Jennifer Fish, our Director of Admissions. We received your online application. Unfortunately we have accepted our freshman class for the fall semester and we have several hundred students wait-listed. However, Ms. Fish was quite impressed with your letter detailing your family circumstances and your academic achievements, and your interest in our School of Foreign Service. Suffice it to say your background is atypical for students with this focus. Your story about the gentleman who wants to provide you with a scholarship was also quite interesting.

Since one of our goals is maintaining a diverse student body, we are taking the unusual step of granting you a personal interview. Given the time constraints we need to do this right away. I offered to travel to your home and conduct the interview, and Ms. Fish agreed it would be the most efficient thing to do. (Actually I get tired of sitting at my desk, staring at the Gothic spires of Healy Hall, and I don't mind an excuse to take a drive in the Virginia countryside.) I'm not sure where Buckingham County is located, but your description of it being in the Bermuda Triangle between Richmond, Charlottesville and Lynchburg was quite clever. I'd like to conduct your interview as soon as possible. Please call me at the number below and we'll make the necessary arrangements. I'm looking forward to meeting you. Please have your transcript forwarded immediately. I await your call.

Jonathan Cox, Admissions Counselor

"Tina, come look at this," Sierra called to her friend, who was propped up in her bed, paging through *Seventeen*. "Georgetown wants to interview me."

"You were just born lucky," Tina reacted. She struggled to a sitting position, threw her feet on the floor and rocked forward to gain the necessary momentum to stand up. She read the message over Sierra's shoulder. "Are you really going to let him come to your house?"

"When he sees where I live he'll really feel sorry for me. I'm not even going to clean it."

Tina eyed her message from Chris. "You heard from your boyfriend."

"I need to write back to him," she said. She started typing.

Chris,

I think it's time to stop using all these silly abbreviations and start writing like a college student. Georgetown's coming to interview me! I can't believe it! I talked to Mr. Chase twice yesterday. He's going through with it. Sorry about your dad. We all have our fathers.

Later, Sierra

Fred walked out of the head shop with his new purchase and climbed into the Astrovan that served as a corporate office, mobile home and drug den. His business partner, Ted, was getting off the phone. "Check this out, man. Some rinky-dink hospital had a mattress fire and they want to give us fifteen hundred bucks to clean it up."

"Whoa." Fred hadn't expected the ad they'd taken in the Yellow Pages to pay off so handsomely. It read simply, *Ted & Fred's Professional Cleaning*, without explaining what Ted and Fred cleaned so professionally. This generalist approach, combined with the low overhead they achieved by living in their van, gave Ted and Fred a significant leg up on the competition.

"Guess we know who the brains of this outfit is," Ted said. He suspected he had a few more brain cells than his friend, who was busy getting his new bong ready for a test drive. "All we've got to do is haul off some carpet and ceiling tiles, and scrub the walls and throw a little paint on them. And get this – they're giving us a kid to help."

Fred frowned. "A kid could seriously interfere with our work habits."

"Nah. We'll bribe Junior with a little weed and get him to do all the work. The place already smells like smoke, right? We'll toke up while he busts his butt, and every couple of hours we give him a little herbal refreshment to keep him motivated."

Fred shook his head admiringly. "Man, you've got it figured out."

"I told the dude we need a deposit up front," Ted revealed. "He's giving us half the money tomorrow."

"Shit, man. Nine hundred bucks buys a lot of product."

"Half of fifteen is seven-fifty," Ted did the math for him.

"Yeah, whatever. This calls for a little celebration."

"Everything calls for a celebration. Pass the bong, man."

Fred shared their newest corporate purchase. "This is gonna be the easiest job we never did."

"Let me see that clicker, VM," Sierra took the remote from her sister.

"You're not putting on HGTV again, are you?" Viola May asked her. She knew the answer. Home and Garden Television was the only channel her older sister ever watched.

"I'm not into *Saved By the Bell* reruns. How can you watch the same old shows over and over?"

"Zack's cute, that's how."

"Get a life, VM. He's just some actor who doesn't know you exist. Those shows are so old he's probably got grandchildren by now."

"He does not. His name is Mark Paul."

Sierra switched channels. HGTV was her refuge, a parallel universe. The people on this channel hired architects and landscapers and interior designers. They laid winding cobblestone paths and dug little water features and filled them with exotic fish. There weren't any trailers on HGTV. You never saw the king of the castle passed out in a recliner with an empty bottle of Colt 45 in his lap. You didn't see a '77 Gremlin parked out front, or a bar next door. She'd been tempted to submit her parents' names to the show where they come and give your house a free makeover. She wondered what the team of designers and decorators would think when they pulled up in front of the trailer. She imagined the stylish women and prissy little men executing an abrupt U-turn and making snide comments as they sped away.

HGTV was featuring a couple who'd spent eight years turning an old schoolhouse into a dream home, with a spiral staircase and a bell tower. "Watch this, VM," she wanted her sister to pay attention to how other people lived. "Maybe someday I'll have a place like this and you can come visit me."

"Oh, sure you will, Jolene. And maybe someday I'll marry Zack."

Chapter 27

When you have an organization that needs top-to-bottom reform, sometimes it's hard to decide where to start. After much thought Zenia decided to start in the Riverside Center's stomach. She'd gone to the kitchen to meet with the food service director, Helen Bowles. Helen's mushy gray fare was uninspired even by institutional standards, and Zenia was excited that her new role would allow her to address this problem. Helen was prepping for dinner, and she put Zenia to work peeling potatoes while they talked.

"Helen, if you're like me, you've probably got some ideas about how we can improve things around here," she opened her little heart-to-heart.

The dietician continued slashing potatoes. "Like what?"

"Like serving healthier food."

Helen paused in mid-peel with a look of irritation. "The meals I serve are plenty healthy. I do miracles with the budget Chase gives me."

"The inmates at the city jail eat better than this, Helen. That lunch you served yesterday was pathetic. I couldn't eat the kielbasa because I don't eat meat. I couldn't eat the slice of white bread because I only eat whole grains. I don't eat desserts because I don't believe in empty calories. So all I had was a plate of watery cabbage."

"That's your problem, honey. I don't see how it's any business of yours."

Zenia thought her authority in the mater was obvious. "I'm the clinical director now. What these kids eat is part of their treatment, and since I'm in charge of the treatment, that puts me in charge of the food. I want to introduce more whole grains and fruits, and a vegan option."

"You've got one small problem, honey. Me. You need a registered dietician to sign off on the menus. If you think I'm going along with your kooky ideas, you're got another thought coming. You don't know beans about nutrition."

"I do so know beans about nutrition," Zenia said in a hurt voice. "I've been studying health foods all my life. I read Adele Davis when I was sixteen."

"We studied her, too. She was the mother of all health nuts. She died of stomach cancer. Her publisher had to pay off all the people who got sick following her advice. Folks in my business get doctorates writing about her mistakes."

"Her advice certainly never hurt me."

Helen aimed her potato peeler at her. "Look at you! You're skin and bones! You're a walking corpse! Wake up and smell the coffee, Zenia."

"Health isn't about looks," Zenia tried to correct her misconception. "It's about finding the proper spiritual and physical balance. And I'm not going to wake up and smell the coffee because I drink herbal teas. I plan to offer a selection of them in the dining room."

"Chase says give 'em Kool Aid, so I give 'em Kool Aid," Helen explained her beverage selection.

"That's just sugar water, Helen. They're human beings, not hummingbirds. If we're going to serve these young people flavored water we might as well flavor it with something healthy, like Kombucha tea."

"Like what?"

"Kombucha tea. It's very popular in the Far East. It's made from a special fungus. It promotes awareness and psychic healing."

"Honey, if you think I'm giving these kids fungus water you've got another thought coming." The dietician's eyes narrowed. "Didn't I see you scarfing down a candy bar this morning?"

"The Goo Goo Cluster represents the perfect balance of yin and yang," she shared a recent insight. "The chocolate and nuts are the yang, or the male principle, and the caramel and marshmallow are the yin, or female principle. Frankly, Helen, I think you serve too many yangs."

"Frankly, Zenia, I think you're full of shit. Go bug someone else. I've got work to do."

"But we haven't agreed on the menu changes."

Helen brandished her peeler like a switchblade. "Get the hell out of my kitchen!"

"We'll continue this discussion later. And it's not your kitchen."

"The discussion's over. Stay out of here or I'll show you my meat cleaver."

"You're being a little harsh, aren't you, Helen?"

"OUT! OUT! OUT!"

Kate was whipping up a marinara sauce over her island stovetop while Andrew and Miss Beauregard perched on stools and nibbled cheese and crackers. "I've got a terminal disease," she said casually as she sautéed garlic and onions.

Miss Beauregard's hand went to her mouth. "Oh, dear. Is it cancer?"

"No, Miss Beauregard, it's called responsibility. I have a compulsion to rescue people. The world is full of needy people and obviously most of them are going to continue being needy despite my efforts, but I still feel like I have to give it a try. I've spent the past two days looking for a missing 16-year-old who apparently wants to stay missing. I'm not even sure what I'd do with him if I found him."

"I've got mixed feelings about Russell, too," Andrew confessed. "We've turned this kid into a fugitive just because he was selling a plant that grows wild everywhere there's dirt."

"Suppose I give him a psychological evaluation that concludes he's better off at home?" Kate proposed. "Do you think the judge would take it into consideration?"

"First we've got to find him."

"I don't know where else to look," she said in frustration. "I've talked to his mother and his landlord and his teachers and his friends. I've gone to shelters and flophouses and checked all the usual hangouts. Apparently he's got a support system that no one knows about."

Andrew helped himself to another slice of Havarti and flipped a scrap to Gilda. "Could it be someone he met at the hospital?"

"The only one he was close to was his roommate, Chris Dewberry. But Chris went home, and he's got very proper parents. They're not the kind who would shelter a runaway."

"But Chris might have known what Russell was up to," Andrew pointed out. "Guys talk, especially when they're thrown together in hardship situations. If Russell was planning to run off, Chris probably knew about it."

Kate opened a can of diced tomatoes and poured them in her skillet. "I guess it wouldn't hurt to give him a call."

Miss Beauregard reached for the cheese. Her stool wobbled and Andrew steadied her. "We're going to have to get you a seatbelt or cut off your liquor, Miss B."

"I only drink to make people like you seem more interesting, Andrew."

"Whew, you're getting feisty in your old age. I'd better watch myself or you might remember you can evict me."

"I remember it constantly," she assured him. "I should sell that old monstrosity of a house and get a nice little place like this."

"You can't sell your house, Miss B! I'd be out on the street."

"I'll sell it to you. Then you won't have to put up with the old bat upstairs."

He grinned. "I don't know. The old bat's growing on me."

She patted his hand. "Flattery will get you everywhere, dear."

It was eight o'clock and Zenia was still at the hospital. None of the staff members had been able to make time to meet with her, but she'd enjoyed circulating and making her presence known. One thing she hadn't gotten around to doing was filling the empty beds. She wasn't sure how the intake process worked, and she was afraid to ask because she didn't want to seem incompetent. Instead she'd devoted herself to arranging discharges. She'd sent four patients home and she'd scheduled two more to leave Wednesday and another on Thursday.

She was patrolling the long corridor that ran the length of the second floor when she spotted Molly Potterfield sitting on the floor of her bedroom, hugging her knees and looking glum. She went in and sat down on the floor beside her. "Why are you looking so unhappy, Molly?"

"Everything. This place. My home. My life. I tried praying about it, but I don't know whether to pray to Jesus or the goddess Kore."

This was exactly the kind of conversation Zenia enjoyed having with her young patients. "I felt the same kind of spiritual confusion when I was your age," she consoled her. "I looked at the different religions and spiritual traditions and they all seemed to have something valuable to offer. I just didn't know which way to go. And then one day I came up with the solution."

Molly studied her with interest. "What?"

"I embraced them all. I became a Christian, a Jew, a Buddhist, a Hindu, a Muslim, a Scientologist, a Rastafarian and a lot of other things."

"But isn't that kind of confusing? I mean, don't they believe different things?"

"Actually it's very liberating. If you consider all religious points of view equally valid you can weave the various traditions into your own beautiful tapestry."

"But where do you go to church?"

"I don't. I have my own rituals. They're quite touching, actually."

"I don't think you'd get along with my stepfather. He's a preacher."

Zenia placed a comforting hand on her shoulder. "I get along with everyone, Molly. That's why Mr. Chase made me the clinical director. I'm a natural leader who can bring people together."

"Please leave me alone," Molly requested. "You're making me even more confused."

Zenia gave her a little hug and hopped up. "We'll continue this conversation another time. I have some more insights I think you'll find very helpful."

She left the hospital congratulating herself on her first day as clinical director. She was born for this job.

Chapter 28

Chris's father had pressured him into interviewing for a job at the Colonial Williamsburg Foundation. Luckily the Foundation had concluded he wasn't quite right for the position. Chris suspected it had something to do with his reply when the man had asked his opinion of the restored village. "It's like Disneyland for history geeks," he'd put it in a nutshell. The interview had gone downhill from there. Since no one was around to celebrate this small triumph he decided to send Sierra a report. He brought up his Facebook and he saw a long message from her called *How to Blow a College Interview in One Easy Lesson.*

Hi Chris -

The admissions officer from Georgetown came to see me this morning. It was a disaster.

I sent my family away and left the place in its usual state of ruin so it would make the right impression. He sounded young on the phone, so I decided it wouldn't hurt to give him something to look at besides my transcript. I know what you're thinking – big mistake. I put on the skimpiest pair of shorts I could find and a pink oxford shirt. I went braless and tied up the shirttails so my stomach was showing. You get the idea – a bouncy preppy. He was young all right. He looked like he belonged in a boy band. His name was Jonathan and he had these cute little wire rim glasses and highlights in his hair. I could tell he was grossed out by the place as soon as he came in. All I had to do was convince him I was a flower in a garbage pail and needed to be transplanted to Georgetown.

Everything was going fine until he asked why I hadn't done any volunteer work. He said Georgetown looks for students who want to contribute to society. I told him I was too busy worrying about myself to worry about society. It didn't sound right and I knew it was the wrong answer. He said even if I didn't have time for volunteer work, if I'd done something like band where I had to master an instrument it would show I could stick with things and work in a group. I guess you get Brownie points for playing the guitar.

He looked me in the eyes and he asked, "Sierra, if we admit you to Georgetown, what can you offer the university community? What can you offer our other students? What can you offer your professors? What can you offer me?" He was giving me this Look and I thought he was coming on to me. I unbuttoned my shirt and I said, "I can offer you this." Okay, so now I know it was a huge mistake, but look how far it got me with Mr. Chase. He stared at my boobs and he turned red. He said, "That's a very interesting offer, but it's not what I had in mind." He begged me to button my shirt before my father came home. I asked if I flunked the interview. He said, "Quite probably." I started crying and I said I'd do anything to get into Georgetown. He said, "You've already made that clear. I can't ever remember an applicant demonstrating their passion for higher education more graphically." Then he let out this gurgling noise that sounded like he was choking and he said, "Why don't we start over? But this time, try baring you soul instead." We talked for an hour, but I don't know. They've got tons of people on the waiting list and the only reason they were interviewing me was the lady in charge liked my letter. I don't know if he's going to tell her what happened.

I'd feel like an idiot telling Mr. Chase I've changed my mind and I want to go to Virginia Tech. What if Georgetown lets me in and he's already paid for Tech? I've got to go through with this thing. So how does it feel having an idiot for a friend?

Later, Sierra

Chris wrote a reply.

All my friends are idiots, so don't give yourself credit for being special. In fact, my parents raised one themselves. So how come you're showing everybody your boobs but me? Your friend Tina doesn't have a web cam, does she? Just kidding.

Amusingly yours, The Talented Mr. Dewberry

Kate had accepted a lunch invitation from Miss Beauregard, and they were having crab cakes at her kitchen table. She hadn't known either of her grandmothers, and this opinionated, gin-guzzling senior citizen fascinated her. She wasn't the cookie-baking surrogate granny she would have chosen, but she was coming to appreciate her.

Their conversation turned to the phone call she was planning to make to Chris Dewberry. When the older woman heard his name she gave her a surprised look. "He's not related to David Dewberry, is he?"

"If you're talking about the history professor, yes. Chris is his son."

"Just a minute, dear." Miss Beauregard hurried off and returned brandishing a trade paperback. She pressed her dog-eared copy of *Battle in a Bottle: the Battle of Drewry's Bluff* reverently in Kate's hands. "This tells how my great-great grandfather saved Richmond," she said proudly. "You don't suppose he'd sign it for me? Maybe I can get him to speak at one of our UDC meetings."

Kate flipped the book over. The photo showed the professor in the same wrinkled seersucker suit he'd worn to her office. "I'd be glad to introduce you to Dr. Dewberry, Miss Beauregard. I'm sure you two would enjoy reliving the War of Northern Aggression over mint juleps."

"Why don't you give him my phone number?"

"I'm going to Andrew's office to call Chris. Why don't you come along, and when we're through, if his father's home we'll put you on with him."

"Really?"

"Dr. Dewberry's hardly an unapproachable celebrity. I'm sure he'd be flattered to talk to someone who's read his book."

"Read it! I've practically memorized it."

"You'll find him very interesting," she predicted.

The Department of Social Services was a warren of cubicles populated by workers who ranged from the young and eager to the old and battle-scarred. Kate knew many of these people from her work at Riverside, and she greeted them as she made her way to Andrew's workstation. Andrew saw the two women coming. "Uh oh, double trouble. What have I done to deserve a visit from the Monarch of Monument Avenue?"

Miss Beauregard waved her book. "The father of the young man you're calling wrote a book about General Beauregard!"

"Calm down, Miss B. You look like a groupie waving a bra at a rock concert."

"That didn't sound like a compliment, Andrew."

"Depends on the groupie."

He pulled up chairs for the two women, and Kate got Chris on the line. She punched the speakerphone so Andrew and Miss B could participate.

"Chris, I'm at the social services office with Russell's social worker," she said. "We also have a friend here who's a big fan of your father's."

"My father has a fan?" Chris sounded dubious.

"We'll get to that later. How are you doing? Do you have a minute to talk?"

"Sure. Are you checking up on me to see if I've pulled a Lizzie Borden yet?"

"I like this guy already," Andrew whispered.

"Actually we're calling about Russell. Did you know he ran away Friday morning?"

"Russell's gone?"

Andrew spoke up. "I'm Andrew Boone, Chris. I'm Russell's social worker. I took him fishing and he ran off. I don't know if it was spur of the moment or something he'd been planning. Did he say anything to you about running away?"

"Just a minute, I need to get something off the stove," he left them hanging. He returned and continued the conversation. "I knew he was pissed about going to foster care. I figured he might do something."

"We've been looking all over for him," Kate said. "We've reached a dead end. We thought you might have some idea of where he would go. He hasn't called you, has he?"

"No. What are you going to do when you find him?"

Andrew had a hunch this might get passed along to Russell. "I've done a one-eighty on this thing, Chris. I'm going to try to convince the court to send him home."

"But he won't get a very sympathetic hearing if he stays on the lam," Kate explained. "They let him plead to a misdemeanor before, so they've already given him one break. If the judge thinks Russell's being uncooperative he could send him to a correctional center instead of giving him probation. That's why we're anxious to get in touch with him."

"What do you want me to do?"

"If you hear from Russell, ask him to call us," Andrew requested. "He probably doesn't want to talk to me, but he might talk to Kate. She's not working at Riverside any more so she's a neutral third party. We just want to help him see things more clearly and try to negotiate a solution that's in his best interest. Will you pass that along if you hear from him?"

"Sure."

Kate signaled Miss Beauregard. "Your father's number one fan would like to talk with him."

"Dad's at work," Chris said. "Who's this big fan?"

Miss Beauregard leaned toward the speaker. "It's Miss Beauregard, dear. You sound like a sweet young man."

"You sound like a dear old thing yourself," Chris replied diplomatically.

"Your father wrote an absolutely brilliant book about my great-great grandfather. I want to invite him to address our UDC chapter."

Andrew got her attention. "For a month's free rent I'll go to your meeting dressed as General Beauregard," he whispered

She made a face. "Tell your father he'll be hearing from me."

"Okay, I'll let him know."

"And please call us if you hear anything about Russell," Kate reiterated. "I think you understand how important this is for him, Chris."

"I'll do what I can," he promised. "Nice talking to you."

"Tell your parents I said hello."

"Okay. Bye."

When the parties hung up, two scenes played out. At the Dewberry residence Russell, who'd been listening on an extension, returned to the Chris's room and flopped down on the bed. "Shit. Now I've got to decide if I should turn myself in."

At the Department of Social Services, Kate turned to Andrew. "Chris didn't ask many questions. He knows more than he's telling us."

"Very perceptive, Sherlock."

"Let's go to Williamsburg," she proposed.

Chapter 29

Norman considered manipulation his only God-given talent. He'd manipulated Meg into marrying him, the state into letting him open a treatment facility and his staff into working for peanuts. Given this track record, he was confident he could manipulate Sierra McGuire. He was a 43-year-old professional manipulator and she was a 17-year-old amateur. He'd lure her with the cash, get the picture, and then give McGuire & Associates a shot of pepper spray and recover his money. In the worst-case scenario, if she'd saved a copy of the incriminating picture on her computer, he'd kiss his money goodbye and create a few more draconian economies at the hospital to recoup it.

He needed to gather the necessary cash without raising any eyebrows. The only people who walked out of banks with $200,000 had held them up. He decided he could tell the bank president Riverside was having a banner year and he wanted to surprise his staff with cash bonuses. It was a flimsy story, even an odd one, but the bank relied on his business and the president would know better than to pry. The tellers were bound by confidentiality, so while they would be dazzled by his generosity they couldn't breathe a word to anyone, so his staff wouldn't hear about the fictitious bonuses. He picked up the phone to call the bank and he heard a noise in the hallway. He went to investigate and found Roach standing at his door, wearing a smile.

"What are you doing out here, Roach?"

"Yo, Mr. Chase," Roach greeted him like an old friend. "I'm sorry I cussed you out the other day, man."

"You are?"

"Yeah, man. Ted 'n Fred're cool dudes."

A sea change seemed to have come over this young troublemaker. "What do they have you doing up there?"

"Lots of stuff."

He noticed the boy's eyes were bloodshot. "Working around all that smoke is irritating your eyes. Get the nurse to take a look at them. So you're actually enjoying the work?"

"Yeah, man. Ted 'n Fred rock."

Norman couldn't believe this was the same foul-mouthed brat he'd dealt with the previous week. "I see quite a difference in you already, Roach. It's amazing what a little tough love can do."

"Yeah, man. I'm starvin'. You got anything to eat?"

"No. I'm glad you've seen the error of your ways, but you need to get back upstairs. I've got work to do."

Roach set off for the second floor, leaving Norman marveling at how far a little discipline could go. He decided his own son needed a dose of the same medicine. He resolved to have his boy help Ted and Fred when school let out for the summer.

Roach was sitting on the floor of his smoke-filled room with his new friends. They looked fuzzy. Fred was waving the bong at him. He accepted it, took another hit and fumbled the pipe along to Ted.

"You in ganja paradise, Roachclip?" Ted asked him.

"Yeah, man. I'm blazin'. My brothers' shit ain't half as good as this shit."

"You keep hauling trash and scrubbing walls and we'll keep paying you this way," Ted promised.

Roach was curious about his new mentors. "How long you dudes been usin'?"

Fred smiled. "Since I was twelve. I'm like livin' proof all this bullshit you hear about how this stuff fries your brain's just bullshit, man. I even drive better when I'm stoned. What's that tell you?"

"It's good for you," Roach concluded.

"I was fourteen," Ted remembered. "My brother wouldn't share his weed so I rolled a couple of joints with oregano. The smell drove him nuts. He gave me the real thing to get me to stop."

Reggae music was thumping from their boom box. Roach raised a fist. "Marley rules, man."

"You know what they call white guys into reggae?" Ted shared a little joke he'd heard. "Waspafarians." The others gave him blank looks. "Never mind, dudes. It's like over your heads."

Fred took another hit and passed the bong to Roach. "We don't got like drug problems or nothin'. We just get high. I mean, if we was stoners you think we could run a successful business like this?"

"Shit no, man," Roach saw his point.

"Time to get back to work, little dude," Ted reminded him.

"Can't I just veg with you guys?"

"No work, no weed," Ted went over the ground rules.

"Yeah, yeah, okay." He took another hit. With some effort he achieved a standing position. He wasn't about to blow a deal like this.

It was a slow night at Stony Point Fashion Park. In a boutique called The Pack Rat a young clerk named Brandon was watching as Norman shouldered backpacks and struck poses for his family. In his first two months at the store Brandon had moved dozens of the less expensive bags. He'd always wondered what kind of customers would buy the high-end numbers that cost as much as a month's rent. He finally had his answer: ones with more money than sense. "I want the Rolls Royce of backpacks," this man had announced when he walked in the door. "I don't want some third grader's book bag. I want a backpack that screams power and privilege and says I can afford anything I damn please." Brandon had obligingly trotted out his five and six hundred dollar models and watched curiously as the man and his family narrowed the choice to a Gucci or a Prada.

"I like that one,' Sean voted for the Prada as his father preened in the mirror. "It looks cool."

Norman was having trouble making up his mind. "It looks like it's some kind of fancy nylon," he observed. "I want something leather."

"But the straps and trim are Italian leather," Meg pointed out. "I agree with Sean. The Prada's much more stylish."

"Well I certainly want to be stylish." He slipped off the rucksack and Brandon practically tripped over himself lending a hand. His customer was doing a good job convincing himself that a $500 tote sack was one of life's necessities and he didn't want to say anything that might blow the sale.

Norman examined the pack more closely. It was big enough to accommodate the cash, and there were handy pouches in front for his sunscreen and pepper spray. "You're right," he decided. "This bag has Norman Chase written all over it."

"It's very well-constructed," Brandon pointed out. "You can take it practically anywhere." His customer didn't exactly look like he was outfitting for a Himalayan expedition, but there were only so many selling points for backpacks.

Norman made his purchase and ten minutes later the Chases were enjoying ice cream cones at Baskin-Robbins. "Why do we have to go to Colonial Williamsburg on Saturday?" Sean complained. "I went there in fourth grade. It's boring."

"Because we're doing more things as a family," his mother said. "I think it's nice that your father wants to take us on an outing."

"None of my friends do things with their families."

"Drop it, Sean," Norman snapped. "We're going to Williamsburg and that's final. And you're not spending the summer playing video games. You're going to work."

Sean reacted with a shell-shocked look. "Work? I'm only thirteen."

"You're going to work with me at the hospital on Monday. The job's only going to last a week or two, and after that you're going to start mowing lawns like I did when I was your age."

"Everyone in our neighborhood mows their own or has some fancy lawn service that drives up in a Ford F350 with a John Deere tractor. They don't want some kid who doesn't even have his own mower."

"Maybe your father can buy you a Deere," Meg suggested. "You can pay him back out of your earnings."

Norman practically spat his ice cream out. "My God, woman, do you have any idea what those things cost? Why don't we get him a Porsche and a yacht while we're at it?"

"Good idea," Sean sensed the plan falling apart before it had come together.

"You're going to work with me on Monday and that's that," Norman said. "When the job's done I'll pay you under the table."

Dru pictured this arrangement. "Why are you paying Sean under the table?"

"It means he's paying me squat and screwing the IRS," Sean translated.

Norman looked at Meg. "We're raising a smart boy."

Chapter 30

Chris remembered it was Sierra's graduation day. He went to his computer and sent her a congratulatory message.

Wish I could be there tonight to see your family's faces when you ruin their perfect record of no one ever finishing high school. I'd be there but we seem to have plans tomorrow morning that require me to remain in the Burg of William.

I took Serge and Russell to the blues place I told you about last night. We were the only whites. I played a set with a guy named Sonny Boy Brown. He plays with a slapping, sliding style. Russell was impressed when I went up and played a couple of songs with him. We've all got our schools, and I guess the Blues Shack is mine. Sonny Boy taught me a song called John the Revelator.

Kate called yesterday. She's looking for Russell. He's thinking about turning himself in. My mom invited him to dinner tonight and he's a nervous wreck because he knows my dad's going to ask him a zillion questions. It'll be fun to watch him sweat.

Happy graduation. See you in the morning when your friends drop you off. As we say in the entertainment world, break a leg. But don't. It would seriously complicate things.

Luv, Christopher Robin

"Hello, Raleigh," the bank teller greeted him as he drove through on his way to his evening shift. "How's business?"

"Depends which one you're talking about, Ramona," he said with a wink.

She glanced around to make sure no one was listening. "Things must be going pretty good at that hospital," she said in a low voice. "Your boss is giving you all big bonuses. Don't say anything, but he nearly wiped out all our cash yesterday." She looked pleased she was able to pass along this little tidbit to her friend.

Raleigh felt sure she was mistaken. "That bastard's never given us an extra five bucks."

"Shhh. It's confidential," she whispered. "Everyone's here's talking about it. We had to send over to another branch to get enough money."

The story sounded fishy to Raleigh. "How much are we talking about?"

"Two hundred thousand dollars. But please don't say anything. I could lose my job."

"Two hundred grand!" Raleigh croaked.

"Shhh. He's giving it to you cash, based on seniority."

"Seniority!" Raleigh gasped. "I've been there the longest!" When something sounded too good to be true it usually was. "Are you sure about this, Ramona? It doesn't sound like Chase."

"I swear, Raleigh. He kept saying, 'Boy are my people going to be surprised.' He got it all in twenties and hundreds and he put it in a backpack."

"Twenties and hundreds?" Raleigh puzzled. "In a backpack? I've never seen the guy with a backpack."

"It was a really nice one."

"But Chase treats us like shit," Raleigh was still struggling with the idea.

"Maybe he's trying to make up for it. People turn over new leaves, you know."

"Not this guy."

"Please don't tell anyone. I could get fired."

"Hey, if you can't trust ol' Ral, who can you trust?" He glanced in the mirror and he saw a line of cars behind him. He stuffed the deposit from his bookmaking activities in the bank drawer.

"You're lucky you have a boss like that," Ramona said.

"Yeah, right." Raleigh smelled a rat and his name was Norman.

On Friday evening as Sierra was marching with the senior class Russell was having dinner with the Dewberry family. He'd prepped for this occasion like he was cramming for a final.

"Chris, would you please say grace?" his mother requested. They bowed their heads and Chris rattled through the Catholic formula in one breath.

Before Russell had taken the first bite of his shrimp kabob the professor zeroed in. "I'm curious about your Thoreau project, Russell. What inspired you to emulate him?"

He'd come armed for bear. "I went to the woods because I wished to live deliberately," he quoted Thoreau, "to front only the essential facts of life, and see if I could not learn what it had to teach."

Chris stared at his friend.

"You certainly know your subject matter," the professor conceded.

"Thanks," Russell accepted the compliment.

"They don't call him Henry Junior for nothing," Chris said.

"I find your knowledge of Thoreau very interesting for a runaway," his father continued.

The boys froze with their forks in mid-air.

"Kate Oxley called me this afternoon. We don't appreciate being put in the position of harboring a runaway." He turned to Chris. "You've only been home a week and you're already back to your old tricks. I realize now it was a mistake sending you to that place, but it was my idea, so I'll have to bear responsibility."

Russell stared forlornly at his shrimp, and then he looked the professor in the eye. "None of this is Chris's fault. He didn't know I was coming here. I just showed up at the door. He's been trying to help me figure out what to do."

"It sounds like the blind leading the blind," the professor observed.

Russell stood up. "I didn't mean to cause problems. I'll leave."

"At least stay long enough to finish your dinner, Russell," Debbie urged him.

"Thanks, Mrs. Dewberry, but I'm not hungry. Sorry I got Chris involved in all this."

Chris got up. "I'm going with you."

"Sit down, Chris," his father ordered sternly. "You're not going anywhere. I won't have you running around with someone who's wanted by the law."

"He's not some kind of outlaw, Dad, he's my friend." His mother's eyes were tearing up. He slipped an arm around her. "We'll be okay, Mom. We're just camping at the lake. It's better than staying here and arguing with Dad."

"At least take some food with you," she fell back on her nurturing instincts.

"Dr. Oxley and your social worker are coming here tomorrow at one-thirty, Russell," the professor informed him. "They're trying to work out an arrangement for you. You can't keep running like this."

"We won't be here," Chris told him. "We've got other plans."

"Cancel them," his father said. "This is more important."

"Please don't do anything foolish, Chris," his mother begged him. "At the rate we're going I'm the one who's going to end up in the hospital. When is our life ever going to get back to normal?"

The question hung in the air as the two young men left the room.

Chapter 31

Seven beach-bound graduates were winding their way east through the Virginia countryside. Grady McCutcheon was at the wheel of his mother's minivan, listening to hip-hop on his iPod. Five of his passengers were dead to the world after a night of revelry. The sixth was wide-awake and staring at the rising sun.

As the first light of day cast elongated shadows over the hills and pastures Sierra pulled out a sheet of paper. After the commencement ceremony she'd approached the speaker and asked for the lyrics to a song she had quoted. Pleased that she'd inspired her, the woman had given Sierra her own copy of the speech. When she was out of sight, Sierra saved the page she wanted and ditched the rest in a trashcan. The song was called *Dream Loud*, by Julie Gold. She felt it was speaking to her personally, telling her to go ahead with her plan. When the speaker had said that dreamers needed to be risk-takers, she felt like shouting Amen.

She knew plenty of people would say that what she was doing was wrong, but they weren't in her shoes. She was just using her talents to get ahead. What was worse – taking advantage of a rich man once, or marrying him and taking advantage of him for the rest of his life like some women did?

She'd noticed the world was full of inspirational exhortations. Dream Loud. Reach for the Stars. Just Do It. But some people had unfair advantages, so the others were forced to Dream Louder, Reach Higher and Just Do It Better.

She stared at the road ahead. Her friend Grady noticed she was awake and he let his headphones slip around his neck. "Sure you don't want to go to the beach with us, Sierra?"

"My friends in Williamsburg are expecting me," she said. "I might catch up with you guys later in the week." There would be the small problem of what to do with $200,000 in cash while she was running around the beach, but she was willing to trade her old problems for this new one.

The sun was shining on her face. She closed her eyes and rode blindly into her future.

Chapter 32

On Saturday morning as historical interpreters trickled to work in Colonial Williamsburg, four teenagers trickled with them, wearing outfits Chris had borrowed from the college theatre's costume shop. To her chagrin Sierra was marching to her rendezvous with destiny in a long brown dress, cream-colored apron and muffin cap. Russell and Serge were slightly more comfortable in the knee britches and blousy shirts of the 18th Century working class. Chris was leading the entourage through Merchant Square in a ruffled shirt, brocade vest, knee length coat and tricorn hat. "You guys don't have any fashion sense," he taunted them.

"We don't have delusions of grandeur," Serge saw it differently. "You look ridiculous in that getup, Dewbie."

"I don't have delusions, I have grandeur." He flapped his coattails. "Don we now our gay apparel."

Sierra caught her reflection in the window of the Trellis restaurant. "I hate this stupid hat thingy. I look like the Big Bad Wolf dressed up like Grandma."

"It's not a hat thingy," Chris educated her. "It's a mobcap."

"How do you know?"

"I'm a Colonial cross-dresser. I've got six of them in my closet."

Russell was carrying a cloth sack over his shoulder. It contained the incriminating memory card and bundles of brochures from local tourist attractions. They'd brought the brochures along to give Norman's backpack some bulk once they relieved him of his money, so his family wouldn't notice the difference. "I see you've conveniently left me holding the bag as usual, Dewberry."

"You don't have to do this, Russell," Chris reminded him. "You can still bail out. "

Russell considered it briefly, but he was already in it up to his eyeballs. He'd taken the picture, printed it, participated in delivering it to their victim, and helped formulate the plan for the exchange. It seemed traitorous to leave his friends at this point. "Are you kidding? I wouldn't miss it for the world."

"I need a tankard of ale to brace myself," Serge said.

"If this works out we'll get a keg," Chris promised him.

"What'll we get if it doesn't?"

"About three-to-five, with time off for good behavior," Russell speculated.

They reached the corner of Duke of Gloucester and Henry Streets. Following their plan, Sierra went into the Barnes & Noble on the opposite corner. She made her way upstairs to the café on the second floor and took a seat in a dormer window overlooking the main street. She pulled out the instructions and her cell phone. A young man at a nearby table noticed her. "I'll bet you work at one of the taverns," he said.

"I don't have to be there until 10:30, so I'm killing time," she lied. She turned and faced the street to discourage him from keeping up the conversation.

"Another day, another dollar," he said.

She had a more substantial figure in mind. She could see her three friends sitting on a bench on the opposite corner. Chris was playing a pennywhistle. He'd placed his hat on the sidewalk and passersby were giving him money! She'd never known anyone like Chris Dewberry. She probably wouldn't have gotten this far without him, but she wouldn't be sitting in the middle of Colonial Williamsburg dressed like an 18th Century wench either.

The Chase family appeared, strolling up Henry Street. As they passed her friends Meg and the children paused briefly to listen to the pennywhistle music, and then they continued across the street to the ticket booth. She had a bird's eye view, and she could see Norman haggling with the ticket vendor. She decided to let him buy his tickets before she called him.

"You're charging us $99 just to walk around and look at a bunch of old buildings?" an irritated Norman asked the clerk.

She gave him a patient smile. "You can look at the buildings for free, but you need tickets to go inside and see the exhibits."

"We'll just look through the windows," Norman decided. He turned around, but Meg blocked his path.

"Get the tickets, Norman," she hissed. "We came here to see Colonial Williamsburg. If you can spend $500 on a backpack you can spend $99 on your family."

Norman turned back to the clerk with a look of resignation. "Do you have any discount packages?"

"Only for schools and groups."

"We're a group. See? Count us – one, two, three, four."

The woman eyed him skeptically. "You look like a family to me."

"Yes, but we're also a group. Are you discriminating against us because we happen to be related?"

Meg slapped her American Express card on the counter. "Two adults and two students," she requested.

Norman's cell phone rang. He glanced at the caller ID. "It's the hospital," he said to his family. He left them at the booth and went to the middle of the street, where he was sure they couldn't hear him. "Sierra?"

She was thirty feet away watching him from the bookstore window. "Good morning, Mr. Chase. Are you having fun yet?"

"Cut the crap. Let's get this business over with."

"We have some activities for you first."

He had no intention of letting her call the shots. "I didn't come here to play games," he said. "I've got the money and if you want it you're doing this on my terms. There's no sense turning this thing into some kind of marathon. Let's take care of our business and then go our merry ways."

"You can go your merry way, but if you want the memory card you'll need to do what I tell you." She glanced at the instructions they'd painstakingly developed. "Walk up the street and take a left at Bruton Parish Church. Go to the Governor's Palace at the end of the green and take the tour. When you're done, go to the east end of the village and take the Capitol tour. After that, as you come back up the street you'll see the King's Arms Tavern on your left. You have a 12:15 lunch reservation. When you finish lunch come back to the church. I'll call again at 1:30."

"For future reference, young lady, when you're shaking someone down and they show up with the money, take it and run. You're over-complicating this whole thing. I just might lose my patience and decide not to go through with it."

"You'll be done by two-thirty," he promised him.

"Two-thirty! If you think I'm going on a Colonial death march for four hours you've got another thought coming. Where are you? Can you see me?" He turned in a circle, looking for her.

Sierra drew back from the window. She closed her phone and slipped the phone and the instructions in her apron pocket. She watched as Norman herded his troop in the direction of the Governor's Palace. Her co-conspirators left their bench and followed at a discreet distance. As her they passed the bookstore they looked at her and she gave them a thumbs up.

Debbie Dewberry had never understood how her husband could turn reading *The Washington Post* into an activity that filled any available time. On weekdays it took him an hour, on Saturdays he devoted the morning to it, and on Sundays, with the exception of church, he spent the whole day. She knew she hadn't married the wisest or the sexiest man in the world, but she'd definitely married the best informed.

"I can't understand how they get away with publishing things like this," he complained about something he was reading. "A Fish and Wildlife official claims the U.S. has a catfish population of 1.3 billion. Where the hell do they get this stuff? Are we paying bureaucrats to count fish? How do they know if it's a billion or a trillion? And who cares?"

"Apparently you do," she said. "Shouldn't we be talking about Chris?" She waited for him to weigh in on the subject of their prodigal son.

He shook his head ruefully. "One-point-three-billion catfish," he couldn't get over it.

Russell was staking out the Governor's Palace while Chris and Serge gave Sierra a tour of the powder magazine, where their rendezvous with Norman Chase would take place. In Russell's mind two dramas were playing out. One starred Sierra and Chase, and it was going according to script. He starred in the other one, and the script was still in development. Kate and Andrew were on their way to Williamsburg to convince him to go back with them. He knew what they would say: come back to Richmond and we'll see what we can do. Best-case he'd end up back at home, flipping burgers while he waited a year to get back in school. Worst-case he'd end up in some juvie center with a couple of hundred Danny Roaches. He had a third possibility in mind, starting from scratch somewhere nobody knew him. Ironically, it was the same plan as Sierra's, but he was willing to do it on a more modest budget.

The system seemed willing to forgive him, but they weren't willing to forgive his mother. He knew where this was heading. If he went home a team of caseworkers would try to whip her into shape. He'd be the carrot. When they discovered she was beyond reform he'd be back to square one.

Now that he'd made it to square one-and-a-half, he wasn't going back.

At one-thirty Norman straggled into the Bruton Parish churchyard with his satchel and his family. At the other end of the yard, hidden under a towering magnolia tree's drooping branches, four pairs of eyes were watching him.

"You look tired, Norman," Meg said.

He flopped down on a stone slab beside the church and slipped off his pack. "No, Meg, I'm invigorated. I can't get enough of the Colonial Period."

"I think we're having a nice day."

"Yeah, fabulous. I'm going to grab a little nap." He stretched out and closed his eyes.

Sean read the inscription on the slab. "There's a dead guy under you named James Scrivener."

"He won't mind."

Meg noticed the other tourists were giving him strange looks. "Norman, please get up. People are staring at you."

"Let 'em stare." He started to drift off but his cell phone summoned him back to reality. He glanced at it. "It's those nitwits at the hospital again. Why don't you take a little tour of the church while I see what they want?"

"I'll carry your backpack," Sean offered. He reached for it but he found his wrist in a death grip. "Ouch!" he yanked his hand away. "Jeez, Dad."

In a flash Norman was on his feet and shouldering the pack. "Keep your hands to yourself, Sean."

"Oh for heaven's sake, Norman, don't be so childish," Meg chided him. "Aren't you going to answer your phone?"

"After you people give me a little privacy."

As his wife and children got in the line filing into the church, Norman answered the phone. "Okay, now what?"

"Did you have a nice lunch, Mr. Chase?"

"My patience has worn extremely thin, Sierra. Let's get this over with."

"Your next stop is the Abby Aldrich Rockefeller Folk Art Museum on West Francis Street."

"Folk art? I'd rather have you put splinters under my fingernails."

"It's behind Merchant Square, by the public hospital. When you get there tell your darlings you're not feeling well. Tell them you're going to find a bench to sit on while they go through the museum, and say you'll meet them back at the entrance at two-thirty. When they're out of sight go to the powder magazine, across the street from the courthouse."

Meg reappeared, dragging both children by the collars. She shoved them at him.

"Your children are totally out of control! We were standing in line and Sean was talking about how you call your employees nitwits and morons. Just as the preacher reached to shake our hands Dru said, 'assholes, too.' Every person in that line heard her! I tried to make some lame excuse about how she doesn't talk that way at home and Sean said, 'Yes she does. She's a little potty mouth.' Then they started fighting! I've never been so mortified in my life!"

"Let's go the folk art museum," he suggested.

"You don't like art," she reminded him.

"You don't like folks either," Sean added.

Four observers watched as they left the churchyard and crossed the street, bickering. "These people hate each other," Russell decided. "I guess money really can't buy happiness."

"I'll let you know," Sierra said.

Nearby a man and a woman were pretending to read gravestones while they kept a wary eye on the Chases. Branigan turned to Fisher. "What do you think?"

"He's our guy," Fisher was convinced. "The family's a decoy. Let's take him to Gregor."

Chapter 33

The powder magazine stood in a small field in the middle of the village. Chris and Serge had chosen this little walled fortress for its location and its privacy, but also for its availability. Their classmate Nathan stood sentry at the magazine on weekends. The boys had arranged for a free spirit named Ellie who gave carriage tours to give Nathan the ride of his life, and they'd offered to cover the magazine for him in his absence, telling him they would even come in costume. As Nathan and Ellie rolled off an occupying force seized the magazine. Serge stood at Nathan's post while Russell guarded at the building's only door. Chris and Sierra scurried up the spiral staircase to the second floor. Like the magazine and the eight-foot brick wall surrounding it, this upstairs room was octagonal. A glass partition divided the room, protecting an exhibit on the other side. Sierra went to the window and waved to her friends below. "I feel like a princess in a castle," she said to Chris.

"Someday your prince will come," he promised. He planned to be that prince. Once he worked up the nerve he was going to profess his love. It was an awkward time to do it, but there never seemed to be a good one.

Sierra felt the weight of the moment. "It's hard to believe this is about to happen. Last week it was just a crazy idea." They'd choreographed the exchange with the precision of a ballet. When Chase arrived Serge would send him upstairs and divert any tourists who happened by. If he tried a snatch-and-run with the memory card, Russell would latch the door and trap him inside the magazine. In the unlikely event he made it to the courtyard he would find himself facing the brick wall and an All-State wrestler guarding the only exit. He couldn't make a commotion without attracting unwanted attention. Once he set foot in the compound they had him.

Sierra nibbled her lower lip and watched the gate. Chris stood close to her, wishing he could nibble the same lip. "You look like something in a fairy tale," he said.

She gave him a distracted smile. "I do?"

His heart was pounding so loudly he wondered if she could hear it. "I want to ask you something, Sierra."

"I want to ask you something, too," she said.

A wave of relief washed over him. "Really? You go first."

She hesitated. "I don't usually talk about stuff like this with guys, but I feel like I can trust you. Your friend Serge is really cute. Does he go with anyone?"

*Should I throw myself out the window no*w, he wondered, *or after I torch her money?*

She turned back to the window. "Have you ever felt an instant attraction to someone?"

"Yes, as a matter of fact, I have."

"When you brought him to my house the other day I just had this funny feeling. And this morning when we were in the costume shop and he was standing there in his boxers ..."

"Russell and I were in our boxers, too."

"He works out, doesn't he?"

"I don't know if he works out," Chris said with irritation. "He's on the wrestling team. Sierra, you're messing with me, aren't you? You're just saying this to ..."

"He's here!" she saw Norman approaching the gate. "We'll talk about it later."

"Yeah, later."

Branigan and Fisher were in high spirits. They were about to win Gregor's little surveillance game and the bragging rights that went with it. They'd tailed their suspect from the tavern to the church, then to the museum, and now to the powder magazine. He fit the description their instructor had given them: he was well dressed, equipped with a phone, carrying a bag, and glancing around constantly like he was worried about being followed. Gregor had cleverly accessorized his make-believe courier with a family, but their suspect had eventually ditched his family and taken off by himself. As he strode purposefully toward the powder magazine they quickened their pace and closed the distance behind him. "We've got the luck of the Irish on our side," Branigan whispered.

"I'm Jewish," Fisher said.

"We've got the luck of the Jewish, too."

"God, I hope not," she fervently prayed.

Norman recognized the young man at the gate as the delivery boy who'd come to his house with the picture. He eyed his costume. "Playing soldier now, are we?"

Serge pointed to Russell. "Go over there and do what he tells you," he was all business. "Sierra's waiting upstairs."

"Just a minute," a woman's voice said. Norman turned and saw a conservatively dressed young man and woman heading his way with looks of grim determination.

"You need to come with us," the man addressed him.

"I don't need to do a damn thing," Norman snapped. "I'm through with your stupid games. Tell Sierra if she wants to see me she can get her little butt down here right now."

Fisher and Branigan exchanged puzzled glances. They'd expected some resistance, but they hadn't expected the subject to step out of character and mention the game itself. "Who's Sierra?" Fisher asked him.

Serge knew about his father's role-playing exercises, and he could spot his trainees a mile away. They always worked in pairs, and they went about their business with the earnestness of Mormon missionaries. He recognized that things were spinning out of control. "I know who you are," he said to Branigan and Fisher. "You're making a mistake. This man's not part of your training exercise."

"Who are we?" Fisher challenged him.

"Gregor Tabanov's students," Serge invoked his father name. "He's got two exercises going on today, and this gentleman's involved in the other one." He realized this would get back to his father, but it was the only way he could think of to get rid of them.

This piqued Norman's curiosity. "How many chumps are you people shaking down today?"

"Only you," Serge assured him.

Branigan refused to buy it. "We're taking him back to The Farm," he said. "Gregor can tell us if he's the wrong guy."

"I'm not going to any damn farm," a confused Norman insisted. "You people need to get your act together. I'll give you sixty seconds to produce Sierra."

"Who's Sierra?" Fisher asked again.

Serge knew that the success or failure of Operation Scholarship was in his hands. He decided to take action. "Mr. Chase, I need to speak with these two people privately. Could you wait out here? We won't be long."

Norman's patience had worn thin. Even if his blackmailers were bumbling idiots he had to play along, but he refused to give them Carte Blanche. "Whatever you have to say you can say to me."

"Okay." Serge ushered the trio inside and latched the gate behind them. Without warning, he wheeled and planted a fist in the middle of Branigan's face. The stunned agent staggered, but before he could react Serge landed another blow to his solar plexus and kneed him in the jaw. Branigan crumpled in the grass and lay there motionless, bleeding from his broken nose.

Horrified, Fisher recoiled against the brick wall. A strange notion crossed her mind – was this some kind of setup designed to test her own reactions? Deception was par for the course with The Agency. Were all these people Gregor's operatives, play-acting for her benefit? Did they expect her to go for help or protect her partner? *Strategize*, she told herself. *Call Gregor.* She inched her way to the gate, hoping no one was watching her.

From their vantage point above the action, Sierra and Chris had been speculating about the identity of the two strangers when they saw Serge suddenly flatten one of them. Sierra grabbed Chris's arm. "Omigod! What's he doing?"

"I forgot to tell you about his violent streak," Chris said dryly.

Her eyes traveled to the backpack. "Should we go down and get the money?"

"Let Serge and Russell handle it," Chris followed his instincts.

Norman assumed he was about to get the same treatment as Branigan. He slipped off his backpack and offered it to Serge. "I've got the money. Here – let me show you."

"Bring it over here," Russell called from the steps.

Serge saw Fisher creeping for the gate and he pointed a finger at her. "If you leave here now you'll never see your friend alive again," he bluffed. Fisher froze in place.

Norman placed his backpack on the magazine's steps and fumbled with the Italian leather straps. He undid them, removed a cotton sweater and showed them the neatly bundled stacks of twenties and hundreds. Sierra and Chris pressed their noses against the window, straining to catch a look. Even Fisher craned her neck, trying to figure out what was going on.

Now that he'd distracted his blackmailers, Norman slipped a hand in a front pouch, whipped out his pepper spray and dosed the two unsuspecting young men at point blank range. He turned to Fisher. "I think women should get equal treatment," he said as he sent a cloud in her direction. He saw Branigan stirring and he gave him a shot for good measure. Satisfied that Sierra's associates were out of commission, he left them choking and stumbling blindly in the courtyard. Adrenalin pumping, he entered the building and bounded up the spiral staircase. When he reached the second floor he saw Sierra cowering behind another henchman, who picked up a Windsor chair and hurled it in his direction. He ducked and the chair shattered the glass wall protecting the exhibit. He raised his canister and took aim.

"Please don't, Mr. Chase!" Sierra begged him. "We can settle this right now!"

"That's exactly what I'm doing. I'm through with you and all your crap." He squeezed the trigger and exterminated his last two pests. As the room fogged he realized he'd made a major blunder – in his haste to teach his blackmailers a lesson he'd neglected to get the memory card from them. It was too late. He turned and fled the magazine to avoid the effects of the pepper spray, high-stepping over his fallen enemies as he sprinted through the courtyard. He let himself out the gate and hurried up Fisher Street, cursing himself for making such a simple mistake. Out of breath and dripping with sweat, he arrived at the museum and he plopped down on a bench. He hadn't gotten what he wanted, but he'd taught his young extortionists a lesson they wouldn't forget. Hopefully they'd find some other lamb to fleece. He reached for his sweater to wipe his face and he realized with horror that he'd left his backpack on the steps of the powder magazine.

Summoning strength he didn't know he had, Norman ran back up the street. He found Branigan and Fisher choking in the grass. Blessedly, his bag was still on the front steps. He shouldered the pack and felt its comforting heft. Running on empty, he dashed back to the museum and collapsed on the bench a second time, feeling like he'd just finished the

Boston Marathon. He put a protective arm around his backpack. When Meg and the children emerged he was still catching his breath.

Meg eyed him. "You look terrible, Norman. You're white as a ghost and you're drenched in sweat. I think you have a fever."

"Take me home," he whimpered. "Put me to bed. Feed me chicken soup."

"I'll carry your pack," Sean offered. He received a withering look.

"That museum's wonderful," Meg enthused. "We'll have to come back again when you're feeling better. It's so nice we're finally doing things as a family."

"Can we go to Disney World?" Dru asked.

"Dad's not a theme park kind of guy," her brother astutely observed.

At the Dewberry home on Powell Street four adults were waiting for Russell and Chris to appear. "Maybe they're running on Eastern Standard Teenage Time," Kate held out hope they were going to show.

Andrew's instincts told him otherwise. "We're being stood up."

"I just don't understand Chris's behavior," the professor said, shaking his head. "He's not the same boy he used to be."

"I have a theory about Chris," Kate decided this might be the time to say what she hadn't at his discharge meeting. "I think he might be more gifted than you realize. I've seen him do some pretty amazing things. One time a staff member brought a banjo to work and showed him a few chords. A half-hour later he was playing it and singing a song he made up on the spur of the moment called *Don't We All Know Billyburg Ain't New Orleans*. It sounded like something a professional songwriter would come up with, and he made it up at the same time he was learning to play the banjo! I'm not saying he's the next Beethoven, but I think Chris is unusually creative. I don't think you should write off his interest in music."

"It's not an interest," the professor reacted. "It's an obsession."

"People think I'm obsessed with fishing," Andrew volunteered.

"You *are* obsessed with fishing," Kate said.

Debbie was listening thoughtfully. "But how do you explain the things he's been doing? Running away from home, refusing to go to college? Chris didn't used to act like this."

"For some reason dissatisfied people produce better art than satisfied ones," Kate shared the rest of her theory. "Chris has a perfectly happy, perfectly safe middle class life. He wants to play the blues, but he doesn't have anything to be blue about. Maybe he needs to manufacture conflict so he has something to hang his art on. He can't write songs about what great parents he has and what a wonderful place his hometown is."

"You've spent a lot of time thinking about him," Debbie noticed.

"Creative people fascinate me. I wish I were one myself. If the other patients at the hospital had been half as interesting as Chris, I might still be there."

"I'd just as soon have an uncreative one," the professor grumbled. "He manufactures conflict, all right. He's a conflict factory."

Andrew glanced at his watch. "I say we go look for them. But let's take your car. If Russell sees my Jeep he'll run the other way."

So for lack of a better plan, they went out cruising.

Norman locked the door to his den. He went over to a small, nondescript table next to his reading chair and lowered his aching bones to the floor. He opened a door camouflaged in the table's base and he dialed the combination of the safe hidden inside. He undid the straps on his backpack, removed his sweater and reached for his money. With a look of panic, he dumped the contents on the floor. The sack was full of color brochures about Colonial Williamsburg.

Chapter 34

The last time Serge's father had summoned him to the deck behind their house for a private conference he had explained the Facts of Life. Gregor was the one in the hot seat then, but now it was Serge's turn. He shifted uncomfortably on the wooden bench and waited for the shit to hit the fan. "I really don't know where to start, Serge," his father said. "Let me lay out the facts, and then you can address them."

"Okay," Serge hoped the facts were as mercifully vague as his human anatomy lesson.

"This afternoon two of our trainees walked in on something unusual going on at the powder magazine."

Serge knew the shit wasn't about to hit the fan; the manure wagon was about to enter the wind tunnel.

"Several young people who weren't employees were pretending to work there. They were waiting for a gentleman named Chase, who showed up with a bag of cash, asking for someone named Sierra. Apparently my students asked too many questions and a young man who fits your description assaulted one of them and broke his nose. This Chase fellow attacked everyone with pepper spray and fled the scene. I've spoken with your friend Nathan, and he's claiming you and Chris were behind all this. I've also spoken with David Dewberry and a social worker named Andrew Boone. Apparently Chris and a young man he met at the treatment center in Richmond took Mr. Boone's Jeep from the Dewberrys' driveway this afternoon. Debbie thinks they've run away because Chris's guitar is missing. Would you like to fill me in on all this?"

Serge knew it was useless to feign ignorance. His only choice was where to begin. "It all started at that hospital where Chris's parents sent him," he said. By the time he reached the end of the story twenty minutes later he realized his father had been taking it all in without interrupting him.

"So this Chase fellow owns this treatment center?"

"That's what Chris and Russell say."

"How did your friends end up with his money?"

"When Chase pepper-sprayed Chris and Sierra, Chris closed his eyes, covered his face with his hat and held his breath, so he didn't get dosed like the rest of us. He helped Sierra out of the building and he saw the backpack on the steps. He switched the brochures for the money. We went to that little sheep pasture on Francis Street and washed our eyes in a stream and stayed there until we could see. Then we went back to the college theatre and changed clothes. That was the last time I saw them."

"What were they planning to do?"

He shrugged, "I guess when saw that social worker's Jeep they panicked and decided they needed to get out of town."

"Serge, the only part of this story I'm having a hard time believing is that the girl wants all this money to go to Georgetown."

"That's what she says. I swear."

Gregor shook his head. "I know you're telling the truth because you've never been a good liar. How did you get involved in this mess?"

"Chris and Russell were telling me about this girl, and the next thing I knew I was helping them."

Gregor stared into the woods behind the house, trying to put it in perspective. "Run through the story again. This time I want you to point out every time you think someone exercised poor judgment."

"The whole thing was bad judgment," Serge saw in hindsight.

"Then tell me every time someone could have made a better choice. Start with your friends at the hospital, if you want."

"Can I go back farther?"

"How far?"

"If Chris's dad hadn't sent him off, none of this would have happened."

Gregor gave him a wry smile. "Blame it all on the sins of your parents. Let's not go back to Adam and Eve."

Miss Beauregard saw a vehicle she didn't recognize pull into her driveway. Andrew emerged from the passenger side. "I've got good news and I've got bad news, Miss B," he called to her over the roof of the car. "Which one do you want first?"

She fortified herself with a swig of gin and tonic. "Give me the bad news, I suppose."

"Someone stole your copy of *Battle in a Bottle*."

"They stole it? Why on earth would anyone steal a book like that?"

"Because they stole my Jeep and it was in the back seat."

"Oh, my," she reacted. "But you said you have some good news, too."

"Your favorite author brought you a replacement copy." He indicated his driver. "This is David Dewberry."

The professor emerged from the Subaru and gave her a courtly bow. "I'm deeply honored, Miss Beauregard."

"The honor's entirely mine, Doctor," she fluttered. She remained seated and received her gentleman caller.

Andrew headed down to his apartment. "While you two are busy being deeply honored, I'm going to go be deeply pissed."

The sun had disappeared in the woods behind the house and Serge and his father were still on the deck. Under persistent questioning Serge had milked every possible moral from the story. "So where do we go from here?" Gregor asked him.

"I was kind of hoping you'd tell me."

"Only five of us know the whole story," his father pointed out. "All Chase knows is that Sierra and some nameless companions have the picture and the money. He doesn't know about Branigan and Fisher."

"Dad, all this calm, rational stuff is driving me nuts. What are you going to do to me? Are you going to tell Mom? Are you going to turn me over to the law? Do I have to pay this Branigan guy's medical bills? Are you going to tell Chris's parents about the money?"

"The government provides its employees with medical coverage. As for your mother, I've spent a lifetime trying to keep her from worrying about my activities. I don't intend to let her start worrying about yours."

"But you're going to do *something*, aren't you?"

Gregor let him wallow in this thought for a moment. "Since we're the only ones who know the whole story, I think it's up to us to make sure justice is served."

"You mean get Chase's money back for him?"

"Did I say that?"

"No. But that's justice, isn't it?"

His father went over to the French doors that led into the house. "Where do you think Chris and his friends went?"

By now the sun was barely visible through the trees. His friends had been missing for hours. Serge imagined them tooling down some country road, watching the same setting sun. "Dad, if I knew I'd tell you. I really don't have a clue."

Part III
Ocracoke

Chapter 35

They were crossing the three-mile bridge that spanned Currituck Sound. Chris was driving, Sierra was riding shotgun and Russell was crammed in the rear seat with backpacks, camping gear and Chris's guitar.

"Joyriding can't be a very serious crime," Chris said to his companions. "Even the name makes it sound like a celebration of life."

Russell had his doubts that an interstate flight with $200,000 of someone else's money was joyriding, but he didn't say anything.

Two hours earlier they'd set out for Virginia Beach, but the turnoff for North Carolina's Outer Banks had beckoned like a beacon in a fog. The Outer Banks sounded remote, and remote sounded excellent. Technically, they were only borrowing Andrew's vehicle. Once they reached their destination they planned to send it back to its rightful owner with a full tank of gas and a note of apology.

They touched the storm-sculpted strand of barrier islands and turned south on the four-lane that ran up and down its length. Chris pointed to a sign. "Look at the names of these places. Duck. Kill Devil Hills. Kitty Hawk. Nag's Head. People used to have wild imaginations." The contemporary and the traditional were at war on both sides of the highway. Elevated, hurricane-resistant cottages towered over low slung, weather-beaten ones, and outlet malls were elbowing Mom & Pop stores aside. At Milepost 12 they saw a sign for Jockey's Ridge State Park, and they pulled into the crowded parking lot to investigate. They saw people abandoning their footwear to hike to the top of the East Coast's biggest sand dune. They wanted to follow suit, but Jeep was missing its top and they were reluctant to leave their valuables unprotected. They decided to take their most cherished possessions with them. Russell grabbed his camera, Chris his guitar and Sierra her cash.

They trekked barefoot through sugar white sand until they reached the crest. They took in a 360-degree jaw-dropping panorama. To the east the Atlantic spread like a vast blue-green blanket. Facing west they saw working boats and pleasure craft plying the placid waters of Roanoke Sound. The Ridge was teeming with activity; people were hang gliding, sand boarding, flying stunt kites, filming each other and watching the sunset. Despite playing host to a crowd big enough to populate a small town, the rolling peaks and dipping valleys looked roomy enough to accommodate the next Woodstock.

Sierra was awestruck. "This is like some other planet. Everyone seems so happy."

They watched an osprey plunge into the sound and fly off with a fish in its talons. "I want to be reincarnated as an osprey," Chris decided. "All they do is glide around and come down occasionally for free all-you-can-eat seafood buffets."

Russell was sitting cross-legged in the sand, watching the sun disappear behind Roanoke Island. "However this thing ends, it was worth it," he finally put his misgivings aside. "And wherever it ends, I'm coming back here. This is the most awesome place I've ever seen."

Roach was sharing his brainstorm with Selena and Molly. "So I wait 'til these dudes are fried and I take their keys and their money. I drive off in their van and tell this place to kiss my ass." He folded his arms and waited for their expressions of admiration.

"Only problem is you get fried with 'em," Selena pointed out.

"I'll fake it. I won't inhale."

"Uh huh," she had even less faith in his self-control than she did in his escape plan.

"Where will you go, Roach?" Molly wondered. "You can't go home. They'll just come and pick you up."

"Shit, I don't know. Anywhere's better than this place."

"I'll go with you," she said impulsively. Everyone else seemed to be checking out and she couldn't think of any reason to hang around. Besides, Riverside Center was her stepfather's idea and he had lousy ideas.

"I don't need no witch," Roach said. "Why don't you just steal a broom and fly away?"

"I'll take off the makeup," she bargained. She was tired of it anyway. "I hate this place. Russell's gone, Chris is gone, Kate's gone."

"Sierra's gone," Selena added.

"Who cares about that slut?" Molly reacted.

"I do," Roach said. "I'd like to slip her twelve inches of the ol' Roach rod."

Selena gave him a look of total disgust. "Roach, you're one crazy-ass boy. Molly'd be a fool to run off with you."

"I'm takin' her with me," he did an about-face. "You'll be the only one left on our unit."

"Least when they send me home the law won't be lookin' for me."

"They can look for me all they want," Roach reacted. "They won't find me."

"Can I think about it some more?" Molly waffled.

"Shit no. You said you want to go with me, so you're goin'."

"Well I don't want the old *Roach rod*," she clarified things.

"Yeah, right," he smirked. "That's what they all say."

"Scuse me while I go puke," Selena left the two of them work it out.

They'd come down from Jockey's Ridge and polished off three baskets of shrimp and hushpuppies at Awful Arthur's Oyster Bar. Chris had been watching the stringy-haired entertainer in the far corner. "I'm way better than that dude. He's just some old hippie who knows a few Buffett songs. He can't pick worth a damn. If he can make a living from music, I can make a fortune."

"Why don't you go play with him?" Sierra prodded him. "You're guitar's under the table."

"I'm not playing with him. He's awful."

"Maybe he's Arthur," Russell speculated.

"I'll open up Crappy Chris's across the street." He looked at Sierra. "Can I borrow enough money to start a restaurant?"

"Funny, Chris."

"How about $53.75?" he slid the check in her direction.

"I can cover that." She reached into her backpack. It was the first time in her life she'd ever picked up the tab for a meal. She thought of her mother, waiting tables at the RonDayVoo. "I'll leave the waitress a big tip."

Chapter 36

On Sunday morning Norman skipped church and set off through the Piedmont country west of Richmond. Storm clouds were gathering over the mountains, and by the time he reached Buckingham a torrential downpour forced him to pull off the road. The storm eventually passed, but a heavy blanket of fog and drizzle settled in. He continued his journey through the concrete gray landscape until he reached the RonDayVoo Lounge. He parked in the gravel lot and knocked on the trailer. He heard unsteady footsteps. The door opened and a rheumy-eyed man with a three-day stubble, fungal teeth and 40 ounces of Colt 45 eyed him.

"Mr. McGuire?" he made a wild guess.

The drunk's gaze traveled from Norman to his Ferrari. "Blackjack," he introduced himself.

"It's a pleasure to meet you, Blackjack. I'm Norman Chase. I'm the director of Riverside Center, where your daughter was in treatment. I stopped by to check on her progress and talk with you about aftercare."

"Jolene's at the beach."

"The beach! Well, well, well – our little girl certainly gets around, doesn't she?" He imagined her in an oceanfront suite, ordering room service at his expense. "I'll bet that little rascal's having the time of her life. Where is she staying?"

Blackjack killed what was left in his bottle and wiped his mouth on his sleeve. "You'll have to ask the missus."

"Where is she?"

"Church."

"When are you expecting her back?"

"Damned if I know."

Norman pulled out his wallet and gave him a business card. "Will you ask her to call me at work tomorrow? I always like to follow up personally on our patients and make sure they're doing well. I can't stress how important aftercare is. The first two weeks are critical. We need to monitor her progress."

Blackjack eyed Norman's wallet. "What'd you say your name is?"

"Norman Chase."

"You're a helluva guy, Norman."

"You look like a helluva guy yourself, Blackjack."

"Tell you what. Let's you and me get in that fancy car of yours and run into town and get some more of this stuff." He waved his empty bottle.

Norman extracted a twenty and tucked it in the man's shirt pocket. "Have a few drinks on me, Blackjack. All I ask in return is for you to have your wife call me. Put the card someplace she'll be sure to see it."

"I'll put it on the toilet seat."

"Whatever."

"Are you fixin' to see Jolene?"

"Absolutely. I want to make sure she gets the treatment she deserves."

Blackjack vaguely remembered something. He went to the kitchen and shuffled through a stack of mail. He found an envelope and handed it to Norman. "When you see her, give her this."

Norman read the return address. "Georgetown University Office of Admission. So Georgetown's interested in her, are they?"

"Hell, I don't know. That girl's got all kinds of crazy ideas."

He stuck the letter in the pocket of his rain jacket. "She certainly does."

A gray gloom had settled over the Virginias and Carolinas and socked in the Outer Banks. Chris was sitting in his sleeping bag on the floor of their motel room, alternately strumming his guitar and scribbling lyrics. Russell was asleep in one of the double beds. Sierra was awake in the other one, listening to Chris. "That's nice, Chris."

"It's reggae."

"Play it."

"Okay, but I've only got one verse and a chorus." He strummed a backbeat and sang quietly, trying not to disturb Russell.

> *The cautious mon, he's seen as wise*
> *in other cautious people's eyes.*
> *The straight and narrow road's appealin',*
> *but the crooked road, she's freer feelin'.*

> *We gonna make it round the bend*
> *throwin' caution to the wind.*
> *We gonna reach our journey's end*
> *throwin' caution to the wind.*

He put his guitar aside. "To be continued."

"I like it." She rolled over and parted the curtain. "It hasn't stopped raining."

"Yeah, I know. The next time let's borrow a car with a top."

"Come on, you guys," Russell complained. "You're ruining my beauty rest."

"If that's your goal, you'd better stay in bed a couple of more months," Chris said.

Russell rolled over and covered his head. "No problem."

"Each day we'll have a different vegan theme," Zenia explained to the two kitchen ladies who were perched on stools, listening to her. "We'll need some things that aren't in the pantry, so you'll have to go shopping. In the morning, when people come in for breakfast, I'll make an announcement about what we're doing."

"Helen's not going to like this," Claudia predicted.

"Helen's on vacation, Claudia," she'd been pleased to discover. "And this is our kitchen, not hers."

"The staff's not going to like it either," Queenie felt sure.

"All we're doing is promoting healthy living. They'll appreciate having more variety in the menus."

"I say they'll be upset," Claudia was skeptical.

Zenia brushed aside their concerns and presented the women with her revised menu. She'd doctored over Helen's plan with White Out and substituted her own selections. The dietician's signature and license number were still at the bottom of the page.

Queenie examined the menu. "Helen's going to kill you, Zenia."

"Then I'll die a martyr for the cause," she said bravely. "I hardly think she'll be upset just because we've made a few little changes. You two need to stop thinking of yourselves as hash slingers and start thinking of yourselves as nutritional educators." Her eyes narrowed. "And if you're thinking about calling Helen, get it out of your heads right now."

Andrew was mourning the loss of his Jeep. Kate had taken him to brunch at the Strawberry Street Café, where a Belgian waffle had failed to revive his drooping spirits. The unremitting drizzle outside complemented his gray mood. "I just got that Jeep three weeks ago. I haven't even made the first payment yet. What did I do to deserve this? Why are the gods angry at me?"

Kate patted his hand. "You'll get your Jeep back, Andrew. I know those two boys. Chris and Russell aren't going to do anything outrageous. They're just having a little adventure."

"Oh, yeah? If they're such great kids, why'd they rip me off?"

"I'm sure they just panicked. These little joyriding episodes usually end pretty quickly."

"Yeah, when the joyriders wreck the car."

"I don't think that's going to happen, but even if they do you've got insurance."

"Would you please stop being such a damned Pollyanna?" he requested. "All this unflagging optimism is getting to me. Let me wallow in misery. I don't even have a way to get to work tomorrow, unless I borrow Miss B's Studebaker."

"You can use my Mini," she offered. "I'll sweeten the pot by letting you stay at my place tonight to make it more convenient."

This managed to get a smile out of him. "Gee, you drive a hard bargain."

"Unless you're worried about scandalizing your landlady, of course."

"She's 112 years old. She's beyond being scandalized."

"Suppose this whole thing had never happened," she offered him some food for thought. "If Russell hadn't run off, I wouldn't have had words with Mr. Chase and walked out on my job. We wouldn't have spent the afternoon together, you wouldn't have invited me over for drinks and one thing wouldn't have led to another. So where's the bad part?"

"You don't take a country boy's wheels."

"Your wheels are fine, country boy. Trust me. Chris and Russell are both good kids. They'll come to their senses sooner or later."

"It's the later part that bothers me."

The rain had stopped and the young road warriors had resumed their southbound odyssey, across Oregon Inlet, past the Bodie Island lighthouse, through the Pea Island National Wildlife Refuge and along Cape Hatteras National Seashore. The scenery had grown increasingly desolate, and then civilization had reappeared in the form of a string of oceanfront villages with odd names like Waves and Salvo. When they reached the Hatteras lighthouse they parked and walked around the black-and-white striped landmark to the beach. Surfers were shooting the East Coast's version of the Banzai Pipeline. Chris stared in awe. "Jeez, those are killer waves. You'll never catch this wussy in a wetsuit."

Russell smiled. "That's a good name for your band, Dewberry. Wussies in Wetsuits."

Feeling more upbeat, they piled back in the Jeep and continued south on Route 12. They stopped at a barbecue joint called Bubba's, where pork was roasting over a hickory fire behind the restaurant. They loaded up on barbecue and Mrs. Bubba's Double Devil Chocolate Cake. "I'm going to name my first child Bubba," Chris vowed after the meal.

"She'll change it when she's 18," Sierra spoke from experience.

"If it's a girl I'll call her Bubbetta."

A half-hour later they reached land's end and cars waiting in line for the Ocracoke Island ferry. They saw a black and white boat chugging their way with a load of vehicles. Sierra looked at the boat and then at her friends. "What's the vote?"

"Caution to the wind," Chris said.

"Ditto," Russell agreed. "Why stop now?"

Twenty minutes later they were standing in the back of the ferry, watching Hatteras Island grow smaller. The veteran commuters had brought along loaves of bread to feed the flock of seagulls trailing the boat. Russell dug out his camera and took a few shots of the birds.

"You don't see things like this in Buckingham County," Sierra marveled.

They docked on the island's north end and followed the other cars along miles of deserted beach until they reached the village of Ocracoke. The little community fanned out around a horseshoe-shaped harbor dotted with restaurants, stores, a Coast Guard station and another ferry terminal. The village was teeming with activity in much the same way Jockey's Ridge had been the evening before. Strollers, bikers and rollerbladers were spilling into the streets, and the air was filled with salt and celebration. They scoped it out and headed back to the oceanfront campground they'd passed a few minutes earlier. As they went by Howard's Pub & Raw Bar Chris pointed to a sign advertising live music. "Howard's Pub could launch my career like the Stone Pony launched Springsteen's. This could be the start of something big."

"Or the end of something little," Russell kept him in perspective.

"I think we're at the end of the road," Sierra said. Ocracoke seemed like its own little island nation, the last place anyone would ever look for them. Lugging around her net worth was getting tiresome and she was ready to find a place to stash it. She looked back to check on her money and she saw Russell smiling. "What are you so happy about, Russell?"

"I really like this place," he said. "It's so different."

Chris caught Russell's eye in the rearview mirror. "I've got you figured out, Moss. You're a nature junkie. You just had to get out of Richmond to discover it."

"Whatever," Russell was feeling too mellow to argue.

"After we set up camp I'm calling my mother," Sierra said. "I want to see if my letter from Georgetown came."

Chris gave her an anxious look. "You won't tell her where we are, will you?"

"What if I do? I can say I've decided to work here for the summer. She doesn't know you guys are with me. The only one who knows we're together is Serge, and he doesn't know where we are."

The mention of his friend's name reminded Chris that he had some unfinished business to take up with Sierra. With nothing to do and paradise to do it in, he had plenty of time to pursue the matter at a leisurely pace. The island seemed ripe with possibilities. "I'm with you, Russell," he voted. "I like this place, too."

Chapter 37

When Riverside's staff and patients shuffled sleepily into the dining hall on Monday morning they saw centerpieces of wildflowers and beets decorating the tables. Zenia was standing in the corner, watching and noting their reactions. As they queued up in the serving line she hopped up on a chair and clapped for their attention. "Good morning, everybody!"

Selena wrinkled her nose. "Whew, this place stinks."

"The kitchen staff and I have a little surprise for you," Zenia said brightly. "This week we're taking a break from our usual fare and serving some vegan entrees. I think you'll discover you feel more energized and centered. Some of you who need to lose a little weight might even shed or pound or two."

"You can shed a pound or two taking a crap," Roach offered.

Her smile faded. "I'd appreciate it if you'd keep your smart aleck comments to yourself, Daniel."

"Then they wouldn't be funny."

She turned away from him. "This week we're going to celebrate a different vegetable each day. Today we're going to Meet the Beet. Tomorrow we'll be Rooting for Rutabagas."

There was a dead silence, which Maurice eventually broke. "Exactly how are we planning to meet the beet?" he posed a question that was on several minds.

Zenia glanced at the kitchen workers for support and she saw them slinking away. "For breakfast this morning we're having beetcakes with peanut cilantro sauce. We're having beetburgers for lunch, and spaghetti with Italian beetballs for dinner."

Instead of the thoughtful response she anticipated, she heard a chorus of retches and yucks. "Let's not act like kindergarteners." Forging ahead, she opened a book she'd brought along for the occasion. "In keeping with today's theme, I'd like to read a short passage from *Jitterbug Perfume* by Tom Robbins." She threw herself into the reading with flair of a Shakespearean actor.

"*The beet is the most intense of vegetables…Beets are deadly serious. The beet is the melancholy vegetable, the one most willing to suffer…The beet is the murderer returned to the scene of the crime. The beet is what happens when the cherry finishes with the carrot. The beet is the ancient ancestor of the autumn moon, bearded, buried, all but fossilized.*"

She closed the book with a flourish. "That's quite a commentary on the lowly beet, isn't it? Any reactions?" To her dismay the only hand that went up was attached to Roach's arm. "I really don't want to call on you, Daniel. But since you were polite enough to raise your hand, I'll let you have the floor."

Roach hooked his thumbs in his belt loops and eyed his audience. "If we don't want to meet the beet, can we beat our meat?"

In the ensuing pandemonium a beet whizzed past Zenia's head and hit the wall. Suddenly beets were flying everywhere, leaving dark stains. She saw the kitchen ladies, cowering behind the serving line.

"Get down from there right now!" an angry voice barked over the din.

Zenia looked in the direction of the voice and saw Helen charging her way. "Helen! You're supposed to be on vacation!"

"How dare you make a mockery of my menus!"

Zenia stepped down from the chair. "I'm not making a mockery of anything." She looked for the kitchen ladies, but her two Judases were hiding. The staff and patients had overrun the kitchen and and were helping themselves to everything except the beetcakes.

"I intend to report you to the American Dietary Association," Helen snarled.

"I don't care what those carnivorous Neanderthals think. They're still living in the nutritional Stone Age."

Helen lunged at her but Zenia sidestepped her and hurried for the exit with her book in hand. "I'm canceling my vacation," Helen called as she left. "And I'm organizing a staff strike until Mr. Chase replaces you with someone sane."

"Good morning, Raleigh," Norman greeted Richmond's only $60,000 gate attendant.

Raleigh tipped his cap. "I see you've got a helper with you today."

"This is my son Sean," Norman introduced him. "Sean's helping with the cleanup from the fire. We're going to show him what an honest day's work is like."

Raleigh, who'd spent fifteen years sitting on a stool and chain-smoking, nodded knowingly. "We'll show you what real working men do."

"Great," Sean had always wondered about this.

A few minutes later as father and son walked up the main corridor, they saw Zenia hurrying the opposite way. "How are things going, St. Clair?" Norman asked her.

She skidded to a stop. "Wonderful! I'm still feeling my way with a couple of the staff members, but you know how that goes."

"Have you filled all the beds?"

"Not completely. I've been focusing on other priorities."

"Other priorities?" Norman wasn't aware there were any. "We're not searching for the Holy Grail, St. Clair. The world is full of problem kids. They're roaming the streets in hordes. I want to see some butts in these beds. If we don't have 100% occupancy by the end of the week I'm laying off some people, starting with you."

"I'll work on it this afternoon," she promised.

Norman decided his acting clinical director could use a lesson in the economics of the business. "Do you know what they pay us for taking care of these kids?"

She thought of Roach. "Not enough."

"Exactly. But they pay us more than our costs. That's what makes this a business. When beds are empty it's not a business, it's a charity. And despite what some people think, we're not running a charity. Am I making myself clear?"

"We're a business, not a charity," Zenia repeated.

"And you and I," he impressed on her, "are partners in this little venture. You're the partner responsible for making sure we don't cross that ugly little line between business and charity. Fill those beds, St. Clair."

"I just..."

"I don't want to hear any lame excuses."

Zenia turned to the young man slouching beside him. "This must be your son," she said, noticing they had the same beady eyes and condescending expression.

"Sean's doing a little work for us. Say hello to St. Clair, Sean."

"Whassup, St. Clair?"

Zenia decided to make herself scarce before her employer discovered the mess in the dining hall. She excused herself and rushed off.

Sean had been watching their exchange with interest. "Boy, you sure told her."

"You've got to be firm with these people, Sean. If I left things up to them we'd be living in a coldwater flat and riding around in a '72 Pinto." He dispatched him to the second floor with orders to report to Ted and Fred.

Norman accepted a stack of phone messages from the receptionist and retreated to his office. Following his custom, he divided the messages into two piles: one for the people who wanted things from him and the other for the people he wanted things from. He took the first pile and dropped it unceremoniously in the trashcan. There was one message left, and he called the number.

"Virginia Tech Office of Development," a male voice answered. "This is Ed."

"Ed, this is Norman Chase calling from Richmond."

"Oh, hello, Mr. Chase! I didn't expect to hear from you so soon. I'd like to talk about the article we're proposing for our alumni magazine."

"I don't know about all this hoopla, Ed," Norman played hard to get. "I try to keep a low profile and let my work speak for itself."

"I thought that's probably the kind of man you are, Mr. Chase. I was talking with our president about you the other day. I said, you know, someone who's spent his life helping troubled kids isn't going to want us making a big fuss over him."

"You've got my number, Ed. But I've learned I've got to put up with a little rah-rah for the sake of these kids. They're the important thing around here."

"I understand completely. We'd like to put your picture on the cover of the magazine. We were hoping to get a shot of you in front of your treatment center."

Norman imagined this portrait gracing the coffee tables of wealthy alumni around the nation. "That's entirely up to you," he said. "I'm not exactly a cover boy, but you people know what's best in that department."

"I know this might be rushing things, but would it be possible for us to come this week? Actually Wednesday would work best for us. I'll bring some of our communications majors to conduct the interview and take the photos. Then maybe you and I can grab some lunch. I'd like to have some one-on-one time with you."

"Wednesday's fine."

"We really appreciate this, Mr. Chase. We'll do a first class job."

"I can tell you're a professional, Ed." *A professional butt kisser.*

"Thanks. I'm looking forward to meeting you. See you Wednesday."

"Anything for the Hokies." Norman hung up and smiled to himself. All this publicity had the potential to fill his beds for months, even years. He'd probably get a few pesky calls from fat cats wanting him to hire their worthless offspring with degrees in anthropology, but if the cats were fat enough he could always put them to work mowing the grass and policing the grounds. The phone rang and interrupted his thoughts.

"I've got Amanda McGuire on line two," the receptionist said. "She says you're trying to get in touch with …"

He punched the button and cut her off. "Hello, Mrs. McGuire!" he sang out.

"Blackjack said you want to talk to me."

"I certainly do! How are you?"

"Okay."

"We need to provide aftercare for your daughter, Mrs. McGuire. We want to make sure she's building on the progress she made during her time with us. Blackjack tells me she's at the beach. Frankly, I'm concerned about her running around unsupervised. We need to touch base with her and make sure she's okay."

"She called last night. She's stayin' there all summer."

"All summer! Well, well. We do need to see her right away. You don't want her to end up back where she started, do you?"

Amanda remembered the night her daughter was arrested for soliciting behind the lounge, and the tongue-lashing the judge had given her at the hearing. "Lord, no."

"If she can get in so much trouble at home, just think of what she can get into at Virginia Beach! We can't have her running wild down there."

"She's not at Virginia Beach. She's on some island."

"An island?"

"It's in Carolina. Starts with an O."

"An O, an O," Norman racked his brain. "Outer Banks?"

"No, it's funny-soundin'."

"Ocracoke?"

"That's it."

"What's she doing in that godforsaken backwater? They don't even have condos or golf courses. It's a waste of valuable real estate."

"I don't know nothin' about that."

At least Ocracoke was a small island and there weren't many hiding places. "You didn't tell her I'm coming see her, did you?"

"I didn't know you was."

"Good. If she calls again, don't say a word. The element of surprise is very therapeutic, so let's just keep this between you and me."

"Well, all right, if you think it'll help her."

"Oh, it'll help her all right."

"You know best about all that."

"Now where did she say she's staying?"

"Some campground."

"She should be easy to find."

"Tell her I said hi."

"I certainly will. And you tell that charming husband of yours I said hello."

He was on a roll. He left the hospital and went back to the store than had sold him the pepper spray and looked for a more potent weapon. He found the perfect persuader: a Taser gun. Soon he was flying east in his Ferrari, hitting bumps and going airborne. He grabbed his cell phone and called Meg, who was crawling through Richmond's traffic in her Lexus, driving Dru to a ballet lesson. "Something urgent's come up," he said. "I'm on my way to North Carolina."

"Since when do you have emergencies in other states?" she asked suspiciously.

"This is a business emergency, Meg. It's too complicated to explain."

"I don't like the sound of this, Norman. I don't like it one bit."

"Whether you like the sound of it or not, I'm on my way. I'm spending the night at the beach house, then I'm heading to Ocracoke in the morning."

"Ocracoke?" This struck her as an odd place to have business. "Did you drop Sean at home?"

"Oh, shit. I left him at the hospital. I forgot he was there."

"Norman, this is unbelievable! First you insist on exposing him to all those ruffians, and then you drive off and leave him there!"

"There's no need for hysterics. The boy's perfectly fine. I'll have one of the staff bring him home."

"Forget it. I'll get him. When are you coming home?"

"I don't know."

"This is ridiculous! You're dashing off to another state and you won't even tell me when you're coming back?"

"It's called a business trip. People take them all the time."

"Not like this."

"I'm in an unpredictable line of work," he reminded her. "It also happens to be a very lucrative one and you share generously in the lucre, so I'd appreciate a little cooperation."

"You're deserting your family and you want my cooperation?"

"I'm not deserting anyone. You're overreacting as usual."

"Overreacting? You want hear overreacting?" She sent her cell phone sailing out the window and watched the Lincoln Navigator behind her crush it to smithereens.

Norman heard the line go dead.

Chapter 38

Howard's Pub was a hurricane of activity 19 hours a day, 365 days a year. Buffy and Ann Warner were at the eye of the storm, making sure their deliveries showed up, their kegs were tapped and their patrons forked over whatever they didn't spend on food and drink on souvenirs and T-shirts as they stumbled contentedly out the door. Occasionally they failed to stumble and the pub's owners found them blissed-out on the rooftop deck, where they'd gone to watch the falling stars and take in the island's only ocean-to-sound view.

Buffy was a former West Virginia state senator, and Ann had worked in the state's economic development office. They'd dropped out of politics and fled from the mountains to the sea, purchasing Ocracoke's historic Island Inn and reinventing themselves as innkeepers. A few years later they traded the rustic for the raucous, selling the Inn and buying Howard's, the quintessential beach bar. Buffy had affixed his legislator's license plate to the pub's ceiling, where it took its place proudly with scores of other mementos from his patrons' previous lives, reminders of roads not taken.

He was unpacking a set of glasses in the kitchen when Chris unexpectedly stuck his curly locks in the door. "Are you Buffy? They told me you were back here. If you've got a minute I'd like to talk with you."

Buffy looked up from his chore. "What are you selling?"

Chris held up his guitar case. "Myself."

"Thanks, but we don't need any."

"I was wondering if you've got your entertainment lined up or if you could use someone else? I'm a singer-songwriter." He'd never introduced himself this way before and he liked the way it sounded.

"Oh, yeah? What do you sing-songwrite?"

"A little of everything."

"Okay, audition."

"Here? Right now?"

"No, at Carnegie Hall in February. Come on, let's get it over with." Chris pulled out his Martin. "What do you want to hear?"

"I don't give a shit. You can sing *The Theme from Gilligan's Island* for all I care. Entertain me."

"Okay. This is *Lovesick Blues* by Hank Williams. It's sort of half-blues, half-country. We're talking Hank Senior, not Hank Junior."

"You don't have to tell me about Hank Williams. He died on a railroad track in my home state."

Chris popped his capo on the second fret and played the song in E. He was two verses into it when Buffy waved him to a halt.

"Tomorrow night, three 45 minute sets, two 15 minute breaks."

"Tomorrow night?"

"Tuesdays are slow. If you do okay I'll give you a weekend. I can tell you're not a professional because we've been talking more than a minute and you haven't asked about the money."

Chris had forgotten money was involved. "What do you pay?"

"A hundred bucks and all the free Cokes you can drink."

"Great. You want to hear something else?"

"Give it a rest, kid. Write your name down and we'll put it on a sign outside."

"I'm Chris Dewberry," he realized he hadn't introduced himself. "Do I need to sign a contract or anything?"

Buffy studied him with amusement. "This ain't Dollywood, Chris. Show up at eight-thirty, play three sets and we'll pay you."

Chris packed his guitar, and when he looked up Buffy was gone. He poked around the main dining room and he saw a mike and an amp in a corner. He gathered that this was his performance space. He didn't have three sets of stage-ready material, but the patrons would come and go and by ten-thirty the barflies who were left wouldn't remember what he'd sung the first time around, so he could recycle it. He imagined himself parked on the stool with his guitar, and he smiled. All his life his father had been telling him to get his act together. Now he really had to do it.

Sierra decided to overnight the memory card to Norman Chase and hope he would consider their contest a draw. They would be back to the original deal: he would have the incriminating evidence and she'd have her college money. She saw a FedEx sign in the window of the Ocracoke Variety Store and she climbed the steps and went in the old wooden building. It looked like someone had figured out how to squeeze the contents of a Super Wal-Mart into a 7-Eleven. She helped herself to a shipping envelope, gave the memory card a farewell kiss and sealed it in the envelope. She printed Norman's name and home address on the label, but she left the sender's information blank. She paid for overnight delivery and went off to take care of her next chore, the more delicate matter of what to do with a bag full of money.

She was strolling around the harbor when she saw an historic marker commemorating Blackbeard's relationship with the island. Inspired, she decided to bury her treasure like the pirates did. She purchased a small Styrofoam cooler and went off searching for a hiding place for her treasure chest. The Ocracoke lighthouse caught her eye, and she walked around the harbor and into the residential neighborhood where the 200-year-old white tower stood sentinel. She followed a boardwalk to the lighthouse and explored the patch of sand behind it, hidden from prying eyes by the lighthouse on one side and a dense thicket of underbrush on the other. Using the lid as a shovel, she dug a hole and arranged her bundled bills in careful rows in the cooler. She helped herself to a little pocket money, put the chest in the hole, covered it with sand and smoothed the spot until it was indistinguishable from the surrounding area. She paced it off carefully so she could find it again when she returned. Satisfied, she hurried off to find her friends and tell them what she'd done.

Back at the Ocracoke Variety Store the clerk noticed the sender's information was missing from Sierra's envelope. She knew FedEx wouldn't accept the shipment without a return address, so she printed *Ocracoke Variety Store, Ocracoke, NC, 27960* in the blank spaces.

Russell watched a weight-challenged older couple climbing out of a charter boat called the Miss Iris. The captain hopped up on the dock and gave them a hand. He glanced at Russell. "Come over here and make yourself useful. Grab these two chests and show me how much muscle you've got." Russell jumped down in the boat, and with effort he wrestled the heavy coolers onto the pier. The captain flipped them open and let his clients inspect their catch. "Want me to clean 'em up for you?"

"Nah, give 'em to the local soup kitchen," the man waved dismissively. Sunburned and tired, they waddled off to their Lincoln.

The captain looked at Russell. "What the hell's a soup kitchen?"

"A place where they feed hungry people," Russell explained.

"We call 'em restaurants."

"For free," he added a clarifier.

The captain considered the two chests of fish, and he looked at Russell. "What are you doing for the next 20 minutes?"

"Same as I've been doing for the last twenty. Nothing."

"You want to help me take these around to the restaurants?"

"Sure."

"We don't have much time. I've got another charter at one."

The Lincoln exited the oyster shell parking lot in a cloud of dust. "They didn't seem to care about their fish," Russell noted.

The captain shrugged. "If folks want to pay $400 for a boat ride I'm not going to argue."

They hoisted the chests into the bed of his Silverado and set off. As they made their rounds, Russell learned that the captain's name was Ben. More interestingly, he discovered that a college student who was supposed to work as his mate for the summer had bailed on him at the last minute. "What's a mate do?" he went on a little fishing expedition of his own.

"Grunt work."

"Do you have to know anything about fishing?"

"If you can tell the difference between a red snapper and a yellow submarine, you're qualified," Ben assured him. "It's just dealing with people. I can teach you how to bait a hook and gaff a tuna, but I can't give you a personality."

"I'm your guy," Russell applied for the job. "One percent brains, ninety-nine percent personality."

"Why don't you go out with me this afternoon and prove it?"

Russell figured he didn't have anything to lose. "Okay. Thanks."

"Don't thank me yet, kid. We're not catching salmon in Alaska and you're not going to make $10,000 a month. Charter fishing's not what people imagine. We've got plenty of shitty days when the water's choppy and everyone's turning green and making trips to the rail. They're pissed because they're miles from nowhere and there's no escape. Ladies show up in these coordinated outfits with picnic baskets like they're going to a tea party, and they end up covered with fish scales and barf. It ain't a pretty picture."

Russell smiled. It was pretty enough. Besides, they couldn't put him in foster care if he was out in the Gulf Stream.

Chapter 39

Zenia was holed up in her office, contemplating her next move. Helen was stirring up the staff, and she needed to do something to stop her. She cracked the door and saw that the coast was clear. She slipped out of the building and hurried down to the gatehouse. The little shack was belching smoke like a giant incense pot, which was fitting considering the oracle inside. She threw herself on his mercy. "I really need your help, Raleigh."

Raleigh looked up from his racing form. "You're at the top of everyone's shit list."

"That bitch Helen turned them all against me! You'd think people would appreciate the fact that someone here cares about their health."

"Yeah, you'd think that, wouldn't you?"

"This place is stuck in the Dark Ages, Raleigh. We might as well be treating these kids with bleedings and leeches."

"Is that what you're planning next?"

"Very funny." She fanned his cigarette smoke away and drew closer. "Helen's trying to get me fired. I've got to do something to win people back." She gave him a conspiratorial look. "You know those bonuses you told me about Friday?"

Raleigh had already decided the story was bogus. "Yeah, what about 'em?"

"Let me break the news to the staff," she begged him. "It would calm them down. I've noticed a lot of the people who work here like money."

"You're a sharp cookie, Zenia."

"Thanks. I thought if I casually mentioned that we've got bonuses coming it might change some attitudes. It never hurts to be the bearer of glad tidings."

"Never does."

She propped her twiggy arms on the Dutch door. "So what's the scoop? When are we getting these bonuses?"

Helen had already conscripted Raleigh to help get rid of Zenia. He saw this as excellent opportunity to put the final nail in her coffin. He crushed his butt in the ashtray and leaned closer, conspiratorially. "First thing tomorrow."

Her eyes grew wide. "Tomorrow morning? Are you sure?"

"Positive. Chase tells me everything." He held up two nicotine-stained fingers. "We're like two peas in a pod."

"So how much are we getting?"

"Two grand each."

She gasped. "You mean like *two thousand dollars?*"

"Yeah, but don't tell anyone where you heard it. If word gets out that old Ral spilled the beans, Chase might decide to forget the whole thing."

"Mum's the word. You just saved my job, Raleigh."

"Yeah, don't mention it." He saw the ted&fredmobile barreling down the hill. "Better get out of the way. Cheech and Chong are coming."

The rickety vehicle gathered speed and whooshed past the gatehouse and onto Riverside Road. It took the ninety-degree turn on two wheels, rocked back to earth and puttered off, belching smoke.

Zenia did a double take. "Wasn't that Molly Potterfield?" she thought she recognized the occupant in the passenger seat.

"Yeah, probably. Roach was driving."

"Oh, my God! Call Mr. Chase!"

"He's out of town. You're the honcho now. This is your baby."

Zenia gave him a panic-stricken look and took off running up the hill.

Roach had the pedal to the metal, and his terrified passenger already realized she'd bitten off more than she could chew. "Roach, please slow down," Molly begged as they rounded a curve at breakneck speed. "If you keep driving like this we'll roll over."

"I don't need no backseat driver."

"Are you sure you know how to drive?"

"Hell, yeah. I been drivin' since I was eight."

"If we get stopped they'll discover you don't have a license and they'll arrest us," she tried to reason with him.

"They gotta catch us first."

"You think the police can't catch this old thing?"

Against his better judgment Roach cut his speed. "You happy now?"

"Yes. Just keep driving like this."

Roach looked at her. "You look sexy without all that black and purple crap on your face." He watched her steal a peek at her face in the side mirror. "So where you want me to dump you?"

"I don't know. Where do your brothers live?"

"The state pen."

"Great," she was starting to see a problem.

Roach tossed her the wallet he'd removed from Ted's back pocket. "See how much we got."

She counted the bills. "Two hundred-and-forty-eight dollars."

"Good. I need some cigarettes."

"Okay. Just drive slow so nobody notices us."

"You keep bitchin', I'm puttin' your ass out."

"You can't put me out of this van, Roach. You don't own it."

"I do now." He saw some Grateful Dead CD's on the floor. "Hey, we got Ted 'n Fred's tunes. Stick one in."

Zenia found Ted and Fred passed out on Roach's bedroom floor, with lazy clouds of marijuana smoke drifting around the ceiling. Sean was sitting against the wall, wearing a blissful expression. She dropped to her knees and shook Ted by the shoulders. "Wake up! Danny Roach stole your van! The police need your license number!"

Ted covered his owl-size pupils with his forearm. "No big deal. That van's an old piece of crap anyway."

"It is, too, a big deal!" she said. "He's a patient in this hospital and he has a 14-year-old girl with him!"

Fred cracked an eyelid. "Yo, lady in black. Who are you?"

"Zenia St. Clair. I run this treatment center."

"No you don't," Sean rasped. "My dad does."

"Your father's on a trip so it's my baby now."

"Dad's gone?"

"Sean!" a woman's voice cried.

Zenia turned and saw an elegant fashionista tugging a little girl in a tutu. She reached Sean and hovered over him. "What in the world is wrong with you? You look like you've got a secret but you don't know what it is."

"Hey, Mom. I smoked three joints."

Meg gasped, and Zenia stepped up. "You must be Ms. Chase. I'm Zenia St. Clair, the new clinical director."

"I don't care who the hell you are! I demand an explanation for this!"

"I have everything under control," Zenia assured her. "This isn't as bad as it looks. In fact, Sean might be feeling some positive energy we can work with."

"She's right, Mom. I feel it."

"Shut up. I'll deal with you later." She gave Zenia the evil eye. "I'll have you know I own half of this hospital."

"Which half?" Fred wondered.

Zenia was pleased to learn she worked for a woman. "Really? We've got a lot to talk about. We should have lunch. There's a new natural foods restaurant in Carytown."

Meg yanked her son to his feet. "Your father's right, Sean. They are idiots and morons."

Ted flashed a peace sign. "Hey, whoa, uptown lady. Make love, not war."

Determined to make war, not love, Meg headed for the door pulling a child in each hand. Sean gave his new friends a weak wave. "Later, dudes."

Out in the hallway Dru gave her mother a puzzled look. "What's wrong with Sean?

"Your brother's on drugs," it pained her to say.

"Yeah and I like 'em."

"You do not!"

"I'm addicted, Mom."

"You most certainly are not! I should never have let your father bring you anywhere near this horrid place. Now look what he's done! How could he let this happen to you?"

"Where's Dad?"

"*North Carolina*," she practically spat out the words. "On *business*."

A hundred-and-fifty miles away Norman pulled up to his beach house in the village of Duck. Homeowners on the Outer Banks liked to give their vacation digs names, and Norman had christened his cottage Sound Mind, for its sweeping view of Currituck Sound, his line of work and his own mental status. *Cottage* wasn't a very evocative description of the sumptuous three-level retreat, which sported indoor and outdoor Jacuzzis, a walk-in refrigerator and a grill the size of a cathedral altar. He parked his Ferrari next to a pair of jet skis in the garage and took the elevator to the first floor. He poured himself a single malt Scotch, kicked off his Italian loafers and padded out on the wraparound deck. He'd paid a fortune for this view but he was too distracted to enjoy it. His thoughts were on McGuire & Company, down the road whooping it up with his money. He'd always known he was in a precarious line of work, but until this little Jezebel showed up he'd never realized how precarious. She could level his empire as quickly as a category five hurricane could flatten Sound Mind.

He took a swig of Scotch and considered renaming the cottage. If he had a sound mind he would never have entered his line of business.

Zenia was back in her office, centering herself. She'd placed her favorite crystal, a pointed amethyst, on the floor, and assumed the full lotus before it. She closed her eyes and visualized the hospital as a ship riding on a storm-tossed sea. She was at the helm, navigating through the relentless waves. An insistent pounding on the door interrupted her voyage.

"We know you're in there, Zenia!" Helen thundered. "You can run, but you can't hide!"

Zenia hopped up and returned the crystal to its shelf. She cracked the door and saw what looked like a lynch mob. "I'm not hiding from anyone, Helen."

The dietician waved a document filled with signatures. "We've signed a petition asking Mr. Chase to get rid of you. If you're smart you'll quit and save him the trouble. This place is going to the dogs, Zenia. We've got kids leaving right and left and there aren't any new ones coming in."

"It's hardly my fault Danny and Molly ran away," she said defensively.

"What do you expect when you give 'em beets for breakfast?"

"Oh, for God's sake, Helen. Don't be ridiculous. There's no connection between eating beets and stealing cars."

"Give 'em sirloin and see what happens," someone suggested.

"It's a question of leadership, Zenia," Rolina tried to move the discussion beyond beets. "You either have it or you don't."

"And you don't," Maurice added.

"Well if you people think for one minute that I'm submitting my resignation you've got another thought coming. If Mr. Chase wants to fire me, he can fire me. But right now he's out of town and I happen to be in charge."

"When's he coming back?" Helen asked.

"Tomorrow morning." She paused for dramatic effect. "When he gives out our bonuses." The hall was suddenly as quiet as a church. She opened the door and stepped out. "Mr. Chase wanted it to be a surprise, but I might as well tell you. He's so pleased with the progress the hospital's making under my supervision that he's decided to give us all generous bonuses."

Maurice smelled a rat. "I hate to be picky, but how generous? We're talkin' Ebeneezer Scrooge."

"Two thousand dollars each," she reported triumphantly. There was a collective gasp.

"Bullshit," Helen refused to buy it. "You're making up this crap. You're just trying to save your own skinny ass."

"You're wrong as usual, Helen. Wrong, wrong, wrong. Mr. Chase knows we're going through a transition period and he wants to show us how much he appreciates our cooperation. Frankly, I'm worried that if you people go marching into his office yelling and making silly demands he'll have second thoughts. You know how touchy he is. I can certainly understand if some of you are having trouble adjusting to my leadership style, but your timing sucks."

"Maybe she's got a point," Maurice waffled. "It won't hurt us to give this another day or two."

Helen couldn't believe her co-workers were falling for it. "She's lying. You'll see for yourselves tomorrow."

"You're the one who's going to have egg on your face tomorrow morning, Helen," Zenia predicted.

Chapter 40

Tuesday morning found Ocracoke Island blanketed in morning fog and Chris, Russell and Sierra waiting in line for the Swan Quarter ferry. They were sending Andrew's Jeep back to him, and as a small thank you they'd washed it and gassed it up. Chris bought a ferry ticket and drove the vehicle up the loading plank and on to the boat, where other cars quickly hemmed it in. He slipped off the boat and hurried back to his friends. They grabbed some drinks at a snack bar and watched the ferry chug out of port. Chris raised his hot chocolate in a salute to their getaway vehicle as it made its final getaway.

Through the fog Russell made out a figure on the dock behind the tackle shop. "There's the captain. Gotta go."

"I can't believe this guy hired you, Russell," Chris said. "It says a lot about the job market around here."

"I can't believe Howard's Pub hired you. They must have some kind of artistic emergency. There must be an eighth grader with a magic act whose bunny died."

"Keep it up and you won't be the president of my fan club anymore, Russell."

"Just don't embarrass us too much tonight, okay?"

"Are you suggesting my balls are bigger than my talent?"

"I've never examined them that closely, but there's a very strong possibility."

"At least I'm not some guy's *mate*," Chris taunted him. "How'd you get the job – answer his mating call?"

Sierra listened to them trading insults. "I always thought I wanted a brother, but I've changed my mind."

The ferry disappeared, and they listened to its horn blowing in the distance.

The first light of day found Roach and Molly parked in front of a convenience store in Richmond. "Man, they got dumbass laws around here," Roach said in frustration. "A 15-year-old can't even score a pack of Marlboros." His new freedom was proving less free than he'd expected. He'd spent his first night driving around the city aimlessly, alternating catnaps with failed attempts to buy tobacco products. He'd bribed a promising-looking wino to buy him a pack, but the man had taken the money, bought a bottle of Night Train and disappeared in the alley behind the store.

Molly viewed this tobacco quest as pointless. "Why do you need cigarettes, Roach? You went without them at the hospital."

"Except when Russell's mom hooked me up."

Molly felt a pang at the mention of Russell's name. "I wonder where he is now?"

"Probably hidin' out at his mom's place."

"Let's go see him."

"How come?"

She had to come up with some reason he would accept. "So his mother can get your cigarettes."

Roach's face lit up. "Where do they live?"

"On Hull Street, over a shop called the Old Dominion Pawn Palace." This was the only tidbit she'd managed to extract from her would-be boyfriend during their time at the hospital.

Roach jumped out of the van. "I'll ask the dude in there how to find it."

"Okay. Hurry up."

Molly struck him as the type who would put out, so he decided to grab a pack of Trojans while he was at it. He couldn't believe it: a 15-year-old couldn't buy smokes, but he could buy whacker wrappers.

Twenty minutes later they presented themselves at Grace Moss's apartment. In their sleep-deprived state they'd failed to consider the hour or the possibility they were rousting their friend's mother from bed. A tired-looking Grace answered the door. "Yo, Miz Moss," Roach greeted her. "We're lookin' for Russell."

Grace gave them a blank look. Molly could see that she had no idea who they were. "We're Russell's friends from the hospital," she explained. "We ran away, too. We just want to make sure he's okay."

"Don't you kids know what time it is?"

Molly looked past her, hoping to see some sign of Russell. "We're sorry if we woke you up. We just want to see Russell."

"He's not here."

She started to close the door but Roach stuck his foot in the doorway. "You sure? You can trust us. We won't tell the cops or nothin'. I'm the guy who bummed the cigarette off you."

She eyed him suspiciously. "What do you want with Russell?"

He turned to Molly. "Why do we want Russell?"

"We're his friends," Molly said.

"He called last night," Grace revealed. "He's in North Carolina."

This wasn't what they expected to hear. "North Carolina?" Molly repeated.

Grace had taken her son's call in the bar across the street. She barely remembered the details of their conversation, but for some reason the island's strange name had stuck in her head. It reminded her of a vegetable she didn't like and a soft drink she did. "On Ocracoke Island."

Molly turned to Roach. "Let's go find him. We don't have anything else to do."

On a One-to-Ten scale Roach's interest in finding Russell was a minus five, but he vaguely associated islands with pot. "Okay."

"If you kids see Russell, tell him I miss him," Grace requested.

Molly gave her a little hug. "That's so sweet. We will."

Grace sized up her young visitors. "You two make a cute couple."

This rendered Molly speechless. A lecherous smile spread across Roach's face. He put his arm around his traveling companion. "Yeah, we kinda do, don't we?"

There was a naked man in her bed. There was also a golden retriever who'd decided her place was being usurped, so she'd snuggled between them. Kate glanced at her clock radio and realized Andrew was late for work. They'd sat on the deck until two, killing a bottle of wine and a bag of blue tortilla chips, and then they'd fallen into bed and made love. Ever since she'd sipped the fateful Rolling Rock on Miss Beauregard's porch she'd been behaving impetuously. She'd never acted like this before, but she was feeling a giddy freedom she hadn't felt in – well, forever. Somewhere along the line they'd decided they were going to live together. Shacking up! She hadn't even known this man two weeks and she'd invited him to move into her house! But if two single, mature adults couldn't test their compatibility, who could?

She reached over to stroke his hair and the phone rang. She answered with the comforting thought that it wasn't the Riverside Center. "Hello?"

"Good morning, Kate," Miss Beauregard chirped. "The police called a few minutes ago. They found Andrew's Jeep on a ferry in North Carolina."

"North Carolina! Where are the boys?"

"They're still missing," she reported. "The Hyde County Sheriff's Department left a number for Andrew to call. They want him to come get his car."

"He'll be thrilled."

"It sounds like he already is. I hear heavy breathing."

"That's my dog, Miss Beauregard."

"Of course it is, dear. Do you want that number now, or are you preoccupied?"

"Give me the number."

Gregor rapped on his son's bedroom door.

Serge cracked an eyelid and saw his father. "Why aren't you at work?"

"We're going on a trip."

He rolled over. "Huh?"

"I just had a call from David Dewberry. Your friends abandoned the Jeep on a ferry in North Carolina. I think they're on the island where the ferry originated."

Serge had never understood how his father came up with this kind of stuff. "How do you know? They might have ridden over on the ferry and taken off on foot."

"If they were leaving the island and they wanted to get rid of the vehicle, they would have just left it there instead of going to the trouble to put it on a ferry. Get up and throw some clothes on. We're going to Ocracoke. David and Debbie are meeting us there."

"I don't want to help you capture Chris and Russell."

"We're not capturing anybody. The owner of the Jeep isn't pressing charges."

Serge was relieved to hear this. "What'll we do if we find them?"

"Relieve them of their windfall."

"And give it back to Chase?"

"Not necessarily. I've got Branigan and Fisher doing a little research on Mr. Chase as a penalty for blowing their assignment. Apparently he has a rather lavish lifestyle. We're trying to figure out how a man who runs a program for children can afford to live like he does. It doesn't smell right."

"Chris is going to think I ratted him out."

"You'll work it out. You've been friends too long to let a girl and $200,000 come between you. Rise and shine, Serge."

"I'll rise but I won't shine," he bargained.

Meg was slinging items into her overnight bag with a vengeance. When the envelope from the Variety Store had arrived her suspicions had gotten the better of her. She didn't usually open her husband's mail, but she'd wondered what a man who shopped at Neiman Marcus wanted from a general store on Ocracoke Island. When she'd pulled the tab and dumped the contents, a single memory card had fallen out. She'd taken it down the local drug store, popped it in the print machine and screamed at what appeared on the screen: her husband frolicking with a half-naked nymphette. She'd cried for all of thirty seconds before she came to her senses and realized this gift was heaven sent. Now she had the grounds she needed and she could do what she should have done years ago: get rid of the bastard, get herself the mansion she deserved for putting up with him for seventeen years, and live fabulously ever after. She'd kiss his moody tirades and his stupid fix-your-kid business goodbye. She'd use Sean's marijuana episode to show the court that the children's time with their father should be strictly limited and closely monitored. Then with a little luck her son wouldn't grow up to be a clone of his father.

She'd hired the most vicious pit bull of a lawyer she could find. He was already poring over the list of assets she'd supplied and he was getting a court order to freeze them. While her lawyer was taking care of the legal end of things she intended to catch the cheating bastard red-handed with his little beach bunny. Norman didn't know it, but Ocracoke Island was going to be his Waterloo.

Debbie Dewberry emerged from the house where she'd just delivered a loaf of English muffin bread to an ailing member of her church. Her husband was sitting in the passenger seat of their Subaru Forester with his nose buried in the *Washington Post*. "So how's Kay?" he asked without looking up.

"She needs a kidney," Debbie reported. "I'm thinking about giving her one of mine. We're the same blood type."

"This is interesting," the professor read a little item in the *Post* to her. "Every year 800,000 hawks fly over Corpus Christi in a four-day period at the end of September. Can you imagine that?"

"I'm going to talk to Doctor Ambler about it next week."

"They glide on thermal updrafts, so they only fly during the daylight."

"Why do people have two kidneys if they only need one? Ecclesiastes says everything has a purpose, but what's the purpose of a spare kidney?"

The professor glanced up from his paper. "What?"

She started the car. "Nothing. We need to find Chris and deal with him."

"You deal with him." He'd concluded that he and his son had irreconcilable differences. "If we're lucky they'll lock him up somewhere."

"David, how can you say something like that about your own son? It's not going to help Chris to lock him up."

"It would help me. How did we ever raise such an oddball? We're perfectly normal people, aren't we?" She pulled away without answering and he went back to his article. "Nature certainly works in mysterious ways. I wonder what makes all those hawks show up at the same place at the same time?"

"Kay loved the bread. She said if she couldn't find a donor she was going to try to get one on the black market."

"There's a black market for English muffin bread?"

"David, I wish you'd try to be a little more positive about Chris."

"I was trying! I was going to let him go off and be a roving troubadour or whatever he thinks he is, and then all hell broke lose."

"Think of it as a little pothole in the road."

"It feels more like the Grand Canyon."

"David, please."

"All right, all right, I'll be positive. He's a terrific kid. Everything's hunky dory. Are you happy now?"

"All's well that ends well," she said. It sounded more like a prayer than a quote.

Chapter 41

The Miss Iris was skimming over waves on her way out to the Gulf Stream, eighteen miles offshore. Four middle-age business types were tossing back beers and sunning themselves while Russell rode in the cabin with Ben. Like most modern fishing vessels, the Miss Iris was a marvel of technology, outfitted with a bank of monitors that made the cabin look more like a broadcasting booth than a fisherman's lair. It was designed to turn an ancient art into a modern science. As they neared their destination Ben would flip on the monitors and track the schools of tuna, wahoo, marlin and sailfish below while Russell kept the party supplied with the ballyhoo and cigar minnows they were using for bait.

"How did people fish before they had all this stuff?" Russell asked the captain.

"They had their tricks," Ben replied. "They watched where birds were fishing and how high they circled before they dove, and they looked for slicks that meant sharks were feeding."

"How'd you get into this?"

"I'm third generation. When my dad and granddad decided I was serious about it they helped me finance my first boat. What about you? What are you doing on Ocracoke?"

"Problems at home," Russell gave him the abridged version. "I'll tell you about it sometime."

"I reckon you will. Get out there and mix it up with those guys. We're in the hospitality business."

As Russell slid from his chair he noticed a cigar box with the words *Perfect Day* written on it in magic marker. "What's that?"

"Cuban cigars. A gift from one of my regulars. A box of these babies goes for four hundred bucks, so I ration them. I only smoke one at the end of a perfect day."

"What's a perfect day?"

"When everything comes together," he explained. "The weather, the fish, the people, the whole damn thing."

"So how often do you have one?"

"Check it out."

Russell opened the lid and saw the box was half-full. "I hope you haven't had these for twenty years."

"Nah, a year maybe."

He did the math. "So you have a perfect day once a month. Or do you have 12 in a row and then 353 shitty ones?"

"Out," Ben evicted him. "Go make conversation with the customers. It's the only way you'll get tips."

"You're giving me tips about life," Russell said as he left the cabin.

"Take the money instead," Ben offered a final one.

Molly and Roach had gone back to the convenience store to get a North Carolina map. While she was paying for it Roach had helped himself to a case of beer and bolted from the store. They'd peeled out of the parking lot with the clerk chasing them on foot. She felt sure he'd gotten their license number and any minute flashing blue lights would appear. She felt equally sure Roach would try to outrun them. He was chugging beers and pitching the empties in back, and he'd cranked up a Grateful Dead song.

> *Drivin' that train*
> *high on cocaine*
> *Casey Jones you better*
> *watch your speed.*

"You better watch yours, too, Roach," she said nervously.

> *Trouble ahead*
> *trouble behind*
> *and you know that notion*
> *just crossed my mind.*

It was definitely crossing Molly's. Complicating matters, Roach had somehow gotten it in his head that she wanted to have sex with him. Any problems she was having at home seemed trivial by comparison.

Four beers later Roach's social graces hit a new low. "Want to see my dick? I got a really big one."

Desperate times called for desperate measures. "Okay, show me," she knew this would force him to slow down and pull over.

He waved his beer can triumphantly. "I knew it! I knew you're wantin' to make it with me."

Molly saw the Hampton Roads Coliseum on the other side of the interstate. She was in familiar territory. "Let's get off here and park where no one can see us," she proposed. He swerved across two lanes of traffic, narrowly missing an Audi, and shot down the exit ramp. Molly closed her eyes and said a prayer. When she opened them she realized that in her hour of need she'd automatically turned to good old Jesus. So much for the goddess Kore.

"Which way do we go?" he asked her.

"Turn left. We'll go to Sinners Playground."

Roach punched the gas and the van lurched onto the highway. "You a virgin?"

"No," she lied. "How do you think I know about Sinners Playground?" He reached for another beer and she slapped his hand. "I don't make it with drunks."

He put the beer back reluctantly. "So where's this Sinners place?"

"Pine Chapel Road. We're almost there." The old van nearly stalled out as they turned on Coliseum Drive, but it sputtered back to life and chugged up the road.

"So you been to this Sinners place before?"

"Lots of times. Take a left." He turned on Pine Chapel Road and a few blocks later she pointed to a brick church. "Go behind there."

Roach did a double take. "That's a church!"

"Why do you think they call it Sinners Playground? There's a place around back where everyone parks. It's safe. No one hangs around churches on Tuesday mornings."

Roach surveyed the parking lot. There were two vehicles parked in front of a small wing on the right. He'd never done anything like this in broad daylight, and the element of danger excited him. He stepped on the gas and they scooted behind the church.

"Over there," Molly pointed to a large oak tree. Roach followed her instructions. When they reached the tree he parked and killed the engine.

"Okay, take off your pants."

"Girls don't tell me what to do. I tell them what to do."

She put a hand on his thigh. "You're not used to girls like me."

"Hell, yeah, I am." He unzipped his jeans and slid them a few inches down his legs.

"All the way," she ordered. "Your shirt and your underwear, too."

Roach wiggled out of his clothing and Molly gathered the articles in a neat pile in her lap and placed his shoes on top. Without warning she opened the door, jumped out of the van and took off running for the church.

Roach threw open the door and started to give chase, but he realized he was stark naked. He was debating his predicament when she disappeared inside the church. "Come back here, you bitch!" he screamed, but it was too late. Red-faced and cursing, he hopped back in the van, fortified himself with another beer and went screeching around the building and back on to Pine Chapel Road.

Inside the church a trembling Molly dumped the filthy garments in a garbage can, ran into the pastor's study and threw herself in her surprised stepfather's arms.

On Ocracoke a romance of a different nature was unfolding. Chris and Sierra were at the end of Lighthouse Road, sitting on a seawall overlooking Teach's Hole, where legend had it the pirate Blackbeard had met his fate in a bloody battle. Chris was working on a playlist for his gig. Sierra was watching him, curious about his compositions. "How do you write songs?"

He shrugged. "I just kind of make them up."

"But how do you make them up?"

He flipped his notepad and showed her a list. "I think of a title and then I try to make up a song around it."

"*Welcome to Lousyville, Population Me?*"

"I was having a pity party that day."

"*Lessons Learned?*"

"I've only got the title. I figure I better learn some lessons before I write it." He decided the time was ripe to broach The Subject. "You remember that day at the powder magazine, when you were talking about Serge and Mr. Chase showed up and interrupted our conversation?"

Sierra splashed her feet in the water. "Do you really think we should get into this?"

"Definitely." He pointed at her, then at himself. "You and me, Sierra. Any chance?" He'd pared the question to six simple words. He wanted an equally straightforward answer.

As long as Sierra could remember she'd had more male attention than she'd known what to do with. She'd had a boyfriend named Jack once, briefly. He'd spent an evening at her home and then dumped her. She'd decided that romance needed to wait until she'd finished reinventing herself. "I like you a lot, Chris," she said truthfully. "You're amazing. I couldn't have done any of this without you. But I'm not ready for a relationship."

"What about all that crap you were saying about Serge?"

"I was just giving you a hard time so you'd get mad at me and leave me alone. We've both got places to go and we don't need any extra baggage."

"I'll go to Georgetown with you and help you carry your baggage."

"Don't you think you'd better finish high school first?"

She was right, of course, but love trumped logic. "I can work around the high school thing."

"I want to live in another country," she thought this news might discourage him.

"Great! We'll move to Argentina."

"You've got it bad, don't you?"

"I'm pathetic, Sierra! I'm putty in your hands! You don't know what it's like sleeping in the same tent with you. I lie awake at night staring at you."

"Chris, it's pitch black in that tent."

"I can sort of make out a lump where you're supposed to be."

"Boy, you sure know how to grovel," she gave him points for persistence.

"I'm an outstanding groveler! It's one of my many fine attributes."

"My life's too complicated for all that stuff."

"I do complexity! I love complexity!"

"Give it up, Chris."

He slid from the wall into the water and stood there facing her. "I know what this is, Sierra. I've seen all those chick flicks. The girl always starts out playing hard-to-get. Then she realizes he's her one true love and she comes running back. We can save ourselves a whole movie if we fast forward to the end."

She joined him in the water. "This isn't *Sleepless on Ocracoke*, Chris. Shouldn't you be working on your show?"

"I've been playing this stuff in my bedroom for years. I'm just going to get up there and pretend I'm in the bedroom. Even if they hate it, I still get paid."

"That's a healthy attitude."

"I have extremely healthy attitudes! That's another reason I'm Mr. Right."

Sierra wondered what she'd done to inspire such ardent devotion. Impulsively she grabbed him and planted an appreciative kiss on his cheek. Just as impulsively he planted a more appreciative one on her lips. They stood knee-deep in Teach's Hole, looking at each other. "I don't know if you're Mr. Right," she conceded, "but you're definitely not Mr. Wrong."

This vague sentiment was music to Chris's ears. He filed *Not Mr. Wrong* away as a song title. "This is the best day of my life."

"It's not over 'til the skinny boy sings," she reminded him.

Chapter 42

The other visitors at the Pea Island National Wildlife Refuge were gazing through field glasses at the red-winged blackbirds, hooded mergansers and masked boobies. Norman was lounging against his Ferrari, ignoring nature and studying the instruction manual for his Taser. His only knowledge of these devices came from Star Trek episodes where the crew of the Enterprise had set their phasers on "stun" and zapped their enemies into submission. He was pleased to learn that the 300,000 volt jolt he was planning to administer to his young extortionist was capable of passing through her clothing and would render her temporarily confused, unbalanced and paralyzed. He was also pleased to discover that since the weapon worked by applying electricity to nerves and muscles he could touch her anywhere and achieve the desired result. He felt blessed to live in an age when torture devices were readily available.

It was hard to believe that a hand-held device that ran on two 9-volt batteries could yield such dramatic results. When he pulled the trigger the gun produced an impressive crackle and a spark between its electrodes. Apparently the only purpose of this fireworks display was to scare the bejeezus out of the intended victim. Young Ms. McGuire wasn't going to enjoy the experience, but he hadn't enjoyed being relieved of two hundred grand either. The Taser was the perfect weapon, one that would terrify her and render her helpless without really hurting her. He got back in his car, stuck the device in his glove compartment on top of the letter from Georgetown's Office of Admissions, and continued his journey south on Route 12.

The Mini Cooper was making its way slowly through the East Dismal Swamp like a giant yellow water lily drifting across a placid pond, a rolling haiku. Andrew was driving, Kate was riding in the passenger seat and Miss Beauregard was surveying the scenery from the back seat. Andrew and Kate had planned to make a quick dash to Swan Quarter to pick up the Jeep, but they altered their plan when Professor Dewberry called and reported that a friend in law enforcement suspected the boys were still on Ocracoke Island. Miss Beauregard had complicated matters by asking to go along, explaining that she hadn't been there since she was a girl, accompanying her father on duck hunting trips. Andrew wasn't enthusiastic about having his landlady in tow, but she'd offered to pick up the tab for the gas and a night at her father's old haunt, the Island Inn. He glanced in the mirror. "Miss B, are you sure you couldn't have worn a bigger hat? You look like Carmen Miranda's grandmother."

"You can hardly expect me have the latest beachwear when I haven't been to one in years," she defended her fashion statement. She turned back the swamp. "To think our poor boys had to make their way through places like this."

"They were in my Jeep."

"I'm talking about the Confederate Army."

"Oh, *our* boys. How silly of me. Forgive me for living in the Twenty-First Century."

"You're impossible, Andrew."

"I've got some good news for you, Miss B," he'd been waiting for the right time to spring it on her. "You're losing a tenant."

"Are you going back to Rappahannock County?"

"No, I'm moving in with my psychologist. She thinks I need 24-hour observation."

It took a moment for this to register, and when it did Miss Beauregard placed a mottled hand on Kate's shoulder. "Good luck, dear. I certainly haven't been able to do anything with him."

"I'm afraid he may be incurable," Kate replied.

"Don't think you can come crawling back to me if this little arrangement doesn't work out, Andrew," Miss Beauregard warned him. "I'm not running a flophouse."

"You know you'll have a hard time replacing me, Miss B."

"This time I intend to find a higher quality of derelict."

"Impossible."

The three mismatched travelers continued their pilgrimage. The swamp may have been dismal, but they weren't.

Serge and Gregor were waiting in line for the Ocracoke ferry in Gregor's BMW X3. Serge had been handling the driving while Gregor had a series of phone conversations with Branigan and Fisher. He'd listened as his father had instructed his trainees to call this bureau and that agency, and so-and-so in Mexico City. "What was all that stuff you were talking about?" he was dying to know.

"We're doing a little research on Riverside Center," Gregor said. "Their psychiatrist's credentials don't check out. He may be here illegally."

Serge's eyes grew wider. "The guy who took care of Chris?"

"The one and the same. The immigration authorities are planning to question him tomorrow and the state's launching an investigation."

"How did you know something was wrong?"

"Chase's wealth doesn't make any sense. He's not in a line of work where people make that kind of money, and I'm having a hard time believing he came by it honestly. So is the IRS. I've got a feeling the money your friend beat him out of is going to be the least of his worries."

"Aren't you glad I got involved in this?"

"No."

"You're saving some kind of special torture for me, aren't you?"

"Drive," Gregor ordered, and Serge pulled the SUV up a few more spaces. He eyed the van in front of them. "We might have to push that guy on to the ferry."

A stringy-haired, tattooed young man in overalls exited the vehicle and approached them. "Yo."

"Yo, yourself," Serge said.

"You guys got any beer?"

Gregor sized him up. "No. You look like you've had enough." The boy drifted off and made the same call on the vehicle behind them.

Serge looked at his father. "Whenever you complain about the son you've got, just remember the one you could have gotten."

Chapter 43

Zenia was holed up in her office. Norman Chase had failed to show up with their bonuses, and Helen and her posse were demanding her head on a silver platter. She'd heard words like *picket* and *strike*. She placed an emergency call to Raleigh. "Mr. Chase didn't show up with the bonuses!" she reported breathlessly. "No one knows when he's coming back, Raleigh. Now they're talking about going on strike!"

"A strike, huh?"

"Can you believe it? Helen called me a granola dyke right in front of everybody! I mean, not that there's anything wrong with granola or lesbians, but I didn't like the way she said it."

"Guess you're ready to throw in the towel, huh?"

"I'm not a quitter, Raleigh. I'm standing my ground. I still think there's hope for this place. The only thing that has me worried is the census. We've got 27 empty beds. But it's not ethical to bring in new patients while we're in turmoil. Don't you agree?"

"You're absolutely right," Raleigh offered his usual wise counsel. "Just forget about the empty beds and deal with the staff."

"I can't deal with them! They won't even speak to me! And I don't know what to do about those workmen upstairs. They're smoking dope and eating junk food and napping. I think they're too stoned to leave."

"Don't worry about Ted and Fred," Raleigh thought they added a nice touch to the general chaos. "Chase'll handle 'em. You just stay in your office and meditate. I bet you'll come up with some good ideas like you always do."

"But how can I run the center if I stay in my office?"

"Put Garcia in charge. He's a doc."

"Raleigh, what would I do without you? You're a genius!"

Raleigh lit another Camel and considered the possibility that he really was a genius. "If you need any more help ol' Ral's always here for you."

There was revolution in the air and three of the revolutionaries were huddled at a table in the kitchen, planning the work stoppage they felt sure would result in a new clinical director and their long overdue pay raises. Helen and Maurice were throwing themselves eagerly into the task, but Rolina was proving to be a more reluctant guerilla.

"We'll have pickets at the front gate," Helen mapped their strategy. "We'll call the TV stations and see if we can get them to come over."

"Raleigh won't let us picket down there," Maurice knew the security guard wouldn't put up with anything that would interfere with his bookmaking activities.

Helen hadn't considered the Raleigh factor. "You're right. We'll picket the front door."

"Put *union* and *unionize* in big letters on the signs," Maurice suggested. "If Chase thinks we're bringing in a union he'll cave. He won't want to have to spend the rest of his life haggling with labor bosses."

"He'll shit in his pants," Helen said gleefully.

"What if he fires us?" Rolina fretted.

"Don't be such a worry wart, Rolina," Helen scolded her. "We've got to hang tough."

"I can't afford to hang tough. I'm a single parent with three children. I need my job."

"Chase can't fire us," Maurice reassured her. "He can't run the place himself or hire a hundred new people. This strike is a slam dunk."

Rolina still wasn't convinced. "We've been asking for raises for years and he always comes up with flimsy excuses. What if he just strolls past the pickets and goes to his office? This thing could turn into a standoff."

Helen thought about it. "We need to do something dramatic to show him we're serious." Her work in food service had taught her the importance of presentation, even if she was lousy at it. "I know!" she had an inspiration. "We'll hang Zenia in effigy! We'll put a dummy in the tree outside Chase's window. Then we'll set it on fire and get his attention!"

Maurice imagined a scarecrow in black leotards engulfed in flames and Norman Chase gaping at the spectacle. "That's brilliant, Helen."

"I think so," Helen believed in taking credit where credit was due.

"Where will we get a dummy?" Rolina fretted over the logistics.

"That's your job," Helen decided the nurse needed to contribute something besides misgivings.

"I can't make a dummy!" she protested. "I can't even sew a button on a shirt!"

"Then find someone who can. And make it snappy. We need it ready when Chase gets back."

"We'll need a big mob under the tree," Maurice strategized. "When the dummy goes up in flames we'll all cheer."

"You're in charge of gathering the mob," Helen gave him his assignment.

"No problem. Old Massa doesn't know it, but his plantation's about to start a profit sharing plan."

Zenia was a nervous wreck. She was afraid she was going to end up in a fetal position on her office floor, babbling incoherently. Even though it violated her most sacred principles, she decided to ask Dr. Garcia for some medication to help her calm down. She imagined the psychiatrist making his rounds, merrily dispensing pills like a Santa throwing candy in a Christmas parade. If she stood in the right spot, maybe she could catch a few.

She cracked the door and made sure the coast was clear. She tiptoed along the corridor and up the stairs. As she entered the third ward she heard music blaring from the room where the cleanup crew was encamped. She knocked tentatively.

"Come on in," Ted called out.

Zenia opened the door and found the two workers sitting at a table by the window, smoking a water pipe. Their brazenness shocked her, but she reminded herself that Ted and Fred were probably the only people at the Riverside Center who were content, and contentment counted for something.

"Yo, Lady in Black," Ted rasped.

Zenia fluttered over to the glass contraption like a moth to a flame. "How does that thing work?"

"The water cools the smoke and filters out the harmful little toxin thingies," Ted explained the basic science. "It's better for your lungs than smoking joints."

"Plus you get high quicker," Fred pointed out another benefit.

"Thanks to you two I'm probably going to lose my job," she laid the responsibility for the incident with Sean at their feet.

"We didn't turn the kid on," Fred said. "Roach did."

Ted angled the pipe in her direction. "Take a hit."

Zenia had never understood why marijuana, which was manufactured by nature, was such a big no-no, while pills, which were manufactured in laboratories, were a yes-yes. They were offering her a 100% natural product, which seemed preferable to polluting her body with manmade chemicals. When it came to a choice between Mother Nature and Father Pfizer, she'd take Mother. "How do I do it?"

"Take a deep drag and hold it in," Ted instructed her. "Then let it out slowly."

Zenia followed his instructions. She felt the smoke filling her lungs. She thought of the hookah-smoking caterpillar in *Alice in Wonderland*, puffing away and spouting wisdom. She exhaled and watched the little curls and wisps dance on the air. They passed the pipe until the herb was gone. Her limbs felt like rubber. She sprawled in the chair and forgot about her problems.

Raleigh was watching this with his binoculars. St. Clair was history, but all this talk about a strike had him worried. He couldn't imagine Norman Chase giving in to demands, so where was this thing heading? He needed to tell Chase what was going on and get him back right away. His $60,000 salary and his rent-free drive-up window were hanging in the balance.

Doctor Garcia was enjoying his new role as a supervisor. Supervision was proving to be even easier than dispensing pills, and it required no knowledge whatsoever. All he had to do was circulate and encourage people to do whatever they were doing. In return for this service they were paying him the generous salary that would enable him to move the rest of the Garcia clan to the States. When Señor Chase returned he would speak to him about jobs for his fifteen relatives.

He walked through the wards, smiling and nodding approval. He found a group in the arts and crafts room making a large piñata. "La fiesta?"

"Yeah, we're having a roast, Doc," Maurice said. "You're invited."

The doctor raised his hands and blessed the activity. "Fiesta! Piñata!" He left these happy people with the preparations for their party.

He found some equally content teenagers in the recreation room, watching an XXX-rated DVD they'd liberated from the nurse's station. He questioned them about this and they explained that it was the hospital's new sex education program. Tonight's lesson appeared to be quite detailed, so he left them to their studies.

He heard music in one of the rooms and he decided the fiesta must have been starting. He knocked on the door but no one answered. He peeked in and saw Zenia, Ted and Fred taking siestas. He shut the door quietly and tiptoed away.

He pulled a Goo Goo Cluster from his pocket and popped it in his mouth. Life was full of joyful little epiphanies. He had discovered he had a natural talent for supervision.

Chapter 44

Every summer afternoon the Pamlico Sound ferries made fifteen crossings to Ocracoke Island from Hatteras, Cedar Island and Swan Quarter. This afternoon seven of the vehicles that rolled off the ferries weren't drawn by vacations or business matters, but by fate. As lazy stacks of cumulus clouds drifted like cotton balls over the blue-green waters, Norman's Ferrari thumped off the Hatteras ferry and shot up the highway. He had every intention of making his visit to the island short and sweet. The ferries ran until midnight, which gave him time to take care of business and make a timely escape.

Later an Astrovan rolled off the next ferry from Hatteras. The overalls Roach had stolen from a farmer's clothesline were itching him like crazy. He'd sobered up enough to wonder why he'd bothered to follow the directions Molly had highlighted on the map she'd left in the van. He vaguely remembered something about Russell Moss, but whatever it was it seemed less important than finding more beer.

Serge and Gregor were following the van, and when they reached the village of Ocracoke, Serge did a double take. "Holy shit," he pointed to a sign in front of Howard's Pub. "I'd love to see Chris's parents' faces when they see that." The sign read:

LIVE TONIGHT – SINGER-SONGWRITER CHRIS DEWBERRY

A few minutes later David and Debbie passed the sign in their Subaru and failed to notice it. The professor was engrossed in a brochure about the island's British Cemetery and his wife was people watching. "This is such a quaint place," she said. "I feel like we're taking a little vacation."

The professor snorted. "I don't call looking for a car thief a vacation."

"Please don't call Chris a car thief. Kate Oxley thinks he's an artist."

"He's an artist, all right. He's a con artist."

"You're turning into an old curmudgeon, David."

"I'm not turning into a curmudgeon. I've been one for years."

A Jeep Sahara rolled off the Swan Quarter ferry, with a yellow Mini Cooper tailing closely behind. Miss Beauregard was riding with Andrew, taking in view of the harbor. "This place is so built up now," she was amazed at the changes that had taken place since her visit fifty or sixty years earlier.

"What do you remember about the Island Inn?" Andrew wanted to know.

"I remember the lobby was dark."

"Edison hadn't invented the light bulb yet."

"You're merciless, Andrew." She turned and waved to Kate, who was craning her neck, looking for the runaway boys.

Suddenly Andrew slammed on his brakes, forcing Kate to follow suit. She stuck her head out the window. "What's going on?" He pointed to the sign in front of Howard's Pub.

A few minutes later a blue Lexus rolled off the ferry from Cedar Island. The short-cut Meg thought she was taking through Carolina farm country had turned into a tour of Tobacco Road and a two-and-a-half hour voyage across the widest spot in Pamlico Sound. The trip had given her plenty of time to put her marriage in perspective, and her rage had grown to murderous proportions. Her lawyer had ordered a poster-size enlargement of the damning photograph to serve as Exhibit A in their divorce proceeding. She intended to catch her poster boy in flagrante delicto and tell him not to bother coming home.

As evening fell, pleasure boats and fishing boats chugged into the harbor and tied up. Shops closed, restaurants filled and lights twinkled on the water. It was another lazy summer evening in the village of Ocracoke, with a few minor exceptions.

Andrew wasn't about to visit a fishing village without fishing. He informed his companions that the next morning they could sleep in while he went surf fishing. He left them to get squared away at the inn, and he went strolling around the harbor to a tackle shop he'd spotted. He left with a 14-foot telescoping Shimano. He saw a dock behind the store and he decided to take a few practice casts. He started to the end of the pier, where a young man was spraying off a boat. When the boy looked up they stared at each other like they were seeing ghosts. Instinctively Russell dropped his hose, dove into the water and started swimming away. Just as instinctively Andrew abandoned his sandals, shirt and wallet and dove in after him. They surfaced half a basketball court apart.

"Don't be so hardheaded, Russell. I just want to talk with you."

Russell maneuvered toward the dock. "Yeah, right. You just happened to be in the neighborhood."

"You're acting like I'm a bounty hunter. I'm not a cop. I'm not going to drag you back to Richmond. Listen, it's stupid to keep treading water. Let's go up on the dock and talk."

Seeing no escape, Russell swam over to the Miss Iris and pulled himself up. Andrew followed him and accepted one of the towels Russell retrieved from a storage compartment. "I work on this boat," he explained. He sat on the stern and propped a foot on one of the chairs. "Okay, give me the lecture."

"I didn't get very far at the Pony Pasture, so maybe I'd better try listening instead."

"I'm better off than you think. I like this place."

"How do you know? You've been here three days, max."

"Don't you ever just *know* something? I want to live my own life and forget about all the crap."

Andrew noticed the Miss Iris was rigged for deep-sea fishing, with six chairs and a dozen heavy-duty rods. "What do you do on this boat?"

"I'm the mate. We went out in the Gulf Stream today."

"Aren't you the guy who doesn't like fishing?"

"I don't like hanging out on rocks like you do," he saw a big difference between freshwater and saltwater fishing. "I'm making eighty dollars a day, plus tips. I got twenty-five in tips yesterday and eighty today."

Andrew whistled. "You made a hundred-and-sixty bucks today?"

"It helps when they're drinking," he said with a grin.

"Where are you and Chris staying?"

"At a campground up the road."

Andrew eyed the other boats tied up in the harbor. "You've come a long way from Hull Street."

"Yeah, and I plan to stay a long way from it. Can't you get the governor to pardon me or something?"

"I don't think he'll buy it. I saw that your buddy's got a job, too."

"Yeah, if you call it a job."

"I'm here with Kate, Russell. Wild horses couldn't keep her away from that show tonight. We've got my 150-year-old landlady along. She's not exactly a beach bar type, but I guess she will be tonight."

"We didn't steal your Jeep, we borrowed it," Russell tried clarify things. "Did you notice we cleaned it up for you?"

"Yeah, but don't expect a Thank You note."

Russell studied his social worker curiously. "You're not as pissed as I thought you'd be."

Andrew claimed a chair and toweled off his hair. "You're presenting me with an ethical dilemma, Russell. CPS expects me to bring you back, or at least notify the law of your whereabouts. I don't have much enthusiasm for either one."

"That makes two of us."

"I'm not a very good representative of the social services system," he voiced the nagging doubts that had been plaguing him lately. "We rescue kids from lousy homes, but half the time as soon as they turn 18 they go right back to them. Except for the extreme cases, I never know if I'm helping kids or hurting them. I'm a simple guy. I like seeing what I've done at the end of the day. In this kind of work you never know. Most days I'd rather be selling tackle in that shop over there, or going out on the water like you are."

Russell gave him an accusing look. "So if you don't believe in the system, why do you want to hand me over it?"

"I didn't say I don't believe in it. It just doesn't work very well in some cases." He tossed the towel aside. "I haven't been wild about putting you in foster care from day one. But as long as I'm working for the state, I can't ignore you. I guess the only real solution's quitting my job. It worked for Kate. Then I won't have to tell them I found you."

Russell wasn't sure he'd heard him correctly. "So you're setting me free?"

"No, you're setting yourself free. I'm just staying out of it and being the world's worst social worker."

"Man, you're the world's best social worker," Russell saw it differently.

"I'm sure my supervisor would beg to differ. You're playing on my soft spot with this charter fishing thing."

"You want to go out tomorrow? I'll talk to the captain."

"I don't think Miss Beauregard can handle a day on the high seas, and I'm not sure Kate can handle a day of babysitting Miss Beauregard. I'll come back another time."

"Okay. I'll teach you how to fish."

"Right." Andrew started to climb out of the boat, but he turned back. "Oh, yeah, one more thing." Without warning he grabbed the young man's legs and flipped him off the back of the boat. Russell disappeared head-over-heels in the water and came up coughing. "That's for taking my wheels. Tell your buddy Chris I'll be heckling him at his show tonight." He gathered his clothes and his fishing gear and he walked back to the Island Inn wearing wet shorts and a satisfied smile.

Chapter 45

Howard's Pub's headliner entered the restaurant carrying his guitar and he froze in his tracks. Revelers were three deep at the bar, tourists were thronging the souvenir counter, children were playing darts, ring-toss and video games, two large screen TV's and a half dozen others were blaring ESPN, and servers were making their rounds with oysters, hushpuppies and pitchers of beer. Chris lingered at the door, wondering how he could compete with this carnival, or even fit in with it. He saw a screened porch with some rockers and he turned to Sierra and Russell. "You think they'll let me play for the rocking chair crowd instead?" The sound system in the dining room suggested otherwise, but before either of his companions could offer an opinion, Buffy spotted him and flagged him over. Chris danced around an exiting party and made his way to the register.

"Get set up," Buffy said.

"I don't know about this."

Buffy could see he was dealing with a rookie. "They're just a bunch of tourists from Pennsyltucky. They're here for the burgers and beer. You'll be lucky if they even notice you. You see anyone who looks like a music critic?"

He squared his shoulders, grabbed his guitar and turned to his friends. "Gotta go play for the Pennsyltuckians," he said, and he headed over to the makeshift stage.

Russell turned to Sierra. "Let's eat. I'm starving." They claimed the table in front of Chris. Sierra scanned the pub looking for Kate. She knew their former therapist would be surprised to see her there, and she'd already decided that she was going to confess to helping her friends take the Jeep, but leave out the part about Operation Scholarship.

Chris was stalling. He tuned his strings, fiddled with the sound system, shuffled through the miscellaneous junk in his guitar case and fetched a Coke from the bar. Suddenly someone killed the house and he knew the moment of truth had arrived. He looked out over a sea of heads and had an oddly comforting thought: once upon a time every performer had been a first timer. He adjusted the mike. "Hey, Ocracoke. My name's Chris Dewberry. I'm from a little place up the road called Williamsburg, where we run around in funny outfits and charge folks a lot of money to look at us. But it's a living. I'll let you in on a little secret. This is my first gig, so if it seems like I'm not ready for Vegas yet, it's because I'm not. I'm just a guy who likes to play music, and I'll play some for you."

"Play *Piano Man!*" someone at the bar belted out.

Chris looked over and saw a red-faced, beer-bellied man who looked like he'd spent half the day baking on the beach and the other half bending his elbow at the bar. "As soon as I learn to play the piano," he promised. "In the meanwhile I wrote a little commercial for the pub." He lit into a funky chord progression and sang:

> *Welcome to Ocracoke*
> *you'll like it round here.*
> *We've got miles of nothing*
> *And we're open all year.*
> *We're in the middle of nowhere*
> *and we like it like that.*
> *We've got little to offer*
> *And we're proud of the fact.*
>
> *Welcome to Howard's*
> *you'll like it round here.*
> *We've got microbrews, macrobrews*
> *and cure-your-blues beers.*
> *Your mama done warned you*
> *'bout places like this*
> *but if you'd listened to mama*
> *just think what you'd miss.*

He stopped playing. "Welcome to the exact center of the known universe, Howard's Pub and Raw Bar. You're in luck tonight, ladies and gentlemen. Tuesdays are a little slow, so your hosts, Buffy and Ann, are planning to dress up like Sonny and Cher and entertain you with their special rendition of *I Got You, Babe*. But while we're waiting for them to slip into their fringed vests ..." He slid his capo up to the second fret and played the opening chords of *Nobody Knows You When You're Down and Out.*

Russell leaned over to Sierra. "Either a star was born or he just got his ass fired."

As Chris launched into his song, he glanced across the room and nearly fell off his stool. He saw Serge and Gregor sitting in a corner at a table with his parents. His mother waved and he stumbled over his lyrics. The Tabanovs left their table and made their way over to Russell and Sierra. They broke into enthusiastic smiles when they saw Serge, but their smiles faded when he introduced his father.

Focus, he told himself. Gregor motioned for Russell to go with him, and the two of them disappeared up the stairs that led to the rooftop deck. This left Sierra with Serge, an equally unsettling development. They were right under his nose, all shiny blonde hair and flashing white teeth, Barbie and Ken on their first date.

First sets were supposed to shoo out the dinner crowd, and it was working; Pennsyltuckians were heading for the door. Second sets were supposed to entice the drinkers and music lovers to hang around. He couldn't remember what third sets were supposed to do, except end in a paycheck. He finished *Nobody* to a smattering of polite applause. He'd have to make his way through six more blues numbers and three of his own songs before he could find out what was going on. He pictured Russell on the deck upstairs, undergoing an interrogation. With his friend being grilled, his parents watching like buzzards on a tree limb, and a seduction scene playing out in front of him, things weren't looking very good. There was only one thing to do: sing his little heart out. That's why they called it the blues.

Norman never forgot an invoice, and when he saw the name on the sign he remembered billing the state's insurance plan for a Dewberry. He parked his Ferrari in front of the pub, punched the Riverside Center on his phone and got Raleigh on the line. "I need your help, Raleigh."

"I need yours," Raleigh said. "You've got to get back here right away, Mr. Chase. This place is going to hell. We're down to 18 kids."

"That's impossible. St. Clair's been filling the beds."

"No she hasn't. She's upstairs getting high with Ted and Fred."

There was a pregnant silence. "Raleigh, I hope you didn't say what I thought you said."

Raleigh hardly knew where to begin. "Those two guys you hired are potheads. They got Roach stoned, then they got your boy stoned and now they've got St. Clair. Roach took off with their van. Oh, yeah – the staff's on strike."

"Who the hell's running the place?"

"Garcia."

"Garcia! Please tell me this is some kind of a cruel joke, Raleigh."

"It's a joke, all right. This whole place has turned into a big joke."

Norman was torn between rushing back to Richmond and staying long enough to recover his stolen cash. Now that he'd come this far, it seemed foolish to turn back; he could practically feel the money in his grasp. "I'll straighten it all out tomorrow," he promised.

"There might not be anything left to straighten out," Raleigh tried to impress him with the urgency of the situation. "I'm telling you, Mr. Chase, this place is a total mess."

Norman remembered why he'd called. "Didn't we have a patient named Dewberry?"

Raleigh grabbed his clipboard and flipped through the visitor registry. "Chris Dewberry. His parents picked him up the week before last."

"Hold down the fort until I get there, Raleigh," he said, and he hung up.

Norman donned a pair of wraparound sunglasses and a Cubs ball cap and he went into the pub. He saw Sierra sitting with the young man who had delivered the picture to his house and gone berserk in the powder magazine. "Hail, hail, the gang's all here," he muttered. He elbowed his way to the bar, grabbed a napkin and scribbled a note. He gave the napkin and a ten spot to a waiter and pointed to Sierra. "Take this to the little sexpot over there. Don't say where it came from. Just give it to her and make yourself scarce."

"Gotcha." The waiter pocketed the money and dashed off. He crossed the room, dropped the message on the table and continued to the kitchen without breaking stride.

Sierra read the note. It said simply, *I know where the money is and I'm on my way to get it. NC.* Serge went tearing up the stairs and Norman saw his opening. As Sierra scanned the crowd he removed his cap and glasses, stepped away from the bar and let her to catch sight of him. Their eyes locked from across the room. He went outside and ducked behind a car. He watched her leave the pub and hurry in the direction of the village. He retrieved his Taser and her letter from his glove compartment and hurried after her under the cover of darkness.

When she reached Lighthouse Road, Sierra broke into a run. Norman stayed in pursuit, making his way quietly through the soft sand on the road's shoulder. When she reached the lighthouse she sprinted up the boardwalk and he followed her. She came to the spot where she'd buried the cooler and she glanced around nervously. Norman guessed that it was dawning on his blackmailer that she might have just led him to his money.

Earlier in the evening before his friends had arrived at the pub Roach had bellied up to the bar, flashed Ted's ID and been promptly bounced. Abandoning the van, he'd gone off in search of a better ride. After what seemed like hours spent peering in car windows, looking for one with keys in it, he found himself down at the docks, staring at a pleasure cruiser tied up across the street from the Anchorage Inn. He'd seen yachts in Baltimore Harbor, but this was the first one of these floating palaces he'd ever seen up close. He realized the *Reel EZ* was the solution to his problems, a getaway vehicle, hideout and floating bar, all in one convenient package, begging to be taken. Even if the Coast Guard caught him there were probably special prisons for yacht thieves.

He boarded the vessel and peered through its French doors. A bottle of Jack Daniels was on a polished brass-and-wood bar. Things were definitely looking up. He decided to punch out one of the glass panes and help himself to a little refreshment while he figured out how to start the boat. He grabbed a rag from the deck, padded his hand and gave the pane a sucker punch. The glass popped and an alarm sounded. He heard voices from below. He grabbed the bottle so he'd have something to show for his efforts and he scrambled back up on the dock and sprinted for dry land. He glanced over his shoulder. A couple wrapped in a blanket were watching him from the back of the yacht.

He went off in the darkness to have a talk with his friend Jack.

Sierra sensed that someone was watching her. She'd convinced herself it was her imagination when she heard a squeak in the sand. She was heading for the underbrush when two hands grabbed her from behind and pulled her back. She screamed and tried to kick herself free, but her captor clamped a hand over her mouth.

"We need to talk, Sierra." Norman said in her ear. "We can't have a reasonable conversation if you're going to scream your head off, can we?"

Chapter 46

Chris watched helplessly from his stool as Sierra read the note and dashed out of the pub. He was singing Elmore James' *I'm Worried* and using a metal slide to get the whiney effect, alternating the verses with instrumentals.

> *I'm worried, worried as a man can be*
> *I'm worried, worried as a man can be*
> *Worried 'bout my baby, she gone away from me.*

Kate entered the pub with Andrew and Miss Beauregard. She waved to him and he gave her a slight smile. It was the first time he'd laid eyes on the Jeep's owner and he was relieved that he looked halfway friendly. He gathered that the senior citizen was the Dear Old Thing, his father's only fan.

He saw feet tapping and heads swaying. He'd run off the Pennsyltuckians. The beach bums who were left didn't look like they were about to give him any standing O's, but they were getting in the spirit of things. Kate spotted his parents and she steered her little entourage over to their table. The five adults fell into animated conversation, and he knew they were talking about the only thing they had in common: him. He was under a spotlight in one corner and a magnifying glass in the other. The lyrics came around again.

> *I'm worried, worried as a man can be*
> *I'm worried, worried as a man can be*
> *Worried 'bout my baby, she gone away from me.*

Sierra struggled to break free of Norman's crushing grip. "Please let go! You're hurting my arm!"

"After we make a little trade, Sierra," he bargained. "I've got something you want and you've got something I want."

"You don't have anything I want."

"I've got something you definitely don't want." He raised his other hand and showed her the Taser. He squeezed the trigger and let electrodes do their intimidating little dance inches from her face. "I want my money and I want that picture, and I want them both right now."

Terrified, Sierra recoiled from the weapon. "I sent the memory card to your house yesterday," she said quickly.

"To my house?"

"That was our deal - the money for the picture. That's why I sent it to you."

Norman released the Taser's trigger. "Did you address it to me personally?"

"Yes. I sent it FedEx. Please let go of me."

"Don't try running or you'll wish you hadn't."

"Just keep that thing away from me."

"As long as you cooperate." He was pleased that his weapon was having the intended effect. "I resent the way you set me up, young lady. I didn't do anything to deserve this kind of treatment. I help troubled children! I provide jobs for people! I'm through with you and your crap. You've got five seconds to give me my money or you're going to be very sorry. It's your choice."

She pointed to the sand. "I buried it over there."

"Start digging. If it's not there you're going to pay a price."

Sierra paced off the spot where she'd buried it, fell to her knees and pawed in the sand. Norman hovered over her and watched the lid of the Styrofoam cooler appear. She removed it and waved a stack of bills. "See? It's all here. Can I go now?"

Norman saw that his money was still bundled like it was when he'd gotten it at the bank. "I never want to hear from you or your so-called 'associates' again. Is that clear?"

She brushed the sand from her hands and legs. "You won't."

"I have something for you," he pulled the letter from his pocket. "It's from Georgetown."

Her college plans were history, but she reached for the letter.

He pulled it back. "I want an apology first."

"I'm sorry."

"That didn't sound very heartfelt, Sierra."

"What am I supposed to feel sorry about?" she asked in frustration. "You're a rich man! You've got three houses! You can go back to your wonderful life." She knew she probably shouldn't be saying this, but something urged her on. "You're the one who's ripping people off, not me. If you really cared about kids you'd try to help them. You're just a phony. You don't care about anybody but yourself."

It was true, of course, but no one had ever been tactless enough to suggest this to Norman. He pressed the Taser's trigger and watched with interest as his critic jerked and collapsed like a sack of potatoes in the sand. He hadn't even felt a tingle. He dropped the letter beside her and turned back for his money.

He was squatting to get it when a hand grabbed him by the neck from behind and jerked him to his feet. Before he could react his arm was pinned behind his back and he was relieved of his weapon. He heard a crackling sound and everything became a gray confusion. Norman had received a far more substantial jolt than the one he had administered, a full ten seconds. His attacker had calculated that it was enough to leave him feeling like he'd fallen from the top of the 75-foot lighthouse and landed face down in the sand.

Roach was straddling a seesaw on the playground behind the Ocracoke School, working on his bottle of Jack. As long as he could remember there had never been anyone on the other end of his seesaw, but Billy the Kid probably didn't have a lot of people fighting to sit on the other end of his seesaw either. That's how life went when you were an outlaw. He took another swig. He was ready to roll, but before he left the island he intended to let everyone know he'd been there.

He'd polished off half the bottle and he was feeling much better about life in general. He stretched out on the seesaw and let the board tilt back and forth. The moon and the stars moved nearer, then farther, then nearer, then farther. It was the closest thing he'd ever had to a religious experience.

Chris was enjoying his first taste of stardom, even if it was only a nibble. During the intermission between his first two sets his mother had gushed with motherly pride, his father had grunted some fatherly grunts, a patron had made an obscure request (no, he didn't know *The Freshmen* by Verve Pipe) and a girl who looked about twelve had asked for his autograph (*Best Always, Chris Dewberry*). Kate told him he was a natural. When he saw Russell's social worker coming over he braced himself.

"I was planning to heckle you, Chris," Andrew said. "But after three Coronas I've lightened up. When you're rich and famous, remember you got there in my Jeep." He raised his bottle to him and walked away.

"Thanks," Chris said. He was about to open his second set when Russell appeared. "Chase is here, looking for his money," he said in a low voice.

"Shit." He remembered his mike was on and he clicked it off and gave his audience an apologetic shrug. "Where's Gregor?"

"I don't know. He sent Serge to make sure Sierra was okay. He told me to stay put and then he jumped over the rail and slid down the gutter like Spiderman. I've never seen a guy his age do something like that. Anyway, I'm packing it in. We've got a charter at seven and I've got to be there at six to get things ready."

"My folks are taking me back to Billyburg in the morning," Chris gave him the news. "I'm staying at a B&B with them tonight. You can hang on to the tent and the sleeping bag."

"Thanks." Russell smiled. "Just for the record, I think the music thing's going to work out for you."

"Thanks, man. Stay in touch. You can afford a phone now that you've got a job."

Russell saw the check on the table. He grabbed it and headed for the register. "Later, dude."

Chris clicked his mike on. "This is for a friend. It's called *Bob Dylan's Dream*." He strummed a G chord.

> *While riding on a train goin' west,*
> *I fell asleep for to take my rest.*
> *I dreamed a dream that made me sad,*
> *Concerning myself and the first few friends I had.*

Three verses into Dylan's hymn to youth and friendship he saw a crowd clearing around the Piano Man. *Dream* wasn't a dance number, but this wasn't stopping the PM, who was lurching around the room, out of synch with the music and the mood. He turned away from this sideshow and he saw Russell leaning against a post, listening to the song.

As easy it was to tell black from white,
It was all that easy to tell wrong from right.
And our choices were few and the thought never hit
That the one road we traveled would ever shatter and split.

How many a year has passed and gone,
And many a gamble has been lost and won,
And many a road taken by many a friend,
And each one I've never seen again.

I wish, I wish, I wish in vain,
That we could sit simply in that room again.
Ten thousand dollars at the drop of a hat,
I'd give it all gladly if our lives could be like that.

The crowd applauded and Russell gave him a thumbs-up. Chris watched him pay his tab and leave behind the Piano Man, who was escorted out the door by Buffy.

Chapter 47

Sierra saw Norman Chase face down in the sand beside her. It was her chance to take the money and run, but for some reason she couldn't move her arms or legs. She stared at the lighthouse beacon and eventually the feeling started to come back to her limbs and she scratched quadriplegia off her list of worries. She struggled to a sitting position only to discover that she didn't have the coordination to stand up. She made her way on her hands and knees to the spot where she'd buried the cash. The hole was empty. She decided one of her three friends must have put Norman Chase out of commission and taken the money for safekeeping. But what kind of Sir Galahad takes the loot and leaves the damsel?

With effort she crawled through the sand to the lighthouse. Using the stucco wall for support, she stood up. Was the money scattered somewhere in the sand? Recovering her strength she fanned out, searching for it. She spotted the envelope from Georgetown and she picked it up and stuffed it in her pocket. She decided someone had taken the money, so she set off on what promised to be a long journey back to the pub.

When she reached the boardwalk Norman called to her. "Sierra, wait," he bleated. "Please don't leave me here. There's something's wrong. I can't move."

Against her better judgment she turned around. "You'll be okay, it just takes a while for the feeling to come back. The money's gone."

"Gone?"

"Someone took it."

"Your so-called friends double-crossed you."

She refused to consider this possibility. "They'd never do that. That's why we're friends."

"Please help me. I can't move."

She was amazed by this request. "Mr. Chase, you're unbelievable. You attacked me and now you want me to help you. I'm not stupid. I'm not falling for any more of your tricks."

Norman tried to sit up, but his muscles were Jell-O. He fell back helplessly in the sand. "I'm out of tricks. You don't have anything left I want."

It was true; the picture and the money were gone, and now there wasn't anything they needed from each other. There was always the remote possibility that if she rescued him he would reward her. It didn't seem likely that he would reward someone who'd already cost him $200,000, but you just never knew about people. Putting aside her misgivings, she went over and she helped him get up.

Meg saw her husband wobbling up the road, draped over a young blonde. She made an abrupt U-turn and let the halogen headlamps of her Lexus illumine the couple like two prison escapees. Norman and Sierra were blinded by the lights, but when Meg emerged from the car it became painfully clear what was happening. "This is what you call a business trip, Norman?" she shrieked as she pounded on him. "Staggering drunk along a highway with some bimbo? I know all about your affair! How could you stoop so low? Sitting there at the dinner table and telling us in that sanctimonious voice you were going back to work, and then going off to frolic with this - this tramp!"

Sierra extracted herself hastily and left Norman to stand on his own two feet. She resented being called a bimbo and a tramp, but this didn't seem like the best time to argue about it. She eased away.

"This isn't what you think, Meg," Norman offered weakly.

"Oh, please, Norman. I wasn't born yesterday. I saw that picture of the two of you on the floor in your office. Now you're here with her when you're supposed to be away on business. How gullible do you think I am?"

"She's an extortionist," he explained.

"I don't care if she's a contortionist! She can have you! I want a divorce!"

"I don't want him!" Sierra exclaimed.

"It all makes sense if you'll just let me explain," he whimpered.

"I'm through with your explanations, Norman. I'm through with you and your damn training center for hoodlums and hookers. Don't bother coming home. I've changed the locks on all three houses, and my lawyer's going to court to freeze your assets."

"Your lawyer?"

"I'm keeping the homes and the investments, and you can have your nuthouse. You can entertain your harem on that nice Oriental rug I picked out for your office. I didn't realize I was decorating the sultan's pleasure palace."

"Meg, please. You're being totally unreasonable."

"Oh, *am* I? What would a reasonable woman do?"

Sierra knew what she was going to do. Wordlessly she slipped off in the darkness and left the two of them to battle things out.

"She set me up. She blackmailed me," Norman explained. "I paid her off that day in Williamsburg and now I'm trying to get the money back. She seduced me, Meg."

"*She* seduced *you?*"

"Yes! She took advantage of me."

"You've never let anyone take advantage of you in your life, Norman Chase. Kenny Rogers was right - you've got to know when to hold 'em and know when to fold 'em. I'm folding this one. I'll see you in court." A newly empowered Meg returned to her car, executed another U-turn and shot up the highway.

Alone, Norman stood on the side of the road, trying to make sense of this turn of events. Minutes passed before he gathered what was left of his strength and shuffled slowly in the direction of the pub.

Roach had lost track of the time, but he was still oriented enough to know who he was (the outlaw Roach) and where he was (some dumb island). He wandered the streets for what seemed like a minor eternity before he spied his van in front of the pub. As he navigated unsteadily toward it he recognized the man getting in the sports car next to it. He zig-zagged over, waving his bottle. "Yo, Mr. Chase!"

Norman turned and saw the young drunk zeroing in on him. "Roach? What the hell are you doing here?"

"You're the man, Mr. Chase," Roach felt like he needed to let him know.

Norman remembered the boy was on the lam, but it was the least of his concerns. "Beat it, Roach. I'm not in the mood for your crap." Roach drew closer and Norman raised a hand and gave him a shove. "Get out of my face, you little jerk." Gravity-challenged, Roach lost his footing and fell to the ground. Norman was opening his car door when the empty bourbon bottle came down on his head with a loud crack.

Roach watched with satisfaction as his tormentor crumpled to the ground. He helped himself to the Ferrari's keys and replaced them with the keys to the Astrovan. Lowering himself into the car's luxurious interior, he fumbled with the key until he managed to get it in the ignition. The engine gave a mighty roar and he knew his moment of glory had finally arrived.

Chris still couldn't remember what third sets were for, but judging from the folks who were still in the pub when he finished they were for drunks and the performer's friends and relatives. Kate & Company lingered, and they came over to congratulate him. "I'm really impressed, Chris," she said. "You could have a future in this." He hoped she didn't mean he could have a future playing in little out-of-the-way bars. The gig had convinced him he didn't want to spend his life entertaining Piano Men and Pennsyltuckians, and competing with ESPN.

Miss Beauregard gave him a pat on the arm. "Your father is a perfectly delightful man."

"Glad you think so," Chris said.

He was packing up when Buffy approached. Mercifully, his father was at the register settling his tab and his mother was pawing through T-shirts, so if the pub's owner offered a scathing review at least he wouldn't have to suffer it in front of his parents. Buffy pulled up a chair. "So what do you think of this joint, Chris?"

"I love the joint, but it bothers me when people start stampeding for the exits as soon as I start playing."

"If you want a captive audience, play prisons."

"It worked for Johnny Cash," Chris said.

Buffy handed him the paycheck that turned him into a professional musician.

"Thanks." Chris stuck it in his pocket. "So how'd I do?"

"You're good with a crowd," he said. "You're clever without being a wiseass. Ann and I liked your songs, and we don't always feel that way when people do their own material. If you're turning out stuff like that now, I'd like to see what you're doing when you're twenty-five."

It was a more favorable assessment than Chris was expecting. "Thanks. You've given me something to think about on the road back to reality."

Buffy held out his hand. "I'll take my usual hundred dollar consulting fee."

"Really?"

"Get out of here, Chris. Come back when you've got enough of your own material to do a whole night of it."

His parents were waiting at the door and he grabbed his guitar. "Like you'll really be able to afford me then, Buffy."

Deflated and depressed, Sierra wandered the streets of the little village aimlessly. She saw a chair in front of the Island Inn and she went over and collapsed in it. What happened to her money? If one of her friends had taken it, why had they left her with Norman Chase? She was trying to sort this out when Norman's Ferrari came around the curve at breakneck speed, hugging the road like it was on rails. It took the ninety-degree turn and rocketed away. Well at least *he* was feeling better. Maybe he wasn't upset about losing his wife after all.

She rearranged herself in the chair and felt the envelope in her back pocket. She pulled it out, opened it and angled the letter so she could read it by the streetlamp.

Dear Sierra:

We usually send our applicants form letters letting them know they've been accepted or turned down for admission. I decided to send you this personal note instead, but unfortunately I'm not writing with promising news. The Admissions Committee reviewed your application, and they decided you and Georgetown aren't a good fit. As I suspected, one of their concerns was your lack of community service. The university has a long tradition rooted in community, tolerance and service, and we look for applicants who show dedication to these principles. We're willing to overlook it in exceptional cases – artistic or scientific brilliance, for example – but that doesn't seem to apply in your situation.

I'm sure you're wondering where to go from here. I'll offer two suggestions. First, try applying to a less competitive school. We turn down 80% of our applicants, including valedictorians with perfect SAT scores. Second, please consider talking with someone who can help you examine your goals and develop a plan for achieving them. Since you can't rely on your family for this, you might try talking with a counselor. You're an enterprising young woman, and you seemed destined for success.

Best luck,
Jonathan Cox

She crumpled the letter and dropped it in the grass. So much for dreaming loud.

The pleasure Roach had drained from his bottle of Jack paled in comparison to the pleasure his new ride was giving him. There was nothing this baby couldn't do and he was proving it, doing 138 miles an hour on the straight stretch than ran the island's length. If he could catch the Hatteras ferry he could make a clean getaway. If his brothers could only see him now.

The ferry terminal came into view. The damn thing was pulling out! Instinctively, he punched the accelerator to the floor and he flew in the direction of the half-empty boat. He'd seen cars make this kind of jump plenty of times in movies. He added a gulp of salt air to his gulps of liquid courage and he went careening in the direction of the ferry at 157 miles per hour.

Roach had woefully misjudged the boat's speed, and now it was forty feet out in the water. He launched the Ferrari off the end of the dock, and the perfect car shot gracefully into the air and executed a perfect dive into Pamlico Sound. But God takes care of fools and drunks, and Roach just happened to be both, so the air bag inflated as he hit the water and cushioned his landing.

Chapter 48

The alarm went off on Russell's wristwatch. He opened his eyes and looked for Sierra, but she wasn't there. He hadn't seen her since he'd gone to the pub's rooftop deck with Gregor the previous night. Her belongings were still in the tent, so he decided she must be on the island.

He pulled on shorts and a T-shirt, and as the first crack of blue spread across the eastern sky he walked three miles to the village. The only activity was at the docks, where charters were getting ready to go out and vehicles were lining up for the first ferry. He went to the tackle shop and hauled an ice chest filled with bait to the Miss Iris. When he reached the boat he was surprised to find Serge and Gregor waiting for him. They were unshaven and wearing the same clothes they were wearing the night before. "What are you guys doing here?"

Serge nodded at his father. "He wanted to see loggerhead turtles lay their eggs, so we walked up and down the beach all night. We finally saw one, but I'm suffering from sleep deprivation."

"Serge, the only thing you suffer from is sloth," Gregor countered.

"That's not true. I also suffer from gluttony because I when I'm not sleeping I'm eating."

"We're in line for the ferry," Gregor explained to Russell. "We came over to tell you goodbye."

"What happened last night?" he asked them. "Did Chase get the money?"

"He followed Sierra to the lighthouse and had her dig it up," Serge explained. "By the time I got there Dad had everything under control."

"Chase used a Taser on her," Gregor picked up the story. "I decided to give him a taste of his own medicine. I made sure he didn't have any other weapons and I left him face down in the sand."

"Sierra never came back to the campground," Russell sounded worried. "You don't think Chase did something to her, do you?"

"He couldn't have hurt a flea in the shape he was in," Gregor assured him. "Every muscle in his body's going to ache for days."

"She probably got scared and took off with the money."

Gregor picked up a burlap sack. "This is for you, Russell."

Russell looked in the bag. When he saw the cash he felt the same kind of physical shock that he'd felt when he'd heard he was going to a foster home. He stared at the money; this gesture didn't make any sense. "Why is it mine?"

"Because we're out of options," Gregor said. "We've been looking into Chase's business affairs. He didn't exactly come by this honestly, and God knows Sierra didn't. I can't keep it. Chris and Serge don't need it. So while we were waiting for the turtles we talked it over and decided to give it to charity. Serge convinced me you were the appropriate one, so you can thank him. Most young people have safety nets called families. Yours has a few holes, so we're giving you a new one."

Russell closed the bag and glanced around to make sure no one was watching. "This is a hell of a safety net."

"Don't put it in the bank," Gregor advised him. "Banks have to report cash transactions over $10,000 and they'll think you're laundering drug money. I thought about using my connections to set up an account for you, but I don't want to have to tell anyone about this little escapade. Use it sparingly. And don't even think about giving it to Sierra." He saw the ferry loading. "We've got to go. Take care, Russell."

"Are you sure you know what you're doing?"

"No," he said as they climbed up on the dock. "But there's no more time to think about it."

They jogged over to their Bimmer and he watched them pull onto the ferry. He felt the sack's weight. It was heavier than he remembered.

Andrew stepped out on the Island Inn's balcony to check the weather. He saw a young woman curled up in one of the chairs in the yard, looking like she was passed out. He was tempted to check on her, but he was anxious to hit the surf with his new rig, so he decided to leave the chore to Kate. He went inside and shook her gently. "There's a girl passed out in a chair in the yard," he told her. "She might have had too much to drink. You might want to make sure she's okay when you get up. I'll be back at nine and we'll grab some breakfast."

Kate wasn't sure why this girl was supposed to be her concern, so she turned over and tried to go back to sleep. The image lingered like a post-hypnotic suggestion, so she got up, threw on her robe and went outside. She placed a hand on the young woman's shoulder. "Are you okay?"

Her eyes opened. "Kate?"

"Sierra! You're a mess! What in the world are you doing here?"

Tears welled in her eyes. "It's a really long story."

A family from Ohio had chartered the Miss Iris to fish the coastal wrecks offshore. Ben was in full captain mode, regaling them with tales of ancient vessels sleeping in watery graves. Russell had been assigned to keep an eye on bespectacled twins named Dayton and Clayton, who went by Day and Clay. The boys were enthusiastic, and he helped them reel in triggerfish, vermilion snapper and sea bass.

It was only his third day on the Miss Iris, but he'd already gotten the hang of baiting the hooks and removing the fish. As he went about his work his thoughts kept drifting to the money he'd tucked in a hold on the boat. Every time he decided he'd probably just imagined this windfall he looked over and saw the burlap sack. Andrew had given him his freedom and Gregor had underwritten it. Thanks to these two surrogate fathers who were willing to walk the thin line between right and wrong to help him out, his possibilities were endless. He could rent an apartment, buy a car, get new camera gear, take care of his mother and still have plenty to spare.

The little sack was a big fat bag of freedom. But, strangely, he'd felt freer when he'd strolled down to the dock at sunrise before he had it. A new day was dawning and he'd thought he had his life worked out. His job was going to make it possible to support himself and send some money home. He'd imagined himself hanging out at Howard's with the locals, watching the Final Four and the World's Series. According to Ben most of the working folks on the island had two or three jobs, so being a fisherman-photographer wasn't out of the question. But the sack of money had changed everything. He was an independently wealthy 16-year-old. He didn't even like the sound of it.

He heard Clay calling his name excitedly. He saw a small shark on the end of his line and he hurried over to lend a hand.

Confession was supposed to be good for the soul, but Kate didn't know what to make of the penitent in the passenger seat, or the elaborate saga she had related on the ferry ride to Swan Quarter. She was still confused about how Georgetown and the CIA entered the picture, but she'd stopped asking questions. They were sitting in her Mini on the ferry. Miss Beauregard was listening with interest from the back seat, and Andrew was asleep in his Jeep.

"Now I get to turn back into Jolene and wait tables at the RonDayVoo Lounge," Sierra said glumly. "I'd be better off if they'd caught me and put me in jail."

"Oh, pish posh," Miss Beauregard didn't buy it. "Your home couldn't be that bad."

"Yes, it is. I've wanted to move away as long as I can remember. I used to think about running away to Richmond because nobody there knows my family. When I got older I realized I could fix everything by going away to college and never coming back."

"Why Georgetown?" Kate was curious. "It seems like an unusual choice for someone who's never visited the school or known anyone who went there."

"They have the best School of Foreign Service. I want to move to another country and start my life over. I want to live in Europe and make up stories for my children about their nice grandparents back in the States."

"And I thought Chris was the creative one."

"I live in Richmond," Miss Beauregard piped up. "And I'm going to have an empty apartment."

"I can't afford an apartment," Sierra explained her predicament. "I can't even afford to rent a DVD."

"I didn't say anything about rent, dear. I don't need money."

Her words traveled magically through the air and fell on Sierra's ears like pixie dust. She turned around. "Really?"

"I come from southern nobility, you know."

Sierra appraised her. "You do look kind of queenly." Miss Beauregard sat up straighter and regarded her reflection in the window.

Kate wasn't sure she was hearing this correctly. "Miss Beauregard, did you just offer Sierra your apartment?"

"I most certainly did. Andrew's moving out and I need a project. I can't spend the rest of my life fretting over Arthur Ashe."

"Is he your boyfriend?" Sierra asked her.

She patted her shoulder. "I like you already, dear."

"I can be a pain."

"I realize you have a checkered past, but I've turned many young women into Southern ladies."

"I'll try anything," she said.

"I'll make a small contribution," Kate offered. "I'm opening a private practice and I'd love to have you as my first client, Sierra. I think you still have some issues you need to address."

"Like where to go to college?"

"Maybe a little broader than that."

As Kate listened to the teenager and the octogenarian sketch their plans, she realized what they had in common. Neither had a fondness for the present; Miss Beauregard was living in an impossibly glorious past and Sierra was living in an improbably rosy future. Maybe, with a gentle nudge, she could help them discover the here and now. She studied their resolute faces and changed her mind. It was going to take body slams.

Chapter 49

When Norman rolled up to the gate in Ted and Fred's van Raleigh knew the end of the Riverside Center, or possibly even the world, was at hand. He skipped the usual pleasantries. "They're all here," he reported grimly.

Norman gave him a pained look. "Who's here?" he asked wearily.

The security guard checked his registry. "Some folks from Immigration, some bigwigs from the state, parents, social workers, you name it."

Norman gave his little Money Factory-on-the-James a fond look. "It's hopeless, isn't it, Raleigh?" The guard took a drag on his Camel and didn't reply. "You haven't heard anything about that little bastard Roach, have you?" he grasped at straws. "He took my Ferrari."

"The cops called last night. They picked him up in North Carolina." Norman brightened. "Where's the car?"

"Under 15 feet of water in Pamlico Sound. They're pulling it out today and sending you the bill."

He banged his head on the steering wheel. "I should just turn around and leave, but I need some things from my office." He floored the Astrovan, but instead of shooting up the hill like his sports car always did, the tired vehicle issued a cloud of smoke, its own little white flag of surrender, and died. Norman abandoned the van and headed up the hill on foot, clinging to a thread of hope that there was still some way he could rescue things. After all, if a young drug rep could turn a passing notion into a multimillion-dollar fortune, miracles could happen. He crested the hill and saw pickets at the front entrance, so he decided to duck in a side door. As he cut across the parking lot a car from the U.S. Immigration and Naturalization Service drove past him. Garcia was in the back seat. He raised his handcuffed hands and waved.

"Adios, Señor Chase."

"Adios yourself, Garcia."

He slipped inside the building and started up the hallway. An imposing woman who was keeping a vigil outside the clinical director's office blocked his path. He recognized Victoria Hoggsett, the Commonwealth's Secretary of Health and Human Resources, a frightening presence who only showed up when there were ribbons to cut, investigations to launch or facilities to close. Her presence was a death knell. "I've been looking all *over* for you, *Norman*," she intoned in her self-important manner. "I can't seem to get your clinical *di-rec-tor* to come out of her *office*. I don't know *what* on *earth* she's *doing* in there, but it sounds rather *strange*, if you ask me."

Norman put his ear to the door and he heard Zenia chanting.

"I am a seeker of the light, a keeper of the light."

He banged on the door. "Open up, St. Clair. We need you right now."

"I am a seeker of the light, a keeper of the light," she repeated.

"That's all fine and dandy, but I've got the Secretary of Health and Human Resources out here. She needs to ask you a few questions."

"I seek the light, I keep the light," Zenia said. She gave her Tibetan bells a tinkle.

Norman gave his visitor an apologetic shrug. "The stress of the work has gotten to her. You know how it goes in this business, Victoria. One minute things are fine and dandy and the next minute everything goes to hell in a hand basket."

The Secretary peered imperiously over the top of her half-frame glasses. "You *obviously* don't understand the *gravity* of this situation, Norman. Your psychiatrist lacks *credentials*, your clinical *di-rec-tor* is having some kind of *breakdown*, your staff is on *strike*, your wards are in *shambles*, and two strange men upstairs just invited me to get *high* with them. In all my years of dealing with facilities for children I've never seen anything even *remotely* like this."

And you don't know the half of it, Norman thought. "Victoria, I'm sure if you give St. Clair a few more minutes she'll come out and explain everything." He ducked around her and dashed into the safety of his office.

It didn't take a crystal ball to see the future. Allegations would beget investigations, investigations would beget lawsuits, lawsuits would beget financial judgments and financial judgments would beget bankruptcy. This captain didn't intend to go down with his ship. He dialed the combination on his private safe and raked his passport and some other documents into his backpack. He sat down at the mahogany desk where he'd spent so many years billing insurance companies for turning obnoxious 16-year-olds into obnoxious 17-year-olds. He called his broker's private number.

"Everett here," the broker answered.

"Everett, Norman. I want you to do a wire transfer. Write this down. Wire everything in my account to J 312 SR7 01890 000 85. Got it?" He congratulated himself for having opened this numbered account in Switzerland, a Nirvana that didn't tax capital gains, didn't criminalize tax evasion and didn't cooperate with U.S. divorce courts.

"I'm afraid I can't help you, Norman," Everett said apologetically.

"What the hell are you talking about?"

"Meg's lawyer came by this morning with a court order freezing your assets."

"Unfreeze them."

"I'm afraid we can't do that."

Norman banged the phone down. He believed in confronting problems, but as his wife's guru Kenny Rogers had wisely observed, you had to know when to walk away and know when to run. He heard a commotion and he looked out the window and saw Helen barking orders and Maurice hoisting an effigy on a tree limb. Staff members armed with sticks, bats and pickets were cheering him on. He raised his fist to bang on the window and get their attention, but there was a knock on his door. He decided it must be Victoria Hoggsett, so he shoved his backpack under the desk and scattered some papers to make it look like he was working. "Come in."

The door opened and a business-type in a suit, flanked by three young casually attired assistants, entered the room. He flashed a megawatt smile and stuck out his hand. "Mr. Chase, Ed Neill from Virginia Tech. I brought along three of our communications majors – Jessica, Chan and Josh. I hope our timing's not bad." The quartets' attention traveled to the window, where Maurice was energetically dousing Zenia's effigy with charcoal starter.

Norman jumped up and pumped his visitors' hands. "Your timing's perfect, Ed. Something's come up at the last minute and I've got to leave on a business trip. I need a ride to the airport. We can talk on the way."

Ed looked at his students and shrugged gamely. "That's not really what we had in mind, but sure, we can do that."

Norman rummaged through his drawers and gathered a few more odds and ends while his visitors watched the activity outside. Chan's journalistic instincts told him to capture the scene. "May I take your picture, Mr. Chase?"

"Yeah, sure." He saw a patient's file in a drawer. He pulled it out and stared at the name of the young woman who had cost him his marriage, his business and his fortune. He heard a whoosh, and he turned and saw the effigy engulfed in flames and his staff cheering. "We're having a little pep rally before the annual staff volleyball game," he explained to his visitors. "We have a spirited bunch here."

"Boy, I'll say," Ed gaped at the spectacle.

Norman secured his backpack, gave his office a farewell glance and bolted for the door with his alma mater's representatives on his heels.

"Where are you going on your trip, Mr. Chase?" Ed asked as they hurried for the exit.

"I'm thinking about starting treatment center in Switzerland, Ed. I've decided there's no reason to focus exclusively on this country when there are so many needy children in other places."

"Switzerland has needy children?" Josh asked.

"I intend to find out."

Jessica was duly impressed. "You're like another Mother Teresa or something."

"Oh, I wouldn't go that far, but I guess some of us are just born humanitarians."

She pulled a pad and pen out of her purse. "May I quote you on that, Mr. Chase?"

"Be my guest."

They reached the parking lot and Norman made a beeline for a white van emblazoned with the maroon-and-orange Hokie Bird. He paused briefly so Chan could take his picture in front of the hospital. The young photographer carefully positioned him to catch the smoldering effigy in the background. He later he sold this photo to the *Richmond Times-Dispatch*, where it was featured prominently in a three-part investigative series on the Riverside Center. They climbed in the van and took off down the hill, detouring around the ted&fredmobile. Norman waved to Raleigh and gave Riverside a final glance. After fifteen years of proudly rolling up to the institution he founded, he disappeared down Riverside Road for the last time.

Chapter 50

The Dewberrys had stopped in Southern Shores so the professor could pick up Wednesday's *Washington Post*. By the time they crossed Currituck Sound his head was buried in the paper. Debbie was driving and Chris was stretched out in back with his guitar, working on *Dewberry's Talkin' Blues*.

> *She tore out my heart*
> *Threw it in the road*
> *Stomped that sucker*
> *Like a flattened toad.*

His mother glanced in the rearview mirror. "Chris, can't you ever leave a passing thought unexpressed?"

"Yeah, but it's no fun."

His father lowered his paper. "At least sing about something besides flattened toads."

"Ah hah! You were listening. You were only pretending to read the paper."

For the next forty-five minutes he worked quietly, strumming, scribbling and trying out different chords. By the time they reached the Virginia border he'd written a little ditty he called *Huck's Tune*. He sang it softly to himself.

> *I wish I had a raft so I could be like ol' Huck Finn*
> *I'd light out for the territory where I've never been*
> *Pick up Tom 'n Becky and we'd drift through Caroline*
> *Travel cross the water for to see what we could find*
> *Put down on an island where the pirates walked of old*
> *Find one that's still hidin' and relieve him of his gold*

We'll take our bag of booty and hang around the harbor
Livin' large on hushpuppies an' learnin' port from starboard

Huckleberry, Huckleberry, Huckleberry Finn
I understand why you just had to go adventurin'
Huckleberry, you just had to go adventurin'

The raft's imaginary, just a figment of my mind
And I've discovered Tom 'n Becky ain't the wanderin' kind
Still I kind of wish I had a raft to travel on
A water-goin' magic carpet, flowin' like a song

A boy can set out foolish and come home bein' wise
On treasure hunts you never know the nature of the prize.

Huckleberry, Huckleberry, Huckleberry Finn
I understand why you just had to go adventurin'
Huckleberry, you just had to go adventurin'

Just as prophets weren't accepted in their own homelands, musicians didn't get many standing ovations from their own relatives. Chris's parents had been rolling their eyes at his songwriting efforts for years. "That's not bad," his father offered the first favorable review he could remember. "I like the literary allusion, especially the 'light out for the territory' reference. And I like your coda."

"I ain't as dumb as you think, Pa."

He went back to his paper. "Let's hope not."

"What's a coda?"

"You figure it out," the professor said. "You're the songwriter."

Debbie saw the trace of a smile on her son's face. "I like it, too, Chris. I'm not sure what it means, but I'm not sure I want to know."

"Trust me, Mom, ignorance is bliss. Why do you think I'm so blissful?"

The Dewberrys rode back to Colonial times with Debbie thinking about her next mission of mercy, David reading occasional tidbits from the *Post* out loud, and Chris looking for his coda.

It was late evening and the sun was setting over Pamlico Sound. The waters were reflecting a mirror image of Ocracoke harbor, and calm had befallen the village.

The Miss Iris was docked in her usual spot. The Rice family had departed with their sunburned twins and sixty pounds of fish, and Ben had hopped in his truck and headed home, leaving the clean-up chores to Russell. He finished spraying off the fish cleaning station and coiled up the hose. He saw his employer's cap dangling from a nail and he snagged it and took it into the cabin. He was turning to leave when the Perfect Day box caught his eye. He hesitated, then cracked the lid and helped himself to one of the captain's Cubans. He unscrewed the cap, tapped the cigar from its tube and cut off the tip with a fillet knife. Kicking off his shoes, he settled in one of the deck chairs and propped his bare feet on the stern. As water gently lapped the side of the boat he lit his cigar, took a drag and watched the sky behind the Coast Guard station fade from orange to crimson to purple. It was a red sky at night and a sailor's delight.

He thought of Thoreau's admonition to simplify and he smiled to himself. Somewhere on the ocean floor, nestled in some ancient shipwreck, was a burlap sack with two hundred thousand dollars and eight of Ben's heaviest pyramid sinkers.

Things didn't get much simpler than that.

Epilogue

He'd never been spirited away from a concert on a motor scooter before. As Chris rode off in the Mediterranean night on the back of Sierra's Vespa, he leaned into her ear. "Where are we going?" he asked as they hugged a narrow road that snaked down from Nice's Cimiez neighborhood.

"Not far," she said. When they reached the coastal highway she turned east, past the high-walled villas tucked behind pine trees and lush foliage. A few minutes later they rolled into Saint Jean Cap Ferrat, a small village perched on a rock outcropping that plunged majestically into the sea. They parked at a cafe overlooking the water, claimed a table on the terrace and ordered a bottle of Bordeaux. "This is where the Alps meet the Mediterranean," Sierra explained.

"Performers who tour Europe call it the Beautiful Prison," Chris shared a little industry lore. "You're surrounded by all this great stuff but you're living in hotel rooms and you never have time to see it."

"Tonight I'm giving you a Get Out of Jail Free pass," Sierra said with a smile. "Bienvenu à la Côte d'Azur, Christophe."

"I'm impressed with your French."

"I've been sharing an apartment with three French students for a year just so I could say that."

He studied the girl he'd known briefly but so memorably six years earlier. She was a more content-looking, bobbed-hair, sophisticated version of the same beauty whose face had launched a thousand of his young fantasies. Somewhere, tucked in a dusty corner of his bedroom at his parents' house, he still had the topless picture of her. "Do you always run off with singers after concerts, Sierra? How long have you been a groupie?"

"Un groupie de Christophe Dewberry? Six années."

"Really?"

"Chris, I fell for you that afternoon in the gazebo when you played *The Loony Bin Blues*," she confessed. "But at the time I was too wrapped up in myself to realize it. You're the most decent guy I've ever known. The most quotable, too. 'We live on leftover tragedy food.' 'I'm an outstanding groveler, it's one of my many fine points.' "

"I think about you every time I sing *Huck*," he made a confession of his own. "And you know how many times I've sung it?"

"The first time I heard it on the radio I couldn't stop laughing," she said. "I wish you would have warned me. Only a half-dozen people know what that song's really about, and I'm one of them." She gave him a once-over. "You look good. You've filled out."

He held out his arms. "This is what a steady diet of cheese and crackers in green rooms will do for you. Almost as nourishing as the beer and pretzels at the RonDayVoo Lounge."

She smiled at the mention of the now-defunct bar. "I've come a long way from those days. I'm like Blanche DuBois – I owe it all to the kindness of strangers, starting with a guy named Chris who humored me when I was young and crazy."

"It helped that I was young and crazy, too. But you know what? We both had little movies in our heads of where we wanted to be, and now here we are, so maybe we weren't that crazy. Do you plan to stay on this side of the pond?"

She smiled mischievously. "Actually, I'm working on a new movie. You're in it."

He saw the playful look in her green eyes. "Oh, shit. Should I fortify myself with a glass of wine?"

"No, Chris, you're going to need the whole bottle."